"I WON, LIBRARIAN LADY."

Liz, giggling, tried to sit up, but he pulled her back. "I hope you're not expecting some sort of reward," she giggled.

"I have the only reward I want."

"What's that?" She rolled over in the snow to find him dangerously close. Closer than he'd ever been, close enough to kiss. "What's that?" she asked again.

"This weekend, you're pretending to be my utterly devoted girlfriend." His voice was a mere whisper in the silence of the night. "I am sure you will give a stellar performance. A performance worthy of an Oscar."

A shiver that had nothing to do with the temperature slithered around and up and down Liz's insides. "I hope you enjoy it," she whispered back, her gaze locked in his.

"I know I will."

He was going to kiss her, she thought. He was really going to kiss her. She could see it in his eyes, and in the way he tilted his head so that his lips were but a whisper away from hers. She could feel it in the slight tensing of his body. He was going to kiss her. The shiver slithered again. She licked her lips in anticipation.

"Do you know what I'm going to do now?" he asked, his voice dark and promising.

"No," she lied.

Romeo & Julia

Annie Kimberlin

LOVE SPELL BOOKS NEW YORK CITY

LOVE SPELL®

October 1999

Published by

Dorchester Publishing Co., Inc.
276 Fifth Avenue
New York, NY 10001

ISBN 0-505-52341-8

The name "Love Spell" and its logo are trademarks of Dorchester Publishing Co., Inc.

Printed in the United States of America.

For Mark, who helped me rescue a scrawny starving teenage cat.

My deepest regards to Julia Child, who has been an inspiration for so many women. Many thanks as ever to Laurie, and to Pam Baker, and to Sonja, who shared with me the story of her rescued Newfoundland and allowed me to use him as the basis for Burl. Thank you to Joyce who asked me for a school bus driver. And finally, thank you to all the fine folks at CML, none of whom is an Attila.

A portion of the author's royalties supports THE COMPANY OF ANIMALS, a nonprofit agency that distributes grants to animal welfare agencies providing emergency and ongoing care to companion animals throughout the United States.

Write to Annie at P.O. Box 30401, Gahanna, OH 43230.

Romeo & Julia

Chapter One

"Liz, you really need to get a new cat."

Liz Hadley kept her eyes on the open *Almanac* on the desk in front of her and pretended that the statement didn't stab her in the heart. Focusing her eyes more firmly on the words on the page—the large-print edition they kept at the reference desk—she scanned down the list. She resorted to the same-old same-old answer she'd given so many times before. "One of these days I'll get a cat. When it's the right time. Aha. Here it is." She pressed the hold button to reconnect to the patron. "Ma'am, according to the current *World Almanac*, the population of Brazil is 169,806,557. Yes. Is that what you needed to know? You're welcome. I'm glad we could help. Good-bye."

But this time, unlike the times of the same-old same-old, her friend and fellow librarian Cecily scowled at

9

her. "If we all waited until it was the right time, we'd never do anything. Your life is boring. All you do is read and cook. Not that I mind you cooking, of course, since we at the library reap the benefits. And eat them."

"My life isn't boring," Liz corrected her. "It's pleasant. It's uncomplicated. It's the way I like it, and the way I intend it to stay."

Cecily groaned. "You really need a cat, and you need one now."

"I can't, Cec. I just can't." Liz shoved the *World Almanac* back onto the ready reference shelf. What she couldn't do was go to the Greene County Animal Shelter and face all those homeless cats. It would be unbearable. Almost as unbearable as losing Skillet had been.

"It's been what? Six months since Skillet died?"

It was six months, three days and about four hours, to be exact. But Liz merely nodded, staring out past the wintered lawn to the parking lot, where a big yellow school bus was just pulling up. Saved by the proverbial school bus. "Your kids are here. Better take off that scowl and put on a friendly face. You don't want to traumatize the little darlings. They'll be scarred for life and never vote for a library levy when they're tax payers."

"And we'll be out of jobs," Cecily said with a grin. "Oh, the pressure of being a children's librarian." She waggled a finger at Liz. "You're not off the hook yet, oh catless cat person. The conversation is just delayed." She waltzed off, her basket of books on her arm, to greet the busload of kindergartners.

Liz relaxed for a moment, watching the hordes of children, bundled up against the cold, swarm into the library like unruly lambs, only to be herded into the meeting room. She wondered, as she had for probably the millionth time, what her life would have been like if she'd been able to have children or if the adoption had worked out. And she wondered about that three-day old baby girl. And, as she had for probably the millionth time, she told herself to forget it. Children were not in her cosmic picture. To moan and bewail that fact would be pointless. Maybe Cecily was right, she told herself; maybe it *was* time to get another cat.

"Psst!" Kendra, one of the library clerks, frantically motioned to Liz. She had an excited sparkle in her eyes as she pointed toward the parking lot. "Didja see him?" she hissed. "It's Romeo." The clerks had a habit of giving private nicknames to some of the more notorious library patrons. Romeo was famous for his good looks. Kendra motioned to the other two clerks, who were at the checkout desk. Luckily there were no patrons nearby at the moment.

Liz nodded tolerantly and watched with amusement as the bevy of young and nubile clerks flocked to lean over the checkout desk so they could better check out the parking lot. And Romeo. Liz could almost see their pheromones fluttering above them in heart-shaped clouds. They were so young, so one-dimensional. They hadn't yet been kicked in the teeth by life. Well, better let them keep their illusions. Reality would chop them up, mince them up, turn them into puree soon enough.

11

"Hiya, Liz." It was Sally Foster, the kindergarten teacher. "What's cookin'?"

"I'm watching the young ones drool over your bus driver."

"Drooling over Alex?" Sally twisted around to watch the clerks. "You ought to get them bibs. Still," she added cheerfully, "a man more worthy of their drool has yet to walk the earth." Then she turned back to Liz. "So why aren't you lusting after him?"

Liz chuckled at the teacher. "Me? I'm too old to have lustful thoughts."

"That's a load of guano. We all have lustful thoughts. It's what gets us through the bad days." She picked up a book from the reference desk. *"Statistical Abstracts of the United States. Gee. Sounds riveting. I think I'll wait for the movie."* She dropped the book and pinned Liz with a curious stare. "So why *aren't* you lusting after Alex? I mean, have you ever seen the guy? He's Greek-god gorgeous to the nth degree. And on top of all that, he's one of the nicest guys I've ever known. If he'd give me just one bit of encouragement, I'd drop Mel in an instant."

"I thought you'd sworn eternal loyalty to Mel Gibson," Liz said dryly.

"I did." Sally shrugged. "But there is something to be said for gorgeous in the flesh instead of on a screen, even in a kilt. One of those bird-in-the-hand sorts of things." She gave a salacious leer. "I'd love to have either of them in my hand."

"You want a bib of your own? I think I have one here."

"You must be made of stone to not drool over Alex Hogan."

With a smile, Liz shook her head. "I'm not made of stone. I'm just old enough to . . . "

"To what?"

Liz shrugged. "Old enough to know better, I guess."

"More guano."

"Well, I'm almost old enough to be his mother."

"Only if you had a baby when you were ten."

"Say, Sally"—Liz decided to change the subject—"how's Kathryn doing? I haven't talked to her for a couple of days. I keep waiting for her to dump her significant jerk."

Sally frowned. "No dumping yet. At least, not that I know of. I wish she would hurry up and do it. I don't think he treats her very well."

The phone at the reference desk rang, interrupting what was, to Liz, an important topic. She grimaced to Sally as she picked up the phone. "Hartley Public Library, reference desk," Liz said in her professional-librarian voice. "How may I help you? The newest Michaelson book? Let's see." She typed a title into her computer. "I'm afraid there's still a waiting list for it. Would you like me to add your name?"

I'll talk to you later, Sally mouthed and wiggled her fingers in farewell. Liz nodded to her friend as she typed the patron's library card number into the com-

puter. Out of the corner of her eye, she could see that
Sally had wandered over to the checkout desk and was
whispering something to the clerks. She was probably
giving them a tidbit of information about the object of
their collective lust before she joined her class in the
meeting room.

Liz glanced at her watch. It was almost one o'clock.
The phone at the reference desk rang again. Liz picked
it up. "I'm sorry," she told the woman on the other end
of the line after doing a computer search. "All our
copies of *The Sound of Music* are checked out. Probably
because the community theater tryouts are so soon. I
can put you on the waiting list."

As Liz was shrugging into her coat, Kendra waltzed
into the staff room. "You're deserting us, I see. Like a
rat on a sinking ship?" She stopped in front of the file
cabinet and pulled open a drawer.

"You're calling me a rat?"

"Only because you get to go home early."

"Only because I put in extra hours at the book sale,
and this is the best day the schedule would allow me to
take the time off. You know how Attila feels about the
schedule. It was handed down to him on clay tablets."

"Our dear director probably pees according to schedule. Where are those wretched volunteer forms anyway?" Kendra muttered.

"Watch what you say, kiddo. You know this staff
room is bugged."

14

"Hope you have a good book with which to curl up. We're supposed to get bunches of snow tonight."

"Great book. Biography of Julia Child. I can't wait to devour it."

"Aha. Julia. Your hero."

"Yes." Liz swung her scarf around her neck and her book bag over her shoulder. "My hero."

"Personally," Kendra said with an overly dramatic sigh, "I'd give my eyeteeth to curl up with Romeo tonight. Or any night. Or every night. Say, Liz, what are eyeteeth anyway?"

"If you ask at the reference desk, I'm sure they can help you find that information," Liz said in grinning parody of the clerks. Then she reverted to her normal voice. "I'm outta here."

Alex tucked away his notebook and pen and clambered up out of the driver's seat. The new chair plans were great, and he couldn't wait to start on them, but right now it was time to stretch his legs before he turned into an icicle. He pulled the door open and climbed down. Sheesh, it was cold. According to the forecast, Mother Nature was going to throw them a humdinger of a blizzard tonight. Maybe it was a leftover from El Niño. Even the sky looked cold. Alex rubbed his hands together.

His contemplation of the night sky was interrupted by an insistent meow. A cat? Alex liked cats. "Kitty?" he called.

A skinny mackerel-and-white cat stomped regally over to him, demanding his attention, yelling at the top of its lungs, which, considering the fact that it didn't look full grown, wasn't much.

Alex scooped up the cat. "Hello there, kitty. Where did you come from?"

The cat yelled at him again.

"You don't say. Well, wherever it was, they didn't seem to take good care of you. How did you get so dirty? And what happened to your chin? Looks like you've been kicked." The cat turned on the instant charm—rubbing a dirty head under his hand, purring like a freight engine. Alex felt the purring vibrations go all the way through him as the little cat snuggled more firmly into his arms. What a little cutie this cat was! He held the cat out so that he could look it in the face. "Yeah, I'm a sucker for strays," he said. "And you sure look like you could use a home. And a bath." At least the dirt seemed to be on the surface, rather than caked on, and from all outward appearances, the kitten appeared to be healthy. Its eyes were bright and clear, its expression alert, and its nose looked clean. The little cat yelled enthusiastically.

Suddenly, the cat twisted and leaped out of his arms. What? The cat was making a direct line for a woman who was coming out of the library. It was yelling and screaming like a fan at a hockey game.

The woman stopped stark still and stood silently, staring at the cat.

Alex strode toward her. "Hello. Is that your cat?"

The woman didn't move until he was almost to her. Then, without taking her eyes off the insistent cat, she swung her book bag onto the ground and stooped down. "Hello there, sweetie," she crooned. "Where did you come from?" Without hesitation, she picked up the cat in arms that were no stranger to a cat's shape. The cat instantly butted her chin with its head and shot a satisfied smirk at Alex. Then the woman glanced over at him. Her eyes were big and gray, windows to a serious and solemn soul. But her glance was a quick one, returning immediately to the cat in her arms.

"Is that your cat," he asked again, "or is it a stray?" If it was a stray, he would take it home, but what would he do with it right now? He couldn't take it on the bus. Well, he could, but some litigious parent would surely call the school board to complain about it.

She shook her head. "It isn't mine." Her attention was still on the cat purring noisily in her arms. "I don't have a cat." But he noticed a small break in her voice. Her hand expertly rubbed the cat's head. The lady knew how to rub a cat's ears. The cat closed its eyes.

He grinned, more to himself than anyone else. "It looks like the cat thinks otherwise."

She shot him another glance, then returned her attention to the cat, considering. He could see it on her face, in the way her mouth, free of lipstick, pursed slightly. In the way she stilled.

The cat, continually butting her chin, didn't notice

17

the stillness. Or maybe the cat merely thought it wasn't worth acknowledging.

"I'm not sure," she said quietly.

"We can't leave the kitty here tonight, not with a big storm on the way. I'd take it home, but I'd have to figure out how to take it on the bus." Suddenly, the thought of this kitty all clean and fed and warm, purring in front of his fireplace, was very appealing.

"No, we can't leave a poor kitty stranded," she said, considering. "You—oh. You're the school-bus driver, aren't you?" She looked up at him, and this time her eyes actually focused on him. They widened slightly, and the solemnity was transformed into quiet amusement. Her lips twitched slightly. The lady was trying not to smile.

He believed in being straightforward, so he stuck out his hand. "Yes, I'm Alex Hogan, bus driver for the Hartley School District."

She left off scratching the cat long enough to take his hand. Briefly. "I'm Liz Hadley, librarian." The amusement was still there. Then she turned back to the cat in her arms. "And who are you, little kitty?"

"Either a visiting dignitary or a sailor, from the way it's been swearing indignantly."

She held the cat out, turned so she could see its face. "You don't like the way this mean old life's been treating you, eh?"

But the cat, evidently realizing it had found its home,

squeezed its eyes shut in the way cats do when they're feeling secure.

"Well, whatever we do," she continued, "we can't leave you here, little one, smack dab in the middle of downtown Hartley. This bus driver is right. With this cold weather, and a big snow coming, you might not make it for long. You look like you're starving."

That reminded Alex. "I have something in the bus. Just a minute." He jogged back to the bus to riffle through his lunch box and came up with a bit of leftover cheese. He hoped the poor cat liked Muenster.

When he returned to the woman and the cat, he held out the cheese. Instantly the cat struggled to get down. Struggled to get to the cheese. Devoured it in a flash, then looked up and demanded more. Evidently the poor thing did like Muenster.

"That settles it," Liz said firmly. "I'm taking this kitten home."

"You sure?" he asked. He suddenly felt protective of the cat. It was so obviously in great need. "I would take it, if you can't."

She picked up the cat again. "I'm sure. I'm going to take this kitty home and get it all clean and fed and fat."

He touched her arm to make her look at him, so she could see that he was serious. "If you can't keep it, for whatever reason, I *will* take it."

Then she smiled at him. A smile of surety and decision. "I'll keep the cat. I'm used to cats. I've had cats all my life. This one will be fine. Won't you, little kitty? As soon as we get you home and warm and fed."

The cat purred.

She was certainly determined. "Where's your car?" He picked up her book bag. Whoa! What did the lady cart around? Bricks?

She smiled at him. "Thanks," she said. "It's that blue one over there." She led the way, evidently assuming he would follow. Which he did, lugging her bag of bricks. He wasn't sure he liked this turn of events. He wasn't sure he liked this cat going off with someone who was practically a stranger. He should've asked for references. Still, she hadn't hesitated to pick the cat up. She held the kitty as if she knew what she was doing. And the cat seemed to be perfectly at home—and cats were very good judges of character, even teenage cats like this one. And Alex knew where this lady worked—he could always come by to see how the cat was doing. As in tomorrow. And the next day. And the next day. Until he was sure, without a doubt, that the cat was well taken care of.

Sally was right, Liz thought, pulling out of the library parking lot. Alex Hogan was the dictionary definition of gorgeous in the flesh. Along with a down jacket and jeans. He was also nice, and polite as well—carrying her book bag for her, opening her car door. And he even liked cats. Yes siree, a Greek god in the flesh. A very young Greek god, she reminded herself sternly. Besides, she wasn't looking for anyone to share her life with. Of course, she hadn't been looking for a cat either, and now she was driving one home. She'd check the paper's lost-and-found ads for the past few weeks. If she didn't find an ad for the cat, she'd consider the kitty hers. "You certainly seem to be quite comfortable," she said to the cat, which was crouched on the passenger seat, watching her. "Most felines I've known didn't like to ride in the car."

The cat merely settled down more deliberately and turned up its purr.

"Well, kitty, Alex Hogan is gorgeous and nice. A combination more rare than truffles." She sighed deeply and glanced quickly at the cat.

The cat closed its eyes at her.

"I hope the younger generation appreciates him."

Abernathy's was predictably crammed with citizens of Hartley trying to stock up on groceries before the forecasted blizzard hit. Shoppers—mostly women with young children in tow—swarmed through the store like locusts. Liz steered her cart directly to the aisle where cat food was shelved. She studied the assortment. She'd always gotten Skillet gourmet canned food. She'd get the stray cat the same thing. But maybe she'd better mix it with kitten food—the cat certainly wasn't full grown. She hauled a big bag of kitten chow into her cart, along with a twenty-five-pound bag of litter and a new litter box and scoop. She grabbed a cat toy or two. Then a third. Some kitty treats went into the cart. Oh, and a cat food bowl. Then one for water as well. There, she thought at last. That should do it for the kitty; now for herself.

Tonight would be a good night for soup. Soup was always great comfort food when it was cold and snowy outside. She could try that new recipe for baked potato soup. She mentally ticked off the ingredients as she put them in her cart. Potatoes, cheese, bacon and a bunch of green onions. Butter and flour she had plenty of at home, but she'd better get another gallon of milk.

As she pushed her cart of groceries to her car, the snow began to fall, giving the world the look of gingerbread sprinkled with powdered sugar. She raised her face up to feel the delicate flakes. So many people complained about the snow, seeing it as a bother, something to be endured. But she loved it. Maybe someday, in many years, she'd be used to snow and see it as a nuisance. She hoped not.

She turned the wheels of the grocery cart so it wouldn't roll away. Then, before she unloaded the groceries into the trunk, she looked in the window to make sure the cat was still there. *Sure, Liz,* she chided herself. *Where do you think it could go?* But it was still there, curled up on the passenger seat, right where she had left it. Suddenly the thought hit her: She had no clue if the kitten was a girl or a boy. Well, once she'd determined that the kitty was hers, she would make an appointment with Dr. March. The kitty would be spayed or neutered—turned into an it. So the question was really academic, except that it affected the choice of a name. Maybe she should choose a name that wasn't gender-specific.

Alex couldn't get the cat out of his mind. For once, he barely paid attention to the chatter of the children on the bus as he drove them home. By the time he dropped off the last child and returned the bus to the school parking lot the snow was coming down steadily. He checked his bus for lost scarves and mittens, stray book bags and books, or any of the flotsam and jetsam that accompanied elementary-school–children each day. He found one scarf, striped, and one purple mitten. He picked up a few stray pieces of paper. And a candy wrapper smuggled on by some enterprising young soul. Then he climbed out of the bus and closed the door.

There wasn't much stick to the snow yet, but if it kept up for any length of time there might be enough to make a snowman. He used the arm of his jacket to brush the lightly coated white stuff off the back window and climbed into his truck. Yes siree, he had a huge front yard that was perfect for a snowman to live in. A whole snow family. Complete with two-point-five snow children and a snow cat and dog. All he needed was the snow. And the snow was on its way. As for his own family . . . well, he had the dog. Now all he needed was the rest of them. Wife, and kids. And the cat.

Speaking of cats, he thought as he maneuvered his

truck along the snowy streets of Hartley, he'd almost had the cat, too. Until Liz the librarian came and stole it from him. He would've found some way to smuggle it onto the bus. Sally Foster, the kindergarten teacher, would've helped. She was pretty manic about cats. She often said that cats were the ultimate race on the earth. Well, someday his cat would show up. Along with the woman who was going to be his wife and the mother of his children.

Alex pulled into his long curving driveway. When he was halfway to the garage, he heard Burl's basso profundo barking. Burl was announcing to the world that Alex was home. Alex grinned to himself. He doubted the world cared if he was home or not. But Burl did.

"Hiya, guy. How was your day?" he called to the dog as he closed the garage door. From inside his house the dog renewed his deep, powerful barks.

Opening the door, he was greeted by 170 pounds of enthusiastic Newfoundland. The beginning of his family.

Liz closed the kitchen door behind her and set the kitty down on the shiny linoleum. Groceries could wait. "Here you are, kitty. This is home." She set the cat down. She took off her coat and hung it on the hook. "By the way," she said. "Come here. Are you a boy or a girl?" She picked up the kitty again and held it up in one hand while she lifted its tail. "Hmm. You're a she." She set the kitty down again.

The cat took a few steps, looking all around. She

sniffed the rag rug by the sink. She stuck her little head into the bookshelves where Liz kept her collection of cookbooks. She really was not a pretty cat, Liz thought. She was in that adolescent, leggy stage, and out of proportion. Her markings weren't even pretty. She was mostly white, with irregular and random splotches of mackerel. Still, she was a growing kitten. Maybe when she filled out a little she'd be more attractive. She wasn't anything like Skillet, who had had lovely markings. And a dainty and ladylike little meow. Compared to Skillet, this kitty was coarse and ill-bred. Rather, a pure-bred alley cat. Well, this was her cat now. She ought to become acquainted with her.

But what she really wanted was Skillet back again. Skillet had been her best friend for a very long time. And you don't replace best friends. With a sigh, Liz slipped out the door and into the garage to bring in the groceries.

The paper bag made a nice playhouse for the kitty. She rattled around in it, pouncing and stalking imaginary mice. Liz bent down to scratch on the bag. The kitty wiggled her behind for a few seconds before she pounced. This kitty liked to play.

"Here, let me get you some lunch," Liz said. It felt . . . friendly to be talking to a cat again. She washed out the cat bowls, opened the can of cat food and dumped it in. Then she mixed in some dry kitten chow. The kitty, smelling the food, was up on the counter in a shot, yelling and screaming. "Let me stir this up for you first." She tried to hold the kitten away from the food while she mashed the foods together. It was a lost cause. "Oh, all right. Here." Liz set the food on the floor. The kitten attacked. Liz smiled to herself. It looked perfectly natural, having a cat eat in her kitchen. It was something she'd been missing for six months, but until now she hadn't realized just how much. Liz set a bowl of water down next to the food. "Here you go, little one," she said. Skillet never attacked her food. Skillet had perfect feline manners. Skillet was a lady. This cat was an alley fighter. Well, she'd probably had to be.

With a sigh, Liz went out to the stacks of papers waiting in her garage for the recycling truck. For once, she was glad she didn't take her papers out until she had a big pile of them. She thumbed through the stack to find all the classifieds that had come out in the past month, and took them into the warm kitchen. Liz doubted she'd find an ad for the lost cat. She hoped she wouldn't.

"Hah!" she said twenty minutes later. "No one has reported losing you." She scooped up the dirty kitty and held it up so she could look it in the face. "So I guess you're mine through default. I think you're a pretty lucky kitty."

The kitty struggled to get back down to the food. When Liz set her down, she made a mad scramble for the food bowl.

She watched the cat eat, trying to get used to the idea

that she had a cat again. In two minutes her life had changed. Now she had a friend, someone to sleep with at night, someone to welcome her home from work. Someone who wouldn't walk out on her because of something she couldn't do anything about. *Quit being morose,* she told herself. *Life is too short.* Besides, the kitty had cleaned out the bowl of food.

Liz, looking over her shoulder, walked down the hall to her bedroom. Would the kitty follow her? Yes. The kitty galloped down the hallway after Liz, then did another behind wiggle before she leaped up onto the bed to give herself a much-needed bath as Liz changed into her sweats. The kitty left off her toilette a moment to watch as Liz dialed Kathryn's number to leave a message on the answering machine. "Hi, Kath, it's me. I know you're at school now, but please call me when you get home. You're supposed to be my best friend. Don't do this disappearing act."

Bath accomplished, the cat performed another kittenish scamper back into the kitchen, where she jumped nimbly up on the counter next to the sink. She stood up on the windowsill and stuck her nose against the window. "No birds today," Liz told her. "It's the snow. Birds don't like to fly around when it's snowing to beat the band. Wait till spring. Then there'll be lots of birds for you to watch." Skillet, making little chirping noises, used to love to watch the birds. The kitty sniffed the drain.

"Do you like to play with dripping water?"

Liz turned on the faucet, just a bare trickle. The kitty batted at the water a few times, then yelled at Liz.

Evidently the cat knew how to make herself at home. "You're not a bit shy, are you? I'm going to put a little bit more cat food in your bowl, just in case you need a few more bites."

Liz left the cat and went to the bathroom to set up the litter box, another familiar task. Then she went in search of the cat. She was still in the kitchen, still at the cat food bowl, but without exhibiting her earlier frenzy. She batted a piece of food out of the bowl, then shoved it around, then sniffed it, nudged it and finally ate it. Then it was on to another piece of cat food. *She's playing with her food,* Liz thought in amazement.

But when she saw Liz, the kitty started yelling again.

"I guess you're saying thank you."

The cat yelled.

Liz stooped down and held out her fingers. "C'mere, kitty. I want to see you."

The cat strolled over to her. Liz picked her up and stroked her, the little head unfamiliar to her hand, and even clean, this was not a conventionally pretty cat. Still, evidently, this was her new feline. "Looks like we'll have to find a girl name for you. Then we'll take you in to the vet's to get checked out. You'll like Dr. March. She's a great vet. She likes kitties."

The cat snuggled into Liz's arms and purred. It was a loud and raucous sound, like everything else about this kitty. Nothing subtle here.

Liz had intended to do laundry this afternoon. Laundry and read her biography of Julia Child. Instead, she found herself following the kitty all over the house. Watching her explore, discover, investigate. She pulled out one of the new cat toys, a bitty catnip-filled mouse. The kitty shoved her face into the mouse, trying to roll on it. Liz set up the second cat toy—a ball in a track. Kitty left the catnip mouse and came to investigate this new thing. And all the while the cat purred and purred.

Finally, Liz glanced at her watch. It was four o'clock already. She had to call the animal hospital.

"Hartley Animal Hospital."

"Hi Jessie this is Liz Hadley."

"Hiya, Liz. What's cookin'?" Jessie was a good friend of Sally Foster's. They both thought it was cute to ask Liz what was cooking.

"I seem to have acquired a cat."

"Good for you." Jessie sounded cheerful. "Sally says that every life should have nine cats."

"This kitty is a stray. She's about nine or ten months old. I found her outside the library." A vision of Alex the bus driver flitted across her mind. It tried to stay, but she shoved it aside. She didn't have time for images of Greek gods. Especially young ones. "Actually, Sally brought her kids for a class visit today, and the school bus driver found the cat. I ended up taking her home." She watched the kitty creep slowly and stealthily toward the catnip mouse. "I'd like to bring her in to get checked out. She was dirty and ravenous, and she has a cut on her chin, but now that she's eaten and cleaned herself up, she seems to be in pretty good shape—considering she was found in the middle of downtown. Still, you never know. I work tomorrow. Can I bring her in on Saturday?"

"Let's see." There was the sound of an appointment book page turning. "Yup. Can you be here at ten-thirty?"

"That would be good."

"Okay, we're on. You know Melissa's emergency number and her home number, in case something comes up between now and then."

Yes, Liz knew all of the veterinarian's phone numbers. When Skillet was so sick, the last year of her life, Liz had put all of the numbers on her speed dial. "Thanks, Jess."

"Anytime. Say, what did you name her?"

The cat wiggled her scrawny behind. The cat pounced. The toy mouse was doomed.

"I'm not sure. Naming a cat is an important thing. You can't do it casually."

"Then I'll just put down 'new kitty' in the appointment book. When you name her, let us know."

"Thanks, Jess. See you Saturday." But Liz's mind wasn't on Saturday. She was watching the cat. She was thinking of names. Skillet was so named because she loved to crawl in the cupboard and sleep curled up in Liz's cast iron skillet. But this kitty . . . Let's see. Long legs. Very demanding, as if she were royalty. Or at least upper class. Playful.

The cat left off playing and, sticking her tail straight up in the air, trotted into the kitchen. Liz followed. The kitty made her way to the food bowl again and, predictably, yelled. She wanted more food. With a grin, Liz poured another handful of dried cat food into the bowl. "But this will have to be it until supper. I hope you don't have worms."

But the kitty used one now white paw to scoop a piece of food out of the bowl and whap it, sending it across the floor like a hockey puck in the playoffs. Instantly the kitty was after it, chasing the piece of food all over the kitchen. "You silly kitty." Liz chuckled. "Didn't anyone ever tell you not to play with your food?" The cat, intent on her game, ignored her.

Liz watched, amazed. "I'm going to name you Julia, after Julia Child." Liz grinned. "Hey, Julia, what do you think of your new name?"

Julia looked up at her and yelled.

"Say, Burl, you sure you want to go for your walk today?" Alex stood by the door and looked down at his dog, beginning one of their long-standing games. Burl looked at the door and wagged his tail expectantly.

"Have you looked out the window?" he teased. "The snow is really coming down."

Burl was convinced that this was a terrific day for a walk.

"Okay." Alex made his voice sound resigned. Burl gave him a quick glance and went back to staring intently at the door. The dog loved his walks. Alex reached up and took the leash off the hook. Instantly Burl bounced up and down, flinging his tail around and around.

"Sit." The big dog sat. "Good boy." Alex snapped on the leash.

Together he and his big dog tramped down the driveway to the quiet country road where they walked every afternoon, rain or shine. Just like the mailman; neither rain nor sleet would deprive Burl of his daily walk.

But today the early snow was pushing it. Under a coating of the white stuff, Burl was beginning to look like a Great Pyrenees. Alex tried to wipe it off. Burl shook his massive body. The snow stuck anyway. Alex reached down to scoop up a handful of snow. He packed it into a snowball, then tossed it up in the air. "Yo, Burl, think fast."

The great big ungainly dog leaped joyfully after it. The snowball dissolved in Burl's mouth. He swished his tail and looked expectantly at Alex for another snowball. He was rewarded with another. And another.

"Say, Burl, we almost acquired a cat today."

The dog glanced up at him, then back down at the snow. Burl loved snow. Burl wanted to catch another snowball.

"Do you like cats? I guess I just assumed you'd like a cat. Do you know what cats are? The only cat you know is Woody, and he's atypical for a cat."

Burl grinned a doggy grin and, using his nose,

shoved some snow at Alex. It was an unsubtle hint. Alex took it.

"Okay, that's enough for today," Alex said at last. "Snow's getting too deep and it's still coming down. Maybe we won't have school tomorrow." It was a cheerful thought. He enjoyed snow days as much as the kids did. They spent the day making snow forts. He spent the day in his workshop. Unless he made snowmen.

Once back in the kitchen, Alex led Burl to a small rug and told him to sit. Burl sat. Alex shrugged out of his coat and hung it up to dry off on a hook. Then he rustled up a towel and dried Burl as best he could. The Newfoundland grunted and groaned with pleasure. Burl loved being toweled dry.

Next, Alex lit the fire in the fireplace and stood in front of it for a moment to warm up. "So, what shall we have for supper, eh?" he asked Burl.

But Burl's answer was interrupted by the phone.

"Is this Alex Hogan who makes cradles?" a young-sounding woman asked breathlessly.

"Yes."

"I saw one of your cradles at a craft show a few months ago. And now—well—I just found out I'm pregnant, and more than anything I want to see if you'll make a cradle for me." The young woman spoke in rushes and starts. She sounded excited.

Carrying the phone, Alex headed into his workshop. "Let me look at my workload for the next couple of months." He ran a finger down his list of assignments. "When is your baby due?"

"The end of July," the young woman said. "Can you have one ready by then? The one I saw was the most beautiful thing in the world. It was perfect. There was a SOLD sign on it, or else I'd have gotten it then."

"I'm glad you liked it," Alex said sincerely. It was always nice to hear that people liked what he made. "I should be able to have a cradle for you by the end of July. I make several styles of cradles. Let me send you a flyer. It has photographs and size information about each of them. Then you can pick the one you want."

"Oh, yes, please." The woman sounded breathless with excitement. Alex smiled to himself as he pulled a cradle flyer from a folder and wrote the woman's name and address on it.

"This flyer will go out in tomorrow's mail. When you get it, look it over, and if you have any questions about the pricing or the shipping costs, you can get back to me. Oh, and congratulations."

"Thank you, Mr. Hogan. This is our first baby and we're—my husband and I—are so excited."

Alex turned the phone off and set it down thoughtfully on his worktable, the table where he kept track of orders and business things. He breathed in the smell of his workshop—the smell of wood shavings and wood oils. It was a special smell, a smell full of hope and the good things in life. The walls were hung with chair backs, seats, headboards. All ready to be turned into cradles for newborn babies, and rocking chairs for their mothers to rock them in. Sing to them in. Nurse them in.

Someday it would be his baby in a cradle made by his hands. His baby who was sung to, by his wife. And the arms of the rocking chair he had made would encircle the baby and the mother, protecting them, comforting them, like his arms. Someday.

With a sigh, he wandered back into the kitchen to rustle up some dog food for Burl and some leftover vegetable soup for himself. It was a good night for soup.

Liz scrubbed the potatoes and set them in the microwave to bake. Then she set her soup pot on the stove and made a roux of melted butter and flour. She stirred it continuously while it cooked slowly, very slowly, as she'd learned from Julia Child's cookbooks. When it was ready, she poured the milk, whisking it vigorously so it wouldn't lump, making a white sauce of which Julia Child could be proud. She hummed to herself while she whisked. This was going to be a good soup. A good soup for a snowy night. She glanced out the window. The snow was still coming down.

The feline Julia sat on the counter next to the stove and watched her carefully. "You want to learn to cook like your namesake, do you?" Liz asked her. "You know, she didn't learn to cook until she was in her thirties."

Julia yawned, showing her little sharp white teeth. Then she settled down into a sphinx crouch to observe.

"First you make the white sauce, using lots of milk." The microwave dinged; the potatoes were done. "Then you let the potatoes cool for a moment," she told the cat, "so you can chop them up without burning your fingers. When you're a cook, you have to be careful not to burn your fingers."

Julia looked suitably impressed with this bit of kitchen wisdom.

"When the sauce is thickened, you stir in lots of shredded cheddar cheese." Liz ripped open the bag of cheese and poured it in the sauce, using her other hand to hold Julia back. "Yes, I remember you like cheese. I'll save a bit for you, don't worry." She handed Julia a bit of shredded cheese. Julia attacked it vigorously. This little kitty had the appetite of a wolf. "Now we're going to skin the potatoes and chop them up. Some green onions. You can watch, but you have to stay over here, and not get in the way of this very sharp knife. Curiosity, you know."

Julia the kitty watched Liz chop the potatoes and green onions. She was especially interested in the frying bacon. And in the crumbling of it. And in stirring it into the soup.

The end result was a pot of lovely baked potato soup, and a well-fed kitty. And only Liz to enjoy them. Still, leftover soup, of which there would be plenty, would keep. Tomorrow she'd take it to the library in her Crock-Pot, and the staff could snack on it all day.

Before she sat down to her soup, Liz brought in wood

from her screened-in porch. One of the things she loved best about her house, she thought as she stacked the wood, was the old fireplace. She loved settling down in front of a blazing fire with a good book. Rachmaninoff on the CD player. Or a Gregorian chant. Skillet was always curled up on her lap and purring. Liz glanced over at her new cat. Julia was stalking the catnip mouse.

"C'mon, Julia, let's eat in front of the fire."

Julia was willing. Especially the eating part.

Alex got the call at shortly after ten that night. There would be no school tomorrow for the Hartley School District. The kids, Alex thought, remembering his own childhood, would be thrilled. He, however, would be busy in his workshop. He had a special cradle to finish for his sister's baby, due any day now. And he could sleep in tomorrow. He could sleep until, oh, maybe six, or even seven—assuming Burl didn't wake up at his usual five A.M. What bliss. But, thinking of Burl—

"C'mon, Burl, you big old guy. Time to go out."

He held the door open. The snow by the back door had drifted almost up to Burl's stomach.

Alex stepped out into the yard, sinking into the deep, deep snow. In the yard it was up to his knees and still coming down. This was one real blizzard—but without the wind. The night was silent with snowfall. He held his arms outstretched and tipped his head back. He watched the flakes pelting down until the sight of them made him dizzy.

He looked around his yard, making sure all was well. This was going to be a bad night for strays. It was a good thing he'd found that cat. It was another good thing that Liz the librarian had taken the kitty home. He wondered how they were doing. He'd have to call the library tomorrow to make sure she still wanted the kitty. If not . . . well, he and Burl would have themselves a cat. Then all they'd need would be a wife and two-point five children. Nah. Make that three children. Or even four or five.

"Burl, are you finished?"

Yes, Burl was finished, and ready to go back inside.

As Alex and Burl were shaking off the snow, the phone rang. Alex slid into the kitchen in his socked feet to answer it. "Hello."

"Hi, Alex, this is Carl Petersen." Carl was the shop teacher at the high school, who did a bit of woodworking as a hobby. "You know the community theater production of *The Sound of Music?* I'm doing the sets."

"*The Sound of Music.* My sisters got the video one Christmas and watched it incessantly. They used to sing along with all the songs. It drove me crazy."

Carl chuckled. "Well, I need some help. I was wondering if you could come up with something simple that would work for a puppet stage. Nothing elaborate. As long as it looks expensive from a distance."

Alex thought for a moment. "I think I could do that. I need the exact dimensions and any other requirements. When do you need it?"

"Not for several weeks. Tell you what—I'll write up the dimensions and things, and in the next day or two, I'll send them over to the bus garage."

"Great," said Alex. Community theater was a big event in Hartley. "Do I get a pair of free tickets out of this?"

"Sure thing," Carl promised.

"It's still coming down out there, Julia." Liz let the curtain fall back over the living room window and went to rub her hands in front of the fire. "You don't know how lucky you are that the school-bus driver found you." She didn't want to say his name. Sally was right; he was too cute for words. Sure, she'd seen him in the library, but never as up close and personal as today. He looked as if a great body would be under his parka. And those golden curls, and a face like an angel. Yes, indeed. If there were angels in heaven, they'd all look like Alex Hogan. Like *young* Alex Hogan she reminded herself firmly. *Young* was the operative adjective here. She had to remember that he was a mere babe. Oh, he was a babe, all right.

"We're not going to think about the school-bus driver." She said it out loud, as if doing so gave the words more power. She opened the fireplace screen and, with the poker, rearranged the logs so they'd burn down before she went to bed.

This statement of obviously dubious conviction did not impress Julia. She was busy being fascinated by the tassels hanging from the corners of the cloth covering the small table that sat under the living room window. She reached out a cat paw to tentatively touch a tassel. The tassel twitched. Julia whapped it, sending it swinging.

Liz reached out and scooped the cat up into her arms. "You haven't been listening to a word I've said," she told the cat.

Julia closed her eyes and turned on the purring charm.

"It's almost time for "Mystery." Do you like Public Television? Maybe, being an alley cat, you've not been initiated into the more refined viewing pursuits. You probably grew up on "The Simpsons." Well, all that's in the past. You're about to be educated. "Mystery" is my Thursday-night ritual. Now it shall be yours as well." She chatted to the cat while she turned on the television and tuned in PBS for the latest televised installment of a British novel.

Julia was not interested in watching television. She wiggled out of Liz's arms and leapt gracefully onto the floor. She dropped into a stalking crouch. Those poor tassels were going to be history.

Liz sighed. Julia and Skillet were like yin and yang. Like fire and water. Like earth and air. Like Bach and Led Zeppelin.

But late that night, Liz woke up. Julia was curled up on her pillow. Liz reached out one finger to stroke the smooth head. The kitty gave a soft *mrrow,* then started her purr. Liz closed her eyes again and snuggled down into the pillow. It was nice to go to sleep to the sound of a cat purring.

Chapter Two

"Attila, thy name is mud!"

"Cursing the name of our valiant leader again?" Liz asked. She shifted her Crock-Pot to one arm and held the staff door open for Cecily.

"He's not valiant. He's a varmint," the children's librarian muttered darkly, stamping her snowy feet on the doormat.

"Let me guess: You're trying to stamp him out."

"Bingo." Cecily left off her stamping and followed Liz into the staff room.

"Looks like we're the first ones here," Liz said, setting the Crock-Pot on the counter and shrugging off her coat.

"Hey," Cecily said, "whatcha got there?"

"Baked potato soup. I got the recipe from a librarian in the Columbus system."

"For us?"

"Who else?" Liz answered cheerfully.

"Liz, you're an angel."

The staff door opened, bringing in a blast of cold air. "Hi, all," Kendra called. "I think it should be illegal for us to have to work today. What was Attila thinking?"

"Attila doesn't care," Cecily answered. "It's his day off. He's probably holed up in his lair, devising new and improved tortures for us. I bet the snow is all his fault."

Liz rolled her eyes. "Come on, you guys. Even Attila can't control the weather."

"Don't tell him that," Cecily warned her. "He thinks it goes along with being the library director. It's in his goals and objectives for the year."

"What's in the Crock-Pot?" Kendra asked hopefully.

"Baked potato soup."

"You made it?"

"Sure did."

Kendra sighed in rapture. "Liz, you're my hero."

The phone rang, on the staff line. Cecily answered it. "Liz, it's for you. Senior staff member of the day has its privileges."

"Hi, Liz," said the voice on the phone. "It's Carol. I'm going to be late today. School is closed, and I have to find a place to park the monster children. Okay?"

"All right, Carol. See you when you get here. Just drive carefully. The roads out there are still nasty."

The door opened again, bringing in a gust of snow and more staff.

"Oooh!" one of the young and nubile clerks squealed. "Liz, did you cook again? You're a gem. What is it today?"

"Baked potato soup. And it needs to stay warm, so put the lid back on."

Another day at the library had begun. While the clerks checked in the books from the overnight drop, Liz and Cecily sat down to deal with the reference desk schedule. "Carol'll be late, so we have to make some changes."

"Since school is closed we won't have the morning kindergarten class coming for their visit," Cecily said. "I can work that hour on the desk." She chuckled softly. "The clerks won't be able to ogle Romeo," she said with a grin. "Their whole day will be ruined. It's a good thing you brought soup."

Liz smiled to herself. She wouldn't have minded ogling Romeo herself. Of course, she'd have had to do it surreptitiously.

"What's that Cheshire cat grin for?" Cecily demanded.

"What grin?"

"That silly grin on your face. What's it for?"

"The clerks not being able to ogle the bus driver," Liz lied.

"Poor little children," Cecily agreed. "Still, he is worth the ogle time. Don't you think so?"

"I'm too old to ogle."

"You're never too old to ogle."

"So if you take the ten o'clock hour on the reference desk—" Liz tried to distract Cecily from thoughts of the school-bus driver. She also wanted to distract herself from those very same thoughts. She pointed to the schedule in front of them. "And if I take the nine o'clock hour, we'll be okay. I can't imagine Carol being later than that. And if she is, we'll just have to cope."

But they didn't have to cope. Carol was only half an hour late. "I sent the monsterlets to play with little Shannon Casey."

"Doesn't she have the chicken pox?" Cecily asked. "The rest of the class was here yesterday afternoon. They told me all about it."

"Yeah. Shannon was the first in her class to get it, so it's going to go around. This way, my kids'll get it now and it'll be over and done with. I hope." She sat down heavily in her chair. "I think we should make a rule: If the weather's bad enough to close school, the library should be closed, too."

"Attila would never buy it," Liz cautioned. "After all, what would parents do with their kids on snow days if they couldn't bring them to the library?"

"Think of the snow-day-suffering of the poor little children," Cecily added saucily, "if they couldn't come to the library to check out videos."

"Their parents wouldn't have to scramble around to

find sitters," Carol said firmly. "You two are lucky you don't have any of the little critters."

Lucky? Liz thought to herself wryly. More than anything, she'd wanted children. So had Richard. But Richard had wanted something she couldn't give him more than he'd wanted her.

"I have an announcement." It was Kendra, over the loudspeaker. "Before we let the seething hordes into these hallowed halls, we're going to take bets on today's circulation statistics. The prize will be announced after we bully Liz into making it. We hope it will be something chocolate and decadent. So everyone—take your best bet. How many books and videos will we check out today? Write your guess on the board in the staff room. You have fourteen minutes before we open. And to get you in the mood—I just saw the Screech family drive up. Mrs. Screech and all the little Screeches are outside our doors."

Alex ran his hand along the runner of the rocking chair he was making. It was as smooth as silk. It was going to be a good chair. The kind of chair that would last through several generations of rocking babies. His thoughts were interrupted by a loud, gusty snore.

He glanced over at Burl, who had found the biggest patch of sunlight and settled down for a noisy snooze. The big guy was worn out. First thing that morning, Alex had put the snow blade on his little tractor, and he'd plowed the driveways of his elderly neighbors.

Then he and Burl had played hard. They'd leaped and jumped through the knee-deep snow in the back yard. Alex had hurled snowballs and Burl had caught them. They'd gotten soaked to their skins; at least he had. Newfoundlands had water-repellant coats. Maybe this afternoon they'd go outside and make a snowman.

The phone rang. "Hiya, Alex. This is Jessie, from Dr. March's office. I was just going over Burl's records, and it looks like he's due for his shots this month. We just happen to have an opening tomorrow at ten-thirty. This is sort of a busy month, so I wanted to know if you'd like me to schedule Burl for an appointment."

Alex gave a slight frown. "I'd forgotten his shots were due. Tomorrow at ten-thirty?" He scribbled himself a reminder note. "Sure. We'll be there. And Jessie, thanks for thinking about us."

"No problemo," came the chipper reply. "I know that Karen is sort of manic about her rescue dogs. Actually," Jessie continued in a confidential tone, "she's more than manic. She's downright rabid. If you weren't able to get Burl his shots, which I'm sure would *never* happen, Karen would go on the rampage. It would not be pretty."

Alex chuckled at the thought of mild-mannered Karen Matheson on the rampage. "Okay, Jessie. You don't have to be overly dramatic. We'll be there."

"Oh, good," she said, and he thought he heard a giggle in her voice, as if she was playing a trick on someone.

After he hung up, Alex bent down to stroke Burl's

soft head. "Well, old guy, you get to go see Dr. March tomorrow and get shots."

Burl, without opening his eyes, gave a halfhearted thwap of his tail. Burl loved Jessie and Dr. March.

"Hey, Liz." Kendra stuck her head in the staff room. "You have a visitor."

It was Sally Foster, the kindergarten teacher. "Hi, Liz." She held out a small package. "This is for your new friend. Jessie told me about her this morning."

Liz took the small package. "This paper is lovely." It was silver tissue paper with cats printed all over it.

"Sylvie Novino made that paper for me a while ago. I thought it was appropriate." She grinned at Liz. "Go ahead; open it."

It was a tiny fur mouse.

"What's that?" Cecily came into the staff room and looked over Liz's shoulder.

"Present for Liz's new friend," Sally answered.

"What new friend?"

"Didn't she tell you? She got a cat yesterday."

"A cat?" Cecily screeched. "Oh, Liz, why didn't you tell us?"

"You didn't tell her?" Sally asked.

Liz looked from one of them to the other. "Well, I . . . it never came up. We were busy with the schedule, and then Carol got here . . . "

"So tell us now," Cecily demanded.

"All the details," Sally added. "Jessie just said that

Alex found a cat and you took her home. She told me to pump you for information. So consider yourself pumped."

"Who's Alex?" Cecily asked.

"Our school-bus driver."

"Romeo?" Cecily's eyebrows shot up dramatically. *"Romeo* found your cat?"

"Romeo?" Sally asked, frowning.

"Yeah," Cecily answered her. "That's what the clerks call him. Because he's so gorgeous. Gee, Liz, wait'll I tell them that Romeo is a hero."

Liz rolled her eyes. "It's nothing like that. I mean, he didn't leap a building in a single bound or anything."

"So what happened?"

"There was a stray kitten in the parking lot yesterday. He found her and I took her home. That's all."

"How could that be all?"

"It just is."

Sally scowled. "That's a boring all."

"Life is often boring," Liz said mildly.

"But did he talk to you?" Cecily persisted. "Did he look into your eyes and swear undying love? The clerks will want to know. And if you don't tell them something graphic, they'll make something up. This is such great daydream fodder. It'll keep them going all year."

Sally shook her head. "You've got it all wrong. Alex isn't the type to fall instantly in love. He's waiting patiently for his Ms. Right."

"Well, damn." Cecily pouted. "The clerks will be so disappointed."

"Besides, he's not only Greek-god gorgeous, he's also incredibly nice." Sally looked pointedly at Liz. "You'd like him. He thinks deep thoughts and watches Public Television."

Liz nodded. She remembered how concerned he'd been over the fate of the stray cat. How he'd carried her heavy book bag, and opened the car door for her. "Yes, he is nice," she admitted.

Sally and Cecily pounced. "Then you did talk to him?"

"Of course I talked to him."

"Well, what did he say?"

"We talked about the kitten. I agreed to take her home. He told me that if I couldn't keep her, he would. End of discussion. Oh . . . he also carried my book bag to my car."

Sally's eyes narrowed. "What are you not telling us?"

"Nothing. Only that you're right—he is very good-looking. He also seemed to be very nice."

Cecily snorted. "You're hopeless. The most lusted-after man in this town finds a cat for you and all you say is that he seems to be nice."

"Tell us about the kitten," Sally prompted.

"She's more of an adolescent," Liz said. "Probably nine or ten months old. She's tall and thin. She loves to bash things around. She yells a lot. And she plays with her food."

"What did you name her?"

"Julia."

"Aha," said Cecily. "You named her after your hero, who is also tall and thin and plays with her food. How appropriate."

"Jess said you were bringing her in to the vet's tomorrow morning," Sally said slyly.

"For a checkup, and to start her on her shots. Make sure she's all right." Liz frowned slightly at the smug expression on Sally's face.

"Well," Sally said as she buttoned up her coat, "I have to be going. I hope Julia enjoys the little mousie. Give her a kiss from her Auntie Sally. Oh," she added with a grin and a twinkle in her eyes, "have a good time at the vet's tomorrow."

Saturday morning, before breakfast, Alex was up and outside with Burl, trying to wear him out a little before they went in for his shots.

Speaking of shots, that little kitty needed to see the vet as well. Alex wondered if Liz the librarian had taken the kitty in. And was the kitty a boy or a girl? What had she named the kitty? He should've called the library yesterday to find out. He'd have to call this afternoon. Suddenly, an image of Liz the librarian floated around inside his brain; Liz the librarian holding the scruffy stray cat close. It was a nice image. Very peaceful and quieting. He stood for a moment, letting the image settle itself into his mind.

Burl came up behind him to give him a nudge toward the back door. Time to go in, he was trying to say. Time for breakfast. Alex took Burl in, and the image of Liz came along, too.

Burl waited impatiently for his big bowl of dog chow. Burl always waited impatiently for his food.

As Alex set the dog food down, he glanced at the clock. It was already nine. Time for a shower and breakfast. No telling how many of the roads had been plowed yesterday. He needed to leave in an hour. It was nice of Jessie to call and remind him that Burl needed his shots, he thought. He'd have to remember to thank her.

"And you'll meet Dr. March, and Jessie, and maybe Suzette, and Woody. You'll like Woody. He's a candy-striper cat. He takes care of all the cats and dogs who have to stay overnight at the clinic."

But Julia wasn't listening. She had her full attention on the bowl of cat food. The bowl of disappearing cat food. That cat seemed to inhale her food. It couldn't possibly be good for her digestion. Well, Liz sighed, maybe it was from being a stray and having to eat whatever was at hand whenever it was available.

Liz stepped back to look at the cat. She still looked like an alley fighter—but at least now she was a clean one. The cut on her chin was healing. Julia looked up at Liz. Julia yelled. Liz looked at the bowl. It was empty. Again. Honestly, where did this cat put all this food? Liz filled the bowl yet again. Julia rubbed against her ankles in a show of feline gratitude. Then she attacked her food. This cat sure loved to eat.

That gave Liz an idea. Yesterday she'd put the cat carrier, with its door open, in her living room, so Julia could explore it and feel comfortable with it. Maybe if she put food in it Julia wouldn't have a problem riding in it. A cat loose in the car, even a cat like Julia, wasn't safe. And who knew what other cats and dogs would be at the vet's. A cat carrier was the safest thing.

She brought the cat carrier into the kitchen. She set it down near Julia. Julia, still intent on her food, ignored her. Ignored the cat carrier. "You sure have a one-track mind when you eat, don't you?" Julia didn't answer. "Good kitty; you don't talk with your mouth full."

Liz pulled the door to the Hartley Animal Hospital open and maneuvered the cat carrier inside. Suzette, the receptionist, looked up from the front desk. "Hi, Liz. Is this your new kitty?"

"Hi, Suzette." Liz set the carrier down on the counter and glanced around. There weren't any other clients at the moment. "This is Julia. Named for Julia Child." She opened the door. "Julia, do you want to come out and meet Suzette?"

From inside the carrier, Julia yelled. Then she stepped carefully out and onto the counter.

"Hello, baby," Suzette crooned.

Julia, obviously knowing a good thing when she saw it, turned on the purring charm and did the rubbing act.

There probably hadn't been many good things in her life until now.

"I know we're early," Liz explained, "but I wanted to give us plenty of time in case the roads were messy."

"That's okay," Suzette crooned to the cat. "This gives me a chance to meet sweet Julia." Then she looked up. "Oh, that reminds me." She punched a phone button and spoke into the speaker. "Jessie, Liz is here with her new kitty."

"I want to make an appointment to have her spayed as soon as possible. I need an appointment on a day when I have the next day off so I can stay home with her."

"Sure thing," Suzette said, still nose-to-nosing it with Julia. "Just let me know your work schedule and I'll take care of it."

A few minutes later, Jessie came down the hall, a wide grin on her face. "Hiya, Liz. And this must be Julia."

Julia left Suzette and shoved her face at Jessie. "My," Jessie said to the kitty, "you are a friendly little extrovert, aren't you? What happened to your chin?" Julia purred and pushed against Jessie's hands.

"I think she must have been kicked by some cretin," Liz explained. "She eats like a wolf, and she's terrorized the catnip mouse Sally gave her."

"Poor kitty probably had to catch mice to live on," Suzette said. "It's a lucky thing that Alex Hogan found her."

"You know Alex?" Liz asked in surprise.

"Oh, yes," Suzette said, her eyes shining in rapture.

"Isn't he gorgeous? He has one of Karen Matheson's rescue dogs. In fact—"

"Suzette," Jessie interrupted her with a teasing smile, "let's not drool all over the counter. Why don't you go see if Melissa is ready to see Julia and Liz."

"Sure," Suzette answered. "Sorry. I didn't mean to drool."

"Why," Liz asked when Suzette had gone into the back, "does everyone start to salivate the moment Alex Hogan's name is mentioned?"

"Because we all appreciate beauty, and Alex Hogan exactly fits the breed standard for perfection in the human male."

"What about temperament?"

"Ah, yes." Jessie looked thoughtful, still petting Julia. "The continuing discussion of form vs. function. Alex also happens to have a superb temperament. He's the kind of male who most definitely should be bred. By the way, have you ever heard Tanner Dodge talk about this very thing? No? Well, someday when you're converted to dogs, you'll have to take one of his beginning obedience classes."

"I'm a cat person," Liz pointed out.

"Well, that's okay. Some of my best friends are cat people. And some of my best friends are also cats," Jessie added, scratching Julia's ears.

"She looks about nine months old, wouldn't you say?" Liz watched Melissa March's deft hands examine her cat, looking in her eyes, using an otoscope to look into her ears, checking her teeth.

"Nine months looks about right," the vet agreed. "Her color looks good," she added. "Eyes look healthy; her ears are fine. Her teeth are in good shape. I don't see any problems there. The cut on her chin is superficial, and it seems to be healing without infection."

"She eats constantly," Liz said. "Maybe it's to make up for her time on the streets."

"Cats normally eat until they're full," Melissa said. "Unlike humans," she added with a quick grin.

"She also plays with her food, which is why I named her after Julia Child. I want to get her started on shots and make an appointment to have her spayed as soon as possible."

Melissa hooked her stethoscope into her ears to listen to Julia's heart. She stared straight ahead at nothing as she concentrated, moving the round, flat end from place to place, listening all the while. "Sounds good," she said at last. She held Julia in a standing position while she used her other hand to palpate her abdomen. She frowned.

"What's wrong?" Liz asked hastily.

Melissa didn't answer, her hand still palpating, a frown of concentration on her face.

A thousand possibilities flung themselves around Liz's brain. She'd lost Skillet to cancer. She didn't want to lose Julia, too. Not yet. Not before they'd had a life together.

Finally Melissa looked up, this time with a smile. "I don't recommend spaying her any time soon, Liz. She's pregnant."

Liz felt the earth tilt. Julia was pregnant? "She's only a kitten," she protested dumbly.

Melissa shrugged slightly. "She's around nine months old. This time of year, stray cats often go into heat. I felt at least three kittens. Right now they're about the size of small walnuts. Pretty soon they'll be surrounded by amniotic fluid, and it'll be more difficult to feel them. This may be why she's been eating like a wolf." The vet nodded to the syringes on the counter. "I'd prefer to wait until after the kittens are born before starting her on shots, but I would like to do a blood workup—make sure she doesn't have FIV or leukemia, both of which would be nasty for the kittens."

"Kittens," Liz said faintly.

"At least three of them." Then the vet broke out in a huge grin. "Congratulations, Liz, you're going to be a grandmother."

"Hello there, you great big burly guy," Jessie greeted Burl with a vigorous belly rub. Burl groaned in bliss and swished his tail around. "And hi to you, too, Alex."

"Nice to know where I stand," Alex answered her with a broad grin.

"You want me to rub your belly, too?" There was a twinkle in Jessie's eye.

"No thanks," Alex answered, matching her teasing tone. "I'll let Burl enjoy it all to himself."

Burl's eyes were closed in rapture. Jessie put her cheek on the big dog's head. "You're a great guy dog, aren't you? Emphasis on great, as in big."

Burl started to drool. Alex whipped out a rag and wiped his mouth.

"Say, Alex," Jessie said, still rubbing Burl, "I heard that you rescued a cat the other day."

Alex felt himself blush. "It wasn't a rescue. It was just a stray kitty who was wandering around the library parking lot. I didn't climb into a burning building or anything like that."

"Still, you did the right thing by finding her a great home."

"Her?"

"Julia," Jessie announced smugly. "Liz named her after Julia Child, who is her absolute ideal."

"You know Liz?"

"I think half the town knows Liz. Besides, she's been one of our regular clients since she moved to town a couple of years ago. She lost her cat to cancer a few months ago, which is why we're all so glad she has another cat now. She also brings us edible goodies, so we think very highly of her. She's crazy about cooking, you know, which is probably why she named Julia after Julia Child."

Alex felt a rush of relief. Odd, how he'd had a sense

of protectiveness for this kitten, wanting to make sure it was okay. If the staff at the vet clinic knew Liz, and spoke well of her, that was a good sign.

"Well, speak of the devil," Jessie said casually. "Here're Liz and Julia now."

Alex looked up, and she was there. Liz the librarian, with the kitty, Julia, in her arms. She looked stunned.

"Are you all right?" he asked her.

"What?" she mumbled. "Oh. I'm fine. Fine."

"How's Julia?" Jessie asked.

"She's pregnant," was the faint answer.

Then Melissa was there, a big smile on her face. "Liz is going to be a grandmother," she said proudly.

"But she's just a kitten," Alex protested. Without thinking, he reached for Julia. Liz handed her to him. Julia snuggled in his arms and purred smugly, her eyes closed. He stroked her smooth shiny fur. She seemed to be very well cared for.

"Kittens do have kittens," the vet answered. "Just like children sometimes have babies. Maybe it's not the best thing, but it's certainly not a reason to despair. Hello there, Burl. You're here for your shots, are you?"

Burl ambled over to one of his favorite people and leaned against her, promoting himself another belly rub. "Say, Burl," Melissa said, "do you like kitties? I bet in a couple of months you'd love a little kitten to play with. Whaddya say?"

"When someone is rubbing his belly, he'll agree to

anything," Alex pointed out. Still, the idea of taking one of the kittens appealed to him. Especially a kitten that purred as loudly as Julia did. "So, Liz, if you need help finding homes for the kittens, just let me know. After all, I sort of helped you get into this." He passed Julia, still purring loudly back to Liz.

"All right," she said, faintly, reaching out for her cat. She still looked for all the world as if she'd been sideswiped.

"See," Jessie said a few minutes later, "I told you Alex had the perfect temperament."

Liz was sitting in the clinic staff lunchroom and Julia was exploring the small area. "It never occurred to me that she might be pregnant." She felt off-kilter. She felt as if the planet had just tipped over.

"These things do happen, you know," Jessie said cheerfully, handing her a cup of coffee. "Here, drink this. You'll feel much better. Now, about Alex . . . "

Liz took a sip. "Thanks, Jess. This is good coffee."

"You're ignoring me. Listen. When he's not driving a bus, he makes rocking chairs. We—the clinic staff—commissioned him to make one for Peter and Melissa when they got married. And M'liss, Karen, Sally and I are having him make one for Sylvie and Ray for a baby present. They're lovely. You ought to see them some time. His chairs, not Sylvie and Ray. Rocking chairs are so comforting, don't you think?"

"Sure," Liz said, not really paying attention to Jessie.

"Sure they are, Jess." She was busy watching Julia and trying to imagine three little walnut-sized kittens swimming around inside the skinny feline belly.

Jessie sighed dramatically. "You're hopeless. I give up. I assume Melissa gave you lots of information about nutrition for kitties who are with child. Or should I say, with kitten?"

Liz nodded. "She's so skinny."

"Who, Melissa? Oh, you mean Julia." Jessie set another treat on the floor in front of the kitty. Julia swatted at it, then scrambled after it all the way across the room. "Wait till her kittens are due," Jessie said cheerfully. "We'll have to hang a sign around her neck that says 'Wide Load.'"

Burl was pronounced to be in excellent health and given the appropriate shots. "I remember," Melissa said, scrubbing Burl's head, "when I first met Burl. He'd just been rescued and was in pretty bad shape. His toenails were so long, they curled around and almost cut through the pads of his feet."

Alex nodded soberly. He remembered, too. "Karen said he was so filthy that she had to give him several baths before he was clean."

"And his coat was so matted, we had to clip most of it, then we found sores underneath the mats." She hugged the big dog. "You were a mess."

Burl licked her cheek.

"Yes, I love you, too."

This was one of the many things Alex liked about Melissa March. Not only was she a good veterinarian, but she truly loved the animals she took care of. She treated them as if she valued their friendship, and Alex knew that she did. No wonder Karen recommended her so highly.

As he and Burl were leaving, he saw Liz with the cat carrier in her arms, as if she wanted to hold Julia close, even in the carrier. Liz was getting into her car.

"Liz," he called.

She looked around. The stunned look was gone, replaced by something thoughtful. "Hello again," she called back, watching him as he and Burl crunched over the snow toward her.

Suddenly he felt the need to get to know her better, to not let her drive off again. "I was wondering," he said, "if you don't have anything planned for today, if you'd like to stop somewhere for a bite of lunch." He watched her consider. "I'd like to know how the kitten is getting along," he said.

Chapter Three

Liz blinked for a moment. Lunch? It seemed like such an ordinary thing to be talking about after learning that Julia was with child. *Enceinte.* In a delicate condition. In the blessed state of motherhood. Going out to lunch was so prosaic. Still, he looked so concerned, as if he also had a stake in what happened to Julia. Well, he did; after all, he'd found her first. So, she smiled at last, a wan smile she was afraid, but a smile. "I don't want to leave her in the car in the cold. I'll tell you what: Why don't you come home with me and I'll fix you lunch?" If he was truly the nice person everyone said he was, she was certainly in no danger. And after all, she was too old for anyone to think she had designs on him. Which she didn't, she told herself firmly. He was much too young. Even if he was charming.

"I don't want to put you to any trouble."

"No trouble," she said breezily.

"If you're sure."

"Of course I am. That way you can see Julia in her new habitat. What do you like to eat?"

"I like everything. Even vegetables," he added with a grin.

"Some of my best friends are vegetables. And I cook them," she teased.

He looked uncertainly at his dog for a moment. The dog was in the front seat of his truck, staring out the window, totally unconcerned about what was going on.

Liz sighed softly. Everyone here seemed to love Burl, and Karen's dogs had a reputation for being well behaved. Still, she was unused to dogs in her house. "Why don't you bring your dog as well."

The relief on his face was almost palpable. "He'd be fine waiting in my truck." What a nice man. He was giving her an out. But just the fact that he did give her the out made it impossible for her to take it, no matter how much she wanted to.

"It's too cold for him in your truck."

He rewarded her with a blinding smile. "Ma'am, he's a Newfoundland. He loves cold weather."

It was yet another out. But confirmed cat person though she was, she'd have to cope. "I'm sure he'll be happier inside with us. As long as he doesn't eat pregnant kitties." She wondered if Julia Child had ever had great big dogs in her house. She wondered if her Julia knew what a dog was. Right now, in the cat carrier in her arms, Julia showed no interest in the big fellow, but what would she do if he was in her house? They'd have to wait and see.

"So, Julia," she said driving home through the snowy streets, "he's coming over for lunch. What can I make? Omelets are too cliché. Quiche is too garden party." Besides, she added to herself, Alex Hogan was truly a real man. "He said he likes vegetables. I wonder if he likes vegetable soup," she said to Julia.

Julia, in the cat carrier, didn't answer.

With Burl on the seat beside him, Alex followed Liz to an older neighborhood. An established neighborhood, close to the library, close to the shops. He followed her to her house, a small cottage-type house, set back from the street, with a porch and a trellis. She probably grew flowers up it in the summer.

He frowned as he watched her steer her car through the tracks in her unshoveled driveway. Tire tracks in the deep snow. If she had to work all yesterday she probably hadn't had time to shovel. He lived too far away to drive his tractor plow all the way to her driveway or he'd plow it for her. He did, however, have a shovel in the back of his van. It was part of his winter equipment. He'd stocked his van for winter just last weekend. He parked on the street. No sense in adding more tire tracks to the driveway. They were more difficult to shovel. Besides, he was going to shovel her driveway and he didn't want his van in the way.

"C'mon, Burl. We're here."

Burl clambered out of the van, gave himself a great shake and looked up at him questioningly.

"No, we're not home; we're visiting. You'd better be on your best behavior. Don't put your feet on the table, no matter what the provocation." Though he knew, intellectually, that dogs didn't understand complex sentences, he would swear that Burl understood every thought he had. Every nuance, every shade of meaning. "And don't you even think about chasing the cat," he cautioned. "She's pregnant. We need to take care of her."

Burl looked away, as if offended that Alex would even suggest he'd do such a thing.

"Come in," Liz called from the front steps, where she was holding the cat carrier in one hand, her purse in the other.

Alex hustled up the driveway, though the deep snow. Burl, however, took his own sweet, lackadaisical time. Alex got up to the front steps and reached for the cat carrier. "Here," he said. "Let me take this for you."

"Thank you," she said, surprise in her voice, "but it's not heavy."

"That may be so, but let me carry it for you anyway."

She raised her eyebrows. He noticed they were delicate and the same shade as her hair. The color of well-seasoned rosewood. Rosewood was a hard wood—he didn't think she was a hard woman. In fact, she seemed as soft as pine, and as warm as maple.

"Please," he said. "Let me carry it for you."

Then she glanced down at the cat in the carrier, and her face softened. "Thank you," she said simply.

"Any time." And every time. He believed in carrying packages for women. And bags of groceries. And book bags—even when they were full of bricks. The cat carrier, however, was not heavy at all. "You haven't been formally introduced to my dog. This is Burl the Newfoundland. Burl, this is Liz the librarian."

"Hello, Burl the Newfoundland," Liz said gravely.

Burl waved his tail. Burl loved people.

"Does he shake hands?"

"Yes, but only if you have a cookie to give him as a reward. But I wouldn't recommend you do that now. His feet are wet and snowy."

Burl, knowing he was being discussed, swished his tail agreeably.

"Did you name him after Burl Ives?"

"No," he told her with a grin. "A burl is a growth on a tree trunk that's used to make things such as bowls. They start out rough, but with a little work, they end up being beautiful."

She thought for a moment. "They told me you worked with wood. That makes sense," she finally said. "Well, Burl, you're the first dog who's come to visit me in my home."

"I've warned him to be on his very best behavior."

"As long as he doesn't chase Julia, he should be fine."

"I think he will." But once in the kitchen, he put Burl on a down stay, just to be sure.

Julia, liberated from her cat carrier, made a big show of creeping up to Burl to check him out. He reached his head out to sniff her. She swatted him with her paw. He twitched his tail. She wiggled her behind and pounced. Burl moved his tail slightly, so she missed. Julia pounced again. Burl moved his tail again, grinning a doggy grin all the while. He knew what was going on.

"They're playing," Liz said in wonder.

"It looks that way, doesn't it?"

Julia left Burl's tail and went to rub, purring, up against his head. He reached out with his tongue and swiped Julia, knocking her down. Julia got up, ran back to him. He swiped again, knocked her down again. Again she got up and rubbed against his head.

"I guess Julia has been around dogs before."

"Newfoundlands are not at all aggressive," he explained. "Some of them never even learn to growl. They were bred to rescue people from drowning."

"You sound like Jessie," she said with a grin.

He grinned back. "I'm a dog person. But I like cats."

"I'm a cat person." But that's all she said. Then, "Oh, my. Here. I'm sorry. Let me take your coat." She hung his coat on a hook by the door. "Do you like vegetable soup?"

"Sounds wonderful."

She moved around her kitchen, opening cupboards and bringing out mixing bowls, whisks and measuring cups.

"So," he said, "tell me about Julia's kittens. Isn't she a little young to be pregnant?"

"Evidently not. Dr. March said she could feel at least three kittens. They'll probably be born in about six weeks. Kittens. Imagine that."

"Do you still want to keep her? You didn't bargain on a pregnant cat. You looked a little shocked back there at the clinic. If it's too much—"

"No." The word was sharp and sudden and fierce. She reached out toward the cat, as if to protect her. A mama bear with her cub. "No," she said again more softly. "She's my cat now. Aren't you, Julia?"

Julia, still stalking the swishing tail, ignored her.

"She's my cat," Liz repeated, turning back to her bowl and whisk. "And she'll be just fine."

"Does she need special care? Because she's so young."

"I need to make sure she gains weight properly. That won't be a problem, though. She eats like a horse. I'll probably take her in for more checkups, just to make sure everything is okay. But that's for my peace of mind, rather than her health."

While she worked, he looked around at her kitchen. It was sparkling clean and very functional. A breakfast nook with a built-in table and benches, painted white with bright green accents, was at one end. There was a picture window over the table that looked out onto the backyard. Above the benches, there were built-in shelves that were crammed with books. Cookbooks mostly, and several videos of—he squinted to see the titles—Julia Child. There was also a stack of books on the table. "Is there something I can do to help?"

"Not a thing. Just keep an eye on the critters."

He glanced at the critters. Burl had stretched out on his side. Julia had given up on Burl's tail and was now under his chin, giving herself a bath. "They seem to be fine."

She turned on the oven.

He frowned. "You bake soup?"

She chuckled. It was a warm sound, inviting him to join. "No. The oven is for the muffins."

Muffins. How homey it sounded. The word *muffin* was soft and round, comforting. Muffins were good. He liked muffins. Come to think of it, he liked Liz the librarian. He liked her direct way of looking at him, he liked her calm, and he liked her kitchen. She would be a good friend.

Liz poured the muffins into the tins, aware that he was watching her, yet unbothered by it. Of course, if she were one of the young and nubile clerks, she'd be a mess. It was a good thing she was too old for such non-sense. "Haven't you seen anyone pour muffins before?"

He appeared startled.

"You were watching me so intently as I poured the muffins," she said as she slipped the tins into the oven and set the timer.

"No, I was just thinking. Sorry."

"No need to apologize. We all need to think once in a while. It keeps our brains flexible." She tossed him a smile. "I've even been known to do it myself once or twice."

"Why did you become a librarian?"

The question threw her off-balance. It was not what she expected at all. And his question was not asked flippantly. He looked like he wanted an answer. "Because I can't imagine a life without books. I'm lucky that I have a job that I love so much. Except for the paperwork," she admitted. And Attila, she added to herself. She realized she was holding a knife. It was a sharp knife. Julia Child said to make sure your knives were always sharp. Hmm. Sharp knives and Attila. Now there was a cheerful thought.

She opened her refrigerator and brought out carrots, potatoes and leftover chicken in a good stock. She rinsed the vegetables and began to chop. "Why did you want to become a school-bus driver?"

"It started out to be temporary."

"Temporary?"

"While I built up my business."

"Jessie says you make rocking chairs."

"And cradles. Yes. I sell them at craft shows, and I ship them around the country."

"You said bus driving started out temporary. Is it still?"

He cocked his head. "I may keep it. I happen to love it."

70

She plopped a chunk of butter in a large pan and turned the burner on low. "What do you like about it?"

He grinned a bit shamefacedly. "This may sound corny, but I like knowing I'm keeping the little kids safe on their way to and from school."

"You like kids?"

"Yes, I do. Someday I'm going to have the perfect American family. Two-point-five children, Burl— Newfoundlands are legendary with children, you know—and a cat. And a wife, of course."

Liz could hear the seriousness underneath his light tone. So Alex Hogan was looking for a wife. Now there was a wonderful thought—being Alex Hogan's "missing piece" and waking up every morning next to him. His golden head on the pillow, his tawny skin next to the white of the sheets. She dropped her whisk into the butter. Maybe, she thought as she fished the whisk out, she should introduce Alex to the clerks.

"You want two-point-five children?" she asked. "What is a point-five child?"

He chuckled. Why, she thought, did it have to sound so intimate? Why did she have to be too old to do anything about it? There was simply no justice in the world. Ah, well. Better concentrate on making a good meal. If she couldn't do anything about his children, point or otherwise, at least she could feed the man.

* * *

They chatted easily through the making of the soup, through the buzzer announcing that the muffins were finished. Liz turned away from her stirring to clear the books off the table and swoosh down a snowy table-cloth. Then she set the table with matching soup bowls and bread-and-butter plates from Williams-Sonoma, and tall Pfaltzgraf glasses. She lined her muffin basket with a linen cloth and tipped the piping-hot muffins in.

"Smells good," he commented, a smile breaking over his face. "I haven't had a home-cooked meal in a long time."

"Any time you want home cooking, just let me know," Liz said without thinking. Then she stopped. Oh, no. It sounded like she was being pushy. She tried to explain. "I love cooking. Since I live alone, there's no one but me to cook for." Somehow that sounded worse. She bent her head down to stir the soup again, hoping he thought her red face was from the heat of the stove. "I'm sorry. That sounds forward. I didn't mean anything salacious."

"I know you didn't," he said.

But somehow that was worse. It made her feel old enough to be his mother. Which she was, but she didn't have to remind herself. She felt as if she were twenty-eight, trapped in a forty-year-old body.

"You're sure there's nothing I can do?" he asked.

"Yes, I'm sure, and no, there isn't. So just keep an eye on the critters for me."

"Burl is sleeping, and Julia is washing her face."

But Julia left her washing and stomped over to Liz. She stood on her hind legs and stretched her front feet up toward the top of the counter. Then she sat down and yelled.

"You're hungry. Why is this not a surprise?" Liz asked.

Julia yelled.

Liz opened the cupboard to get the bag of cat food. She'd had Julia for three days, and the bag was almost empty. She'd have to go shopping tomorrow for more cat food. She poured some into the cat bowl. Julia attacked it with a great gusto. Then Liz glanced over at Burl. He had opened his eyes and was watching her every move. He was also drooling.

"He won't try to eat her food, will he?" she asked.

"He'd better not," Alex said. "He's had his breakfast."

"But his eyes are so mournful," Liz said. "He looks so sad."

"He's just trying to win your sympathy. He's very good at it."

Liz looked into Burl's great big dark doggy-brown eyes. He looked so very hopeful, and so hungry. "Does Burl like dried cat food?" she asked. "Can't he have some? Just as a little snack. I'm sure Julia won't mind sharing."

Alex chuckled. "Okay. But just a little bit."

"Let's see. If the kittens are born in about six weeks, then they'll be ready for their new homes in about three and a half months. I'll help you find homes for them," he offered. "In fact, Burl and I would like one of them."

She looked at him in surprise. Then she wondered, *why am I surprised?* He likes cats; he was willing to take Julia. "That would be lovely," she said.

"Then it's settled."

"Then all you'll need is a wife and your two-point-five children." Suddenly, it seemed personal, talking about his having a wife. Liz felt herself envying the woman, whomever she was.

Julia, finished with her food, leaped gracefully onto his lap and curled up, her motor on high. Liz watched for a moment as Alex ran his large hands over Julia's small body. Julia stretched up her chin so he could better scratch. He obliged. His hands were rough from working with wood, but they were also gentle. He'd give a cat a good home. He'd give anyone a good home, she thought. In fact, he looked right at home here, in her kitchen. He looked as if he belonged.

The soup was done. She got out the hot pad and carried the hot pot over to the trivet on the table. "Lunch is ready," she announced, totally unnecessarily.

"It looks very nice," he commented, nodding his head in approval.

Liz felt a blush swarm up her neck and face. "Thank you," she managed. *"Bon apetit!"*

After lunch, Alex insisted on helping with the dishes. "You cooked—let me clean up," he said.

74

"It's no problem," she said.

"Before lunch, I didn't know you well enough to insist that you let me help. But now I do. So, lady, consider yourself helped."

Actually, there wasn't much to cleaning up. Liz opened the dishwasher and peered inside. She rarely used it. "I usually wash dishes by hand, since it'd take me about a week to use up enough dishes for a full load."

"Then we'll do them by hand. Do you want to wash or dry?"

Liz felt her whole self smile. "Whichever you prefer."

"I don't prefer," he said with a grin. "That's why I'm asking you."

After the dishes had been washed and put away, the pot scrubbed and the leftover soup put in a storage bowl, Liz found herself dawdling. She didn't want this to end, she realized. She so enjoyed his company. It had been a very long time since she'd enjoyed a man's company this much. She glanced over at Alex. He was sitting at her table again, next to the window, looking out into her backyard. Then he turned, a glint in his eye, a grin on his Greek-god-gorgeous face.

"I'll tell you what. Let's go sledding." He looked eager and excited. Suddenly, Liz got a fleeting glimpse of what he'd looked like as a young boy. He's still young, she reminded herself wryly. But he's no boy, she answered. Even with all of his charm, there was a mature sensuality surrounding him. Oh dear, she thought. Better not think about sensuality.

"Sledding?" She hadn't been sledding since college, and that was more years ago than she wanted to think about.

"Sure. Haven't you gone sledding at Kedrick Park?"

She shook her head.

"At the back of the park there's a hill. Great for sledding."

She smiled, wanting to join in his enthusiasm, but not sure how. "I haven't gone sledding since I was in college."

"Then it's about time you did. I have a couple of sleds at my house. We can drop Burl off and grab the sleds and go. Burl would love to come, but he gets too excited."

Liz glanced doubtfully at the big dog. He had his great big head on his great big feet and was asleep again. Julia was batting at his tail. Burl excited?

"Get on your warmest clothes and let's go." Alex's enthusiasm was contagious. Liz felt a niggle of excitement slither up her spine.

"Okay," she said.

Chapter Four

Alex changed into his snow clothes, told Burl to guard the house, took the two sleds down from their hooks on the wall and shoved them into the back of his truck. Then he got into the warm cab next to Liz. Liz who looked lovely in her cranberry red parka and scarf and hat. She had the bottoms of her jeans tucked into her boots. She looked ready for action. Almost.

"You don't have snow pants."

"Don't own any," she replied.

He stared at her legs for a moment, thinking. He didn't want her to get wet. He wanted her to have fun. "Okay," he said at last. "This is what we're going to do. Sledding is no fun when you get wet and cold. So you'll wear my snow pants."

"But what about you?"

"I have an old pair that I keep forgetting to toss out," he said.

She frowned. "I don't want to put you to any trouble."

"You wearing my pants is no trouble." He grinned at her. He watched her blush until her cheeks matched the cranberry color of her hat. He shrugged out of his parka and slid off his snow pants. He held them out to her. "They go over your jeans," he said. "They'll keep you very warm and dry."

She slid the snow pants on, somewhat uncertainly. He reached out to help her adjust the shoulder straps. He had to brush back her hair to reach the buckles. The softness of it hit him like a hammer. It sent waves of awareness through him, over him, washing into all the corners of his soul. He realized he was standing closer than necessary to do the buckles. When had he gotten this close? She was looking up at him, her eyes wide and gray, her eyes open, inviting him in, having nothing to hide, no guile, no artifice, no deceit.

Since his teenage years, Alex had put up with girls wanting him for his looks. Most of them made no pretense about it. All they wanted him for was his body. He found them completely unappealing. But Liz was no girl—no little chickie, looking for a good time with the good-looking guy. Liz was a lovely woman, warm, full of depth. Liz was seasoned, like a fine piece of wood, full of body and character. Chairs made of such wood would last a lifetime.

78

"Is something the matter?" she asked, her voice breaking into his silence.

He shook his head. "No," he said. "I was just thinking for a moment." He quickly adjusted the straps for the buckles.

"You seem to do a lot of that," she said, a teasing glint in her gray eyes.

"It's a good thing to do," he agreed.

"So where are these old snow pants of yours?"

"What? Oh. They're inside. I'll be right back." He stopped at the door into the house and looked back at her. "Do you have gloves? Or mittens?"

She pulled a knitted something from her parka pocket and held it up. "Yes, I do."

He nodded. "Then you'll be warm."

She grinned. "I might not be able to move, but I'll be warm."

He smiled to himself. She was very warm. He liked her warmth.

Kedrick Park was at the edge of town. In the summer, large trees gave shade to the dozen or so picnic tables there. A playground was located near the tennis courts. There was a bandshell for free summer concerts by local bands, and the lake was a popular place for ice skating in the winter. And then there were the sledding hills. And a plowed parking lot, full mostly of minivans.

"Lots of sledders today," Liz remarked as Alex carefully maneuvered his truck into the last empty space and nosed it up against a man-made snowbank.

"It's a perfect day for it," he pointed out. "Bright sun, lots of freshly fallen snow. And it's Saturday."

Alex opened the back of the truck and slid out the sleds. He looked at them, doubt clouding his face. "Should we take both of them?"

Liz didn't know enough about sledding to have an opinion. "What do you think?"

He shoved one sled back into the truck. "Nah. We'll just have to share."

"Okay," Liz said brightly, not wanting to appear too eager. "You're the sledding expert."

He locked his truck, slipping the keys deep into his parka pocket. Then, pulling the sled behind him, Alex reached out a hand to Liz. "Ready for your sledding experience?"

He was only holding hands with her to keep her from slipping, she told herself. He was that kind of guy. So she took his hand. It felt big. It felt warm. It felt good. Even if it was just to keep her from slipping. "Let's go," she said with a smile.

The hill was crowded with people of all ages. Some were on their sleds on the way down the hill, alone or in pairs. Some were pulling sleds back up, followed by others trudging up behind them. Some were at the top of the hill, hovering over smaller children; some were at the bottom, holding their arms out to their little ones as they swooped down.

"Howie!" A familiar screeching voice assaulted Liz's ears. "Get back here! You know you're not supposed to go down without your sister!"

But Howie Sherman, known to the library clerks as the oldest Screech kid, ignored his mother as he hurtled himself and his sled down the hill.

"Howie!" his mother screeched after him.

"Howie!" screeched the oldest Screech girl, stomping her feet in a fury.

"Hi, Mr. Hogan," chorused a group of giggling young girls.

Alex smiled down at them. "Hello, Robin, and Kaitlyn, and Angie. Are you having a good time?"

The little girls giggled in embarrassment and glanced at each other, as little girls do when in the presence of their heroes. Evidently, Liz thought, they all had giant crushes on Mr. Hogan. And just as evidently, Mr. Hogan was aware of it and, bless him, treated the girls as young ladies. Angie caught her gaze, and her little eyes widened. "Hi, Ms. Hadley," she said in surprise.

"Hello, Angie." Liz truly liked the little first-grader, who was the stepdaughter of Dr. March.

"Robin and Kaitlyn, do you know Ms. Hadley from the library?" Alex asked.

The little girls nodded, giggling. "She helps us with our homework sometimes," Robin answered.

"That's a good thing to do." Alex grinned down at her. Liz caught the grin and felt her insides start to turn to mush. *Stop it,* she said sternly. *Get a grip. Remember you're almost old enough to be his mother.*

"Are you girls here with your folks?"

"We're here with Kaitlyn's mom," Angie said. "Robin's mom is at work, and Melissa and my dad said they needed some adult time this afternoon."

"And we're with Kaitlyn's brother," Robin added. "But right now he's hogging the sled."

Kaitlyn nudged the other two. "There he is, coming up the hill. Let's go get the sled. It's our turn now." And they were off to waylay Kaitlyn's brother.

Liz watched them go. They were such nice little girls. The kind of little girl she'd have wanted to have.

Alex, holding up a hand to shield his eyes from the brightness of the sun reflecting on the white of the snow, took the measure of the hill. "Looks like we're in a good place to be." He took his gloves out of his pockets. "Ready for your first trip down the hill?"

At his direction, she settled on the sled. Then he climbed on in back of her, his legs on the outside of hers, his arms around her. She closed her eyes for a brief moment. No, she told herself sternly. This is just the way people sit on sleds together. There's absolutely nothing personal here.

"Hold on," he said in her ear. She could feel his

cheek pressed to the side of her head. "Let's go!"

And they were flying.

"Look! It's Ms. Hadley and Mr. Hogan," came a voice from behind them as they were pulling the sled back up the hill.

"Look!" Alex said back to the young boy with a grin. "It's Joshua Martini."

"Hey, Ms. Hadley. I got a good one for ya. Where does the king keep his armies?"

Liz, glad for the interruption, stopped her trudging and wrinkled her forehead in thought. She was seriously out of shape if one little hill made her huff and puff like the Big Bad Wolf. Alex, on the other hand, was seriously in good shape. Not a single huff. "Hmmm. On the battlefield?" Joshua's obsession with telling jokes was well known in town. He'd tell jokes to anyone and everyone. "No? Then where?"

"He keeps his armies in his sleevies!" The little boy chortled and whooped in glee. "In his sleevies!"

From beside her, Alex groaned. "That's a good one, Joshua."

Little Joshua laughed so hard, he fell onto his sled, and with a shove of his feet, he started off down the hill. "See ya later!" he hollered to them.

"What a happy child he is," Liz said, wanting just another few seconds before they continued up the hill. It was much steeper coming up than going down. Must be some law of physics. "I've known him since I came to Hartley three years ago, and I've never seen him in a bad mood."

"How did you meet him?" Alex asked over his shoulder as he started up the hill again.

"He came into the library to ask where the joke books were." She chuckled, an out-of-breath sound. "By now, he knows where they are, but he still asks." Huff and puff. "It's become a ritual between us. I think he just likes the interaction. And he wants someone to laugh at his jokes." Huff and puff. "How do you know Joshua? Is he on your bus route?"

"Yes. And believe me, after he tries his jokes out on you, he gives them to me. That kid knows more jokes than anyone I've ever known. Someone ought to publish his brain." He turned back to look at her with a grin. "You all right there?"

"You can hear me imitate the Big Bad Wolf?"

He reached down. "Let me give you a hand."

"I'm not that feeble," she protested. But she took his hand. It helped.

He grinned at her. "Of course not. You're just not used to the up part of sledding."

"But the sledding down part is so nice. Why don't they make sled lifts?"

Then they were at the top of the hill. "Let's do it again!" she said.

"Even if we have to walk up the hill again?" he asked, a teasing tone in his voice.

"It's worth it. Even without sled lifts."

So they went down again. And again. And again. Each time, Liz reveled in the ride. Reveled in the feel of his arms around her. In the swooshing sound of the sled on the snow. In the slowing slide to a final stop when Alex hopped off and offered his hand to help her stand. Or even when they tipped the sled and tumbled, laughing and tangled together, into the snow. Oh, she liked sledding.

"Your cheeks are all red," he told her. They were once more at the top of the hill, but there was a smile on her lips and a sparkle in her eyes.

She rubbed her cheeks with a mittened hand. "I can't feel them at all," she told him with a grin.

"How does the rest of you feel?" he asked, then he grinned at himself. He already knew how the rest of her felt. He'd had his arms around her. The rest of her felt very nice.

"The rest of me is fine." Then she frowned. "Except for my feet. They seem to be revolting."

He quickly scanned the throng of people. Ah, there they were. "Look over there," he pointed. "One of the local scout troops usually sets up a hot chocolate stand. Can I get you some?"

She closed her eyes for a moment. "That would be lovely," she said. "Nothing like hot chocolate on a winter day."

He shifted the sled rope to his left hand, then held his right out to her. "Let's go." And they started off through the maze of people.

"You're from the library," a young child said to Liz.

"Yes, I am," she answered the child with a smile. "Are you having a good time sledding?"

Liz seemed to smile a lot, he thought. Her smile was a genuine smile, an open smile, an invitation to smile back. And the young child smiled back.

He was amazed. She knew almost as many of the people as he did. He knew the kids from his bus routes, and he knew some of their parents. But she said hello to people of all ages. "How do you know so many people?" he asked.

"They come into the library," she said simply. "Hartley is a town where people use their public library. We don't have to bribe them to come in. They do it on their own." She grinned up at him. "Even if I don't know their names, I know who they are."

"Do you know what they all read?" he teased.

"Sure do," she said saucily. "But don't ask me, because I won't tell you. It's confidential."

He liked the way she was able to be completely and naturally at ease with people. He liked the way she knew who she was, and wasn't afraid to be herself. He nodded to himself as he watched her greet yet another Hartley Library patron. Yes, he liked Liz. He liked the intelligence that shone from her eyes, along with a definite lack of snobbishness. He liked her attitude that the world was peopled with friends she hadn't met yet.

He slammed his truck door and turned to look at her on the seat beside him. "Did you have a good time?" he asked. He knew the answer, of course; no one could possibly miss it. But he wanted to hear her say it anyway.

"I had a marvelous time. Thank you so very much for taking me this afternoon." Her eyes glowed.

"You're so very welcome," he answered lightly. "I had a good time, also."

She sighed and settled against the back of the seat and looked out the window. "To think I've lived here for three winters and have never gone sledding. I never knew what I was missing."

"Where did you live before this?"

"I grew up in Arizona. No snow."

He was puzzled. "What made you want to come to Hartley?" He knew why he was in Hartley. He was here because it was a small city that felt like a small town. He was here because Hartley had a good school system and was a great place to raise a family.

"Kathryn Leslie, you probably know her from school. We grew up together. She talked me into moving to Hartley. Besides, I wanted to experience snow. Up close and personal."

It was said with a grin, but he could tell by the slight tension in her cheeks, by the tone, which was just a hair too cheerful, that there was something more. That whatever it was, was not a topic for discussion. So he didn't push. Instead, he returned her grin as he started his truck. "You sure got up close and personal with snow today. I hope it met your expectations."

"Every one."

Chapter Five

Julia greeted her at the door, yelling and demanding food. Now.

"Okay, sweetie. I'll feed you. Let me take off my—oh. I forgot to give Alex his snow pants." She looked at the unoffending snow pants still on her legs, still keeping her warm and dry. She'd have to return them to him, of course. She'd have to call him to—she didn't know his phone number, but she was a librarian. She would simply treat this as a reference question.

Julia yelled, interrupting her train of thought. Julia was not impressed by kidnapped snow pants. Julia wanted food.

"Okay, okay, little Julia. Give me a second to get these things off." She peeled off her outdoor clothes and hung them over the kitchen chairs to dry. Julia hustled into the kitchen after her, insisting that the world was unfair to poor kitties.

Liz scooped cat food into Julia's bowl. Julia gobbled it up, all the while making little growly noises mixed in with snatches of purr. This was one noisy, raucous cat. She wondered if the kittens could hear Julia's insistent voice. People always said that babies could hear their mother's voices.

Liz leaned against the counter and watched her cat eat. Her pregnant cat. She pressed a hand to her own flat belly. A belly that would never grow a child. It was so grossly unfair! She'd have made a good mother.

Stop wallowing, kiddo, she told herself. *You have a good life. You have a career you love—except for Attila. You have a lovely house in a lovely neighborhood. You even have a new cat. In a couple of weeks you'll have kittens. This is not something to be pitied. Or wasted, pining after something that can never be. So, as the Mary Englebreit character says, snap out of it!*

"All snapped," she said quietly. "Well, Julia, it looks like I'll have to expend all my mothering instincts taking care of you. What do you think about that?"

Julia kept her attention focused on her food.

The phone rang. Liz picked it up.

"Elizabeth, dear." It was her mother. Of course it was her mother. If she wallowed for a moment, then her mother called, probably wanting to add salt to the wound.

"Hello, Mother."

"Why, Elizabeth, you don't sound happy."

"Nonsense. I'm fine. How are you?" Maybe she could distract her mother. "How's Dad? How's the weather out there today? We had a huge storm here the other day and ended up with about a foot and a half of snow. Of course, the library was still open. But the snow looks lovely. And—"

"That much snow? Oh, Elizabeth, you know we worry about you up there, driving in it. You know how many accidents are caused by slippery roads. I know you're a careful driver, but all those other people . . . "

"People up here know how to drive in snow, Mother," Liz said dryly. "They're used to it."

"Yes, but you aren't. Don't you think you've been there long enough? Your father and I think it's time for you to come home."

"This *is* my home, Mother. Besides, I like it here."

"Everyone always asks about you. Why, just the other day I saw Richard with his new wife." Aha, thought Liz. So this was the real reason she'd called. But her mother went on. "They're expecting another baby soon and they both looked radiant. This will be their fourth child, you know. I just can't help think-ing"—her mother's voice grew sort of weepy—"it should have been you. Maybe if you'd seen better doctors . . . "

"I had good doctors, Mother." Liz closed her eyes, thinking it would help shut out her mother's strident tones. It didn't. She could still hear her mother as clearly as ever.

"Well, Richard asked about you. He is such a nice man."

"Yes, he is a very nice man." He was. He just wanted children. His own children. She couldn't blame him for that. "Listen, Mother, I have to go now. I have something in the oven. Give my love to Dad, and I'll talk to you later, okay?"

"But Liz—"

"I have to go now, Mother. 'Bye."

"Liz, dear, wait . . ."

Liz replaced the receiver. She hated lying to her mother, but once her mom got started, she didn't quit. First it would be how nice Richard was, then how sad it was for Liz not to be able to conceive. Then, finally, she would start on the Great Tragedy of it all. How all her friends had lots of little grandchildren while she had none. How Liz's childless state was the Great Disappointment of her life. Liz could practically hear the capital letters.

Julia was finished with her food, for now at least. Liz scooped her up and carried her into the living room. The cat in her arms, she plopped down into a comfy chair. Julia cuddled in her arms and turned on the purr charm.

"So, Julia, what do you think my mother would have said if I told her I was going to present her with at least three grandkittens in a few weeks?" She held her hand on Julia's belly, feeling the vibrations of her purring, imagining little walnut-sized kittens inside. They were probably vibrating, too. "Grow well, little babies. Julia and I will take care of you." She wondered if there were kitty Lamaze classes.

The phone rang.

Liz sighed. At least it probably wasn't her mother again. Still cradling Julia, she heaved herself out of her comfy chair and over to the phone.

"Liz!" came a shriek on the line. "You creep! Why didn't you tell me you have a new cat!" It was Kathryn Leslie, elementary school music teacher extraordinaire, best buddy, and fellow cat person.

"Because I just got her a couple of days ago and I had to work yesterday, while you school-type people got to stay home in your warm beds. Then I had to take her to the vet's this morning, and I went out this afternoon and just got home. And that's all I've done. But how did you know I got a cat?"

"That's not all I know. I heard from Mrs. Calloway, who heard from Kaitlyn Elliott's mom that you were sledding this afternoon with Alex Hogan. This was after I'd heard from Sally Foster that it was Alex who gave you the cat. So here you are traipsing around Hartley with the Hunk of the Century, and you don't even bother to tell me about it. So what gives, huh?"

"I'm not traipsing around Hartley. I ran into him at the vet's and . . . he . . . I made him lunch. Then he invited me sledding at Kedrick Park. I really don't call that traipsing."

"But," came the wailed reply, "you could've at least told me." Then she dropped her wail and was her usual cheerful self. "So tell me now about the cat."

"Her name is Julia, and she eats like a horse. Melissa says she's about nine or ten months old. She's not very pretty and looks like a purebred alley cat." Liz propped the phone between her ear and her shoulder so she could pet Julia to keep her purring. "Oh, yeah. In about six weeks she's going to be a teenage mom."

"Really!" Kathryn gasped. "How wonderful! Oh, I can't wait to see her! What are you doing tonight?"

"Nothing, but—"

"Good. I'll be over in time for dinner. You haven't eaten yet, have you?"

Liz laughed out loud. "One of the joys of having best friends is that they feel perfectly comfortable in inviting you to make dinner for them."

"Only when the best friendee is a gourmet cook. So listen, I'll bring the movie and popcorn, and you'll bring the fireplace and the VCR. And dinner. Sound good?"

"Sounds great."

"Do you want *Truly Madly Deeply?* Or *Yentl,* or *To Gillian on Her 37th Birthday?*"

"You're in the mood for a good cry?"

"They're all movies about leaving the past behind," Kathryn explained enthusiastically, "and getting on with your life."

"So you think a little video therapy is in order here?"

Liz teased. "You think someone needs to leave a past behind?"

"And get on with your life. You sure do," came the cheerful reply. "So I'll see you in a few."

"I left my past behind when I came to Hartley."

Kathryn sighed loudly and dramatically. "No, Liz, you packed it up and brought it with you."

"Hi, kiddo," he said into the phone. "It's your big brother."

"Alex!" his sister Sharon exclaimed. "How are you? I saw on the news that Ohio got hit pretty badly by that snowstorm. I bet you gave your tractor plow a workout. And all of your elderly neighbors love you."

Alex grimaced. He'd forgotten to shovel Liz's driveway. He'd have to do it in the morning. "Yes, I plowed their driveways," he said with a grin. His sister knew him very well. "They closed school yesterday, so I spent most of the day working on the cradle for your little *El Niño*." Alex lifted the curtain to watch Burl roll in the snow in the backyard.

"Well, this little *El Niño* is going to make an appearance pretty soon. You're gonna to be an uncle again."

"How soon? Isn't it early?" He dropped the curtain.

"Not much. Doc says the little guy looks pretty healthy."

"Make sure you call me immediately. Are Mom and Dad going to be there?"

"Mom said nothing will keep her away." He could

94

almost hear the smile in her voice. "You know how she is. The benefits of living across town from them. Don't worry, Alex. Everything will be fine. I promise."

"But you're my baby sister. I have worrying rights." He opened the back door and Burl ambled casually in.

She laughed. "Women have been having babies for a few years now. I think we've got the routine down pat. Honestly, you're as bad as Dave. And remember how nervous Arthur was when Shelby had her first baby?"

"Will they be driving in to see the baby?" Alex pointed to the floor and Burl sank down. Alex propped the phone up with his shoulder so he could towel Burl's wet fur. Burl grunted with pleasure.

"Not yet. Their little darlings are getting over the chicken pox. All three of them. Poor Shelby. They're not coming near *El Niño* until that's long gone. Probably Mom and Dad's party. But don't worry. Dave has all his camera stuff packed and ready to go, with about a gazillion rolls of film. In case he runs out." She chuckled. "Speaking of said party, you better be here, big brother, or I will personally—"

"Personally what?" He stopped toweling. Burl lifted his head and gave him a pointed look. He swiped the dog with the towel again, but his attention was on his sister.

"I don't know. But it will be a good one, whatever it is. We didn't see you much at all this summer, and Thanksgiving and Christmas are always so crazy that it's not a good time for nice visits. So you're long overdue."

Alex was silent for a moment, pondering the real reason he'd called his sister. He could chicken out now. Or he could tell her. "I met someone," he began.

"You did!" she squealed. "Who is she? How did you meet her? When are you going to bring her home so we can meet her?"

"Hold on." He laughed. "I don't know how serious it is, or even if it's going to be serious. I just met her the other day."

"But you like her," his sister prompted.

"Yes, I do."

"Why?" his sister asked promptly. "What is it about her that you like?"

"For one thing," he said dryly, "she's the only woman I've met recently who doesn't turn red and stammer when I'm near."

"That's because you're so gorgeous," was the smug reply. "Gets women every time. They're so in awe of your good looks that that's all they can focus on."

"Knock it off," he said, rolling his eyes.

"It's the truth. You don't think Shelby and I watched it happen over and over when we were growing up? You don't think we got sick and tired of hearing all the other girls gush about how studly you were?"

He sighed in exasperation. "That's nonsense."

"It isn't, you know. But I'll change the subject. So if this woman doesn't turn red and stammer, what does she do?"

"She treats me like I'm a normal human being."

96

Sharon chuckled. "Good for her. She's obviously brilliant."

"She's a librarian."

"They're smart, aren't they? Sitting around books all day? So, is she beautiful?"

He thought for a moment. "She's not a beach babe. But she has a classic look. I guess you could say she's striking rather than beautiful. I think she's older than I am." He paused for a moment to think, then he said, "She has that certain air of maturity that younger women lack."

"So what? Susan Sarandon is older than Tim Robbins."

"Who?"

Sharon snorted. "Susan Sarandon and Tim Robbins. Honestly, Alex, if you'd get yourself to a movie theater once in a while you'd know who they are. And Linda McCartney was older than Paul. Age isn't such a big thing anymore."

Alex was silent for a moment.

"You're thinking about this biological clock thing, aren't you?" his sister said. "You think your clock is ticking and you're running out of time."

"It feels like I am."

"Nonsense. You're only thirty. Men can have babies for a long time. Didn't Picasso father kids in his eighties? Or was that Pablo Cassals? Someone with Ps and Cs in his name. Look, you're not over the hill, so quit worrying about it. Oh—I just got it."

"Got what?"

"You think that because this woman is older than you are that she's over the hill? That she can't have babies."

"That's not—"

"Alex, my very dear big brother, I love you, but you're not very smart sometimes. The reason you get married is to have a marriage. If all you want is a little chickie who can bear your young—well . . . " she sputtered. "Well, you're being stupid. There's a lot more to it than that."

Alex leaned back against the sofa and closed his eyes. "Yeah, I know," he said.

"Well, if you know, then don't let it bother you."

"I won't." But he didn't know if he could.

"Okay, I've calmed down now. I apologize. You're not just another dumb stud muffin. I bet you did know all that stuff all along. You just needed me to affirm it, right?"

"Right," he agreed.

"Am I right in assuming you want me to keep this to myself?"

He shuddered. His family did not make it a secret that they couldn't wait for him to get married. "Keep it under wraps. At least for now. At least until there's something to tell them."

"You got it. Look, I gotta go. Literally. The little *El Niño* just kicked me in the bladder. Oh, the joys of the third trimester."

"I love you, little sister."

"Love you, too, big brother."

Burl clambered up onto the couch and planted his big head on Alex's knee. He tried to promote himself a scratch. Alex obliged.

"Well, buddy," Alex told him, "you're lucky you don't have to worry about things such as biological clocks. And that you don't have little sisters who try to boss you around." Burl grunted and waved his front leg in the air so Alex would scratch his belly. "Let's just see what happens, shall we? After all, Liz might not be the right woman. Even if she does have a cat. And she likes to cook. And she's intelligent." Burl closed his eyes in bliss.

After a few more scratches, Alex heaved himself off the couch and into his workshop. He stood before the cradle he was making for Sharon and Dave's little *El Niño*. It was a lovely piece of work, he thought. Sharon and Dave would love it. But when would he make a cradle for his own child?

Chapter Six

Liz woke to a scraping sound. What in the world? She propped herself up on an elbow to listen more closely. Beside her, on the pillow, Julia stretched languorously, making herself look longer than she really was. The scraping sound came again. Then again.

She climbed out of bed and padded over to the window to look out. She squinted against the blinding brightness of early morning sun on snow. Her eyes were scratchy this morning. Then she saw his truck parked at the side of the road. What—Then she saw Alex, bundled up against the cold, shovel in hand. The man was shoveling her driveway.

Liz cocked her head in thought. She was stunned and delighted all at the same time. That was such a thoughtful thing for him to do. She whirled her bathrobe around herself and headed down the hall to the front door.

"Good morning!" she called, sticking no more than her head out into the cold.

He looked up. "Hello."

"You're shoveling my driveway," she said unnecessarily. Then she flinched. What a great conversationalist she must be.

"I figured you didn't have time on Friday, and yesterday I took you sledding, so I decided to do it myself. I hope you don't mind."

Liz opened her eyes wide. Was the man for real? "Mind? Not at all. I think it's wonderfully kind of you." A puff of frigid air made its way down her throat. She pulled her bathrobe tighter. She thought quickly. Milk, eggs . . . Yes, she had enough. She even had strawberry preserves. "Then let me make something warm for you, for when you're finished." Julia shoved her face out the door. Liz scooped her up. "Julia would like it, too."

His grin was as bright as the sun. "I learned early that one does not turn down an invitation of food. Thanks." He surveyed her driveway.

"It should take me about half an hour."

"Great. Come on in when you're finished."

He raised a hand in agreement, then turned back to his shovel and her snow.

She had a half hour. Well, first things first.

She scooted into the kitchen and to the refrigerator for two eggs and a carton of milk. Julia wound herself around her ankles. Liz looked down. "You think you should eat first? Well, we must have consideration for pregnant

101

mommies." She poured cat food into Julia's bowl. Julia eyed it for a moment. "What? Are you becoming a finicky cat?" Julia attacked the food. "I guess not."

Liz reached into a cupboard to bring out her blender. And into another cupboard for the tins. She turned the oven dial to 450. Oh, yes, butter. She measured out three tablespoons of butter and set it in a small bowl in the microwave to melt. Then she broke the eggs into the blender, added a cup of milk and a pinch of salt. She scooped in a cup of flour. The microwave dinged. She poured in the melted butter and turned on the blender. The blender trick she'd learned from one of Julia Child's baking programs on Public Television. The blender whirred for a few moments; then she turned it off. She greased the tins—generously, she reminded herself—then poured the batter. While she waited for the oven to get up to temperature, she swiped the counters clean, then brought out a cut-glass bowl for the strawberry preserves. When the oven was hot, she carefully set the tins in to bake. She adored popovers. They looked so homey and were incredibly easy to whip up.

Julia leapt gracefully onto the counter. Liz picked her up. "You know, I really shouldn't let you up here."

Julia closed her eyes and purred.

"You know you found a sucker, don't you?"

Julia settled deeper in her arms. Julia was a lap cat.

Alex stuck the shovel into the snowbank he'd finished creating, then leaned back to gaze up at the sky. What a beautiful day. A perfect day for doing anything outdoors. The sun was warm, the air brisk. Perfect day for making a snowman. Or a snow family. Liz had a small front yard, so a large snowman would be overwhelming. Still, something like a child or a dog would be nice. No, she was a cat person. He'd never made a snow cat, but that didn't mean he couldn't. He was an experienced snowman builder, a skill he fully intended to pass on to his children.

Well, the driveway was shoveled. Liz had said something about food. Alex smiled to himself. The woman liked to cook, did she? Well, he liked to eat. He carried the shovel back to his truck and slid it in. He turned to study the house for a moment. Probably built in the fifties. It was a nice house, comfortable looking, though it was small. A house for one person, two at most. So Liz didn't look to a day when she might have a family. A thought struck him—maybe she did have a family somewhere. She couldn't be that old, could she? Maybe she was seeing another man. He'd noticed tire tracks from a second car when he was shoveling. But somehow he didn't think so. She was too willing to go sledding with him yesterday to be seeing someone else.

The door opened. Liz, with Julia in her arms, stood in the doorway. "What are you waiting for? Come on in. It's almost ready."

He went. Into her house. Into her home. Into warmth and comfort. "Something smells good," he said.

Her eyes twinkled at him. "I hope you like it."

He glanced around. "Where can I wash up?"

"Second door on the left. There should be a clean towel on the rack."

Her bathroom was very female. Pink soap, pink towels. One of those gold-rimmed soap dishes. Only one toothbrush in the holder. *Stop it,* he told the reflection of himself in the mirror while he washed his hands. *Quit trying to check the lady out. Next thing you know, you'll be looking in her medicine cabinet for a man's razor. Quit trying to rush it. Just see what happens.*

He splashed cool water on his face. Shoveling was hard stuff.

The kitchen was as welcoming now as it had been yesterday. So was Liz's smile. Julia lay stretched out in a spot of sun, in the middle of the floor. He had to step over her. "Hello, Julia," he said.

Julia ignored him.

"She thinks she's queen," Liz commented.

"Isn't she?" he quipped.

"Ha, ha," Liz answered with a smile.

The oven buzzer buzzed. "Time," Liz sang out. Reaching into the oven, she pulled out a pan of cups with—"I hope you like popovers," she said as she set the pan on top of the stove and quickly tipped the cups, one by one, into a cloth-napkin-lined basket.

He was sunk. The woman was wonderful. "I haven't had popovers for—I don't know how long."

"Then it's too long." Liz carried the steaming basket

to the table. "Sit here," she directed him. He sat, still under some sort of gastronomic spell.

"Butter, strawberry preserves. Unless you're one of those odd types," she teased, sliding into the opposite seat, "who eat popovers with honey. I have that also."

He broke open a popover. Steam poured up. He slathered it with butter. "This is excellent," he told her, spooning preserves into the buttery insides. He took a bite. It was heaven.

"Popovers are comfort food," she said.

"Comfort food?"

"You know, food that makes us feel nurtured. Like bread pudding, or homemade soup."

"I like bread pudding. I like soup."

He watched her lick a bit of errant strawberry preserves off a finger. "Let's see. Hot chocolate is comfort food. And pot roast."

"Not for a vegetarian," he pointed out, reaching for another popover. "And certainly not for the cow."

"That's right, I forgot. Well, then, how about hand-mashed potatoes? There's real comfort food for you. Oh, and *pots de crème*."

"Pots de what?"

"It's a kind of custard made with heavy cream." She sighed rapturously. "It's the best. You can almost feel it clog your arteries."

"Then why eat it at all?"

She opened her eyes wide. "Because," she explained, "it's too good to miss. Besides, once in a while it can't hurt you. I've tried making custard with skim milk and those cholesterol-free eggs. Trust me, it's worthless." She set down her butter-encrusted knife and folded her arms primly on the table. He had a feeling he was in for some of her philosophy.

"What's the point," she said, "of eating food that's tasteless, even if it's allegedly good for you? Eating should be a sensual experience. The appearance of the food, the scents, the way it feels in your mouth. All of these should come together to create a pleasurable event. Not just something you do because your body needs amino acids and proteins."

She sat across from him speaking of physical pleasure, yet she did it comfortably. Once more he was struck by the difference between Liz and the other women he had met. Liz was a woman. All the others were girls. Nice, perhaps, but unformed.

"Why are you staring at me?" Liz asked. Then she continued before he could say anything. "Haven't you ever thought about food and the part it plays in our lives? Most people grab some pseudofood at the local burger joint and call it a meal. Maybe they don't know any better. I hope they don't know what they do. Your popover is about to drip strawberry preserves on my tablecloth. And you're still staring." She cocked her head and her gaze met his.

He quickly swiped at the preserves with his tongue. But this time he paid attention to the flavor, the texture of the sweet stuff. "I had never thought about food that way," he said slowly. "I never knew anyone who was passionate about food. I've always thought food was nice and pleasant, and made a mess to clean up." He took another bite of popover, this time allowing himself to concentrate on the buttery flavor.

"Aha." But she said it gently, with a smile in her voice and eyes. "You have a faraway look in your eyes. Can it be that you never really tasted a popover before? Don't you see how much better it is if you eat it slowly, taking the time to enjoy it? Savor it. Take it in your mouth and swirl it around with your tongue." Her eyes were teasing. Her lips were trying to hide a smile.

Alex felt warm. He felt a tightening in his groin. Alex felt good.

"Lady," he said, softly, looking into her eyes, "you sure know how to cook."

"And I love to shop for delicious food. Scrumptious food. And cook it for people who will appreciate it."

"Trust me, I appreciate it."

He watched, fascinated, as her lovely gray eyes grew infinitesimally larger. Suddenly she seemed to be holding her breath, and he knew he was holding his.

Splat! A splot of preserves plopped onto the tablecloth. Julia had landed in the middle of the preserves. She was yelling.

"Oh, no!" Liz cried. She scooped up the cat. "Julia you rascal. Oh, you're getting preserves all over my shirt. Oh, dear." She sent a rueful glance at Alex. "So much for the sensual enjoyment of preserves. Now they have cat prints all over."

Alex chuckled. "At least the butter is safe. And the popovers."

"Well, eat them now. They're no good heated up. Popovers are truly a thing of the moment. Look here, Julia, your street manners don't work anymore. You can't jump up on the table while people are eating. It's rude." She held Julia close and spoke softly to her. "How are you going to teach your babies about manners if you don't have them yourself?" Then she looked up at Alex. "Of course, she probably doesn't have a clue that she's going to have babies. Probably doesn't even know what they are."

Alex helped himself to another popover, broke it open and buttered it generously. "You should have seen Burl when I first got him. He was two years old. Imagine a hundred-seventy–pound dog who had never lived in a house, wasn't housebroken. He didn't know a single word. Not even a name. I don't think he even had a name before I got him."

Liz's eyes grew wide again, but this time he could tell it was from astonishment, not something else. He didn't want to think about what that something else was. "You mean," she said, her voice full of astonishment, "you mean—where did he come from?"

"Some kind soul saw how he was being treated by his owner and called someone who called someone who called Karen Matheson. She, according to Jessie, went halfway across the state to get him. She said it took about five baths to get him clean." Liz was still staring at him. She'd forgotten to pet Julia. So he continued. "His toenails had never been cut. They had curled around and were beginning to cut into the pads of his feet. He had a difficult time walking."

"Why, that's awful!" Liz burst out. "Poor Burl." She scrubbed Julia's head gently.

"Dogs live in the moment, like popovers." He made his tone light. He shouldn't have bogged her down with the story of Burl's earlier life. Even if he'd just told her the tip of it. "He doesn't sit around thinking about it. Dogs are incredibly forgiving." He smiled at her. "He has a name now, and a home."

"You love him."

"Yes. I love him and he loves me. We're family." The beginning of his family.

Liz, ignoring the strawberry preserves, hugged Julia to her. "It's beyond me how anyone could treat an animal that way," she whispered into Julia's fur. Julia wiggled to get free. Liz checked the gash on her chin—it was much better—and released her. Julia leapt down to the floor and began the process of cleaning her feet.

"The sad thing is," Alex said, "that Burl isn't the only dog or cat who's lived like that. Ask Karen to tell you some of her rescue stories. They're enough to break your heart." He looked thoughtful.

What a nice man Alex is, she thought. Sally had said

he was incredibly nice, and she was right. It was a special man who could give his heart to an abused dog like that. What would it be like to be loved by such a man? She imagined he would love fiercely, protectively and loyally. A woman would be lucky above all others to have such love. Well, Liz decided, she'd have to keep tabs on him to make sure whatever young thing he ended up with was good enough for him.

"Will you please eat that last popover?" she asked. "I have more preserves." She stood and moved over to the refrigerator to pull out the jar of preserves. "You'll have to spoon it from the jar, though." She pulled a silver spoon from the drawer and brought it to the table.

He chuckled. "I promise I won't be offended." Then he stopped and truly looked. "Homemade preserves? Ma'am, did you make these yourself?"

She decided to ignore the *ma'am*. "Picked them, too. With these very hands. Last June, Kathryn Leslie introduced me to a strawberry u-pick-it place southwest of Columbus."

"I'm impressed."

"Don't be. Preserves are so easy to make."

He spooned some preserves onto the last popover. "Could you make preserves blindfolded?"

"With one hand tied behind my back." She grinned at him. "You look like you're sure enjoying that."

He smiled a smile that was downright beatific. "I sure am," he said, and took another bite. "I sure am."

She sat back down at the small table. She'd wait till he was finished before she started clearing the table. She didn't want to rush his obvious enjoyment. She liked watching it too much.

"One of the sorry parts of living alone," she said, "is that there's no one to enjoy your food."

"Any time you want to cook for someone, lady, I'll be happy to oblige."

She liked his calling her *lady*. It made her feel feminine. Made her feel as if something a whisper away from intimate was happening between them. But that must be her imagination, because she was much too old for him. Certainly he knew that, and she certainly did. So that part must be wishful thinking. He probably was just being friendly.

She carried the plates over to the sink. "No, stay there. Relax. You've been shoveling snow all morning. Play with Julia. She doesn't look as gaunt as she did when we found her," she said, the *we* coming naturally.

"She looks much cleaner." He chuckled. He reached into his pocket and pulled out his keys. He dangled them, jiggling, enticing Julia to play.

Liz reached onto the shelf over the sink for a cat toy, one that looked like a fishing pole with feathers dangling at the end. "Here. She goes nuts for this."

Alex cast the feathers and Julia, as predicted, went crazy. She leaped and pounced and galloped and gamboled and batted. She had a great time. So, Liz thought, watching them while she cleaned up the dishes, did Alex.

Alex fit into her home so completely. He was so at ease here, as if he belonged. *Oh, no,* she told herself. *Don't go there. You're not going to keep him, so don't even bother toying with the idea. He's not a stray. He has his own home.* But she could feed him. Then he'd keep coming back.

"Do you have plans for this afternoon?" he asked her. Julia pounced on the feathers. He gently pulled the toy out from under her and dangled them again.

"I was going to build a fire, curl up and read a book."

"Sounds peaceful," he said, whipping the feathers from Julia at the last instant. He dangled them just out of her reach. She crouched down and did a little wiggle dance. She leaped.

"It is peaceful."

"Good book?"

"Biography of Julia Child."

"Ah, the French chef." This time he dragged the feathers slowly across the kitchen floor.

"Did you know that she was in Ceylon and China working for the Office of Strategic Services during World War Two? The OSS was the forerunner of the CIA, you know."

He blinked. Somehow he couldn't see Julia Child as a spy. "Did she wear an apron and carry a cleaver?"

She grimaced. "I'm serious. She is a very interesting person. I've learned so much from her cooking shows."

"Then I must thank her, for I, also," he teased, "have benefited from her cooking lessons. Indirectly."

She gave him a tolerant grin.

"Still," he continued, "peaceful as that sounds, reading in front of a fire, wouldn't you like a little more adventure in your afternoon? After all, there's time enough for doing things in front of fires when the sun goes down."

"What kind of adventure?"

She hadn't asked about doing things in front of fires, which was a good thing, because he might have been tempted to tell her. He allowed Julia to catch the feathers. "How good are you at building snowmen?"

"Snowmen?"

"Why sound so incredulous? Haven't you ever built snowmen before?"

"I grew up in Arizona, remember? I've never built a snowman in my life."

Now it was his turn to be incredulous. "Lady, you can't go on living without building a snowman. It's not to be allowed. In fact, I think there just may be a law against it."

She glanced out the window into her backyard. It was a nice backyard, he thought, though rather small for snowmen.

"Let me take you over to my house and we can build snowmen. I have a perfect yard for it."

"But you just spent the morning shoveling snow out of my driveway. You must be worn out."

He flexed an arm. "Still works. I can rest when I'm ninety-four."

She broke into a smile. "You're serious."

"Absolutely. I'm a champion snowman builder. Made dozens of them every winter with my family. Wouldn't be winter without snowmen."

"Don't ever move to Arizona."

"So, will you come make snowmen with me?"

He could see her waver. Could see the hesitation in her face, in her eyes.

"I promise you'll have a terrific time."

What was she weighing? What were her pros and cons? How could he tip the scales in his favor? "Tell you what. I have a fireplace, too. So, bring your book, and if you decide you really don't like building snowmen, you can go inside and read. Deal?"

She broke into laughter. "That would be rude, wouldn't it?"

"Not at all."

She finally shrugged. "Okay."

"Be sure and wear my snow pants. They'll keep you warm."

She started. "Oh. That's right. I'm glad you reminded me. I'd completely forgotten."

He hadn't forgotten. In fact, he'd purposely not mentioned it when he drove her home yesterday, so he'd have an excuse to see her again.

"It'll take me a couple of minutes to get ready. Make yourself at home. Play with Julia. I'll be right back."

First it was sledding, Liz thought as she shimmied into her thermal T-shirt—white with pink flowers—now it was snowmen. The man obviously had a thing about snow. She topped her thermal shirt with a turtleneck, then a plaid flannel shirt. She liked to be warm. Her body wasn't used to this much cold. Before she moved up north, she'd never even owned a winter coat. She pulled on an extra pair of socks. Her mother kept saying, "Elizabeth, you'll freeze up there; you'll be sorry you left Arizona and want to come back." She hefted another pair of socks, considering. For three years she'd proved her mother wrong. Liz had lots of very warm socks.

She hadn't paid much attention to his house yesterday. She was only there for a couple of minutes, and that was in his garage. Now, as they drove up the driveway, Liz looked around his front yard. It was huge, rimmed with a split-rail fence and lined on the side by tall trees. The house sat far back from the road, a one-story, rambling ranch with a huge garage on the side.

"Have you lived here long?"

"Couple of years. I had to practically sell my soul to get the loan, but it was worth it." He held the truck door open for her. "Let me go inside, put some water on, get Burl and some snowman parts. We'll be right out. Unless you want to come in."

He was standing very close to her, so close that if she leaned just the slightest bit toward him—"I'll wait out here. Get acclimated to the snow." She shot him a grin, pulled her mittens out of her pocket, then headed out to the yard to cool off. Then she stopped and turned back. "Why do you need to put water on? And what are snowman parts?"

From across the garage she could see his eyes twinkle. "You'll see," was all he said, so she trudged out into the middle of the snow, the middle of his yard and prepared to wait.

She didn't have to wait long. Alex, followed by his dog, came into the yard carrying a cardboard box, which he set down in the snow next to her. The flaps were closed, so she couldn't see in. Snowman parts? "The first thing you need to know," he announced, with a twinkle in his eyes, "is that there's an art to making snowmen." He scooped up a handful of snow and packed it round and firm. "You start with a snowball, tightly packed, and roll it in the snow to make it bigger. Let me demonstrate. No, Burl," he told his dog. "This one is not for you."

Liz tentatively held out her hand to the dog. It wasn't that she didn't like dogs, or anything like that. She was a cat person. Still, this dog was friendly, she thought, as he sniffed her mittened hand. He was also huge. The big dog looked at her and held her gaze. Why, she realized in amazement, he was doing it on purpose. His eyes were wise and deep. They had expression! She never knew dogs had expressions like cats did.

"You're not listening to me," Alex said.

She broke Burl's gaze. "Sorry. I was looking at Burl. He's a nice dog." As if to prove her point, she

116

reached out and patted his huge head. Burl leaned his furry body against her legs and sighed noisily. "I'll pay attention now. You were saying that it starts small and you roll it around and it gets bigger?" Then she heard what she'd said. She felt a blush creep up inside her thermals. To hide her red face, she quickly reached down and grabbed some snow to shape into a snowball.

"Look, put it on the ground and roll it around."

"The snow sticks to it!" she exclaimed in delight. "I always knew, intellectually, that it happens, I've driven past yards where kids were building snowmen, but I've never actually seen anyone do this up close."

"Here we go, then. I'll go this way; you go that way."

"Hey, Mr. Hogan, can I help?" came a child's voice.

Liz looked up. It was little Joshua Martini. Where did he come from?

"Sure thing, Joshua. Pick a spot."

Rolling snow was harder than it looked, Liz thought as she stood up and stretched her back. All that bending over, and the snowball got heavy as it got bigger. *Well, of course, you ninny,* she told herself. But somehow it didn't seem right that it should weigh so much. After all, one snowflake weighed nothing, and take a gazillion nothings and you still had nothing. At least, you should. Evidently, snow was magic.

Suddenly filled with a joy she hadn't felt in years, Liz bent down and swooped armfuls of snow into the air. "Wheee!" she cried.

"Hey, Ms. Hadley," Joshua called. "What do Alexander the Great and Smokey the Bear have in common?"

She thought for a moment. "I don't know. What?"

"The same middle name!" The little boy jumped up and spun around in the air. "They have the same middle name!"

That's a good one, Joshua," she called to him. Then she added, "Do you live around here?"

"Yeah," he called back and pointed vaguely. "I live over there."

Pretty soon, another child, this one in a bright blue snowsuit, appeared. The child didn't look familiar, Liz thought. Though there were so many kids who came into the library, it was hard to be sure. "Mr. Hogan," the child called. "Can I help?"

Alex, from across the yard, stood up and looked their way. "Sure thing, Alice. Grab some snow and join in."

Next came a couple of teenagers. Liz had seen them at the library doing homework. They wanted to help, too. Then more kids of all ages, and even a couple of parents thrown in. All making huge snowballs in Alex's front yard. Burl wandered around it all, waving his tail, ready and willing to leap after any stray snowballs that might come his way.

Out of breath, Liz stood up by her snowball. It came to her knees. Then she looked around. And stared, amazed by it all.

"Hi, Liz," a woman said, rolling a snowball up to her and stopping. "It's great, isn't it? Such fun for the kids."

118

She was out of breath also. Liz knew her slightly. She read mysteries by British authors.

"I've never seen anything like it," she said.

"Oh, Alex does this every year. Every time there's enough snow. Somehow the kids seem to know that if there's a big snow, Alex will be building snow people and they can help." The woman rubbed her nose with her mittens. "We'll build lots of snowmen, all over the yard. They'll stay here till they melt. And if it snows in the meantime, we'll just build more. Look, one is going up."

Liz stared at the woman. Then she looked where she was pointing. Sure enough, two youngsters had rolled their snowballs next to each other and were lifting the smaller one on top of the bigger one.

"Liz!" It was Alex beckoning to her from a group of kids, all with large snowballs. "Come on over here and see. We're going to put a big one together." He hauled the cardboard box over and opened it up. Out came— what was it all? Liz wondered. Lampshades, electric plugs, pieces of wood, hats, hunks of cloth, with fringe and without. Some evergreen. A purse. A purse?

"Snowman parts?" she asked.

"Yup." And the lampshade became a hat pulled on over a thatch of evergreen hair. The fringed cloth became a shawl. Working together, they built a snow-man, carving carefully and packing snow around the base to make a skirt.

Then another, and another. And when they were all done, it was just as the mystery reader had said. There

119

were seven snowmen, of varying sizes and genders, all lined up in a row. Each one was different, seemed to have its own personality.

"Where's Alex?" she asked, suddenly realizing he wasn't among them.

But then he was there, carrying a tray of steaming— "Hot chocolate," he called, and was immediately surrounded by the snowman builders. All but Liz. She stood back and watched. She had never known a man like Alex Hogan. She doubted she ever would again. Men like Alex didn't come along very often. Men like Alex were as rare as truffles. She had looked up truffles for a patron the other day. And speaking of work, she reminded herself, here she was, forty years old and, like one of the young and nubile clerks, lusting after Alex Hogan. But while they lusted after his body, Liz was lusting after his . . . his what? His spirit? His mind? His soul? Well, the part of him that wasn't his body. Of course his body was nice, also. And right now that body, that spirit, that truffle of a man was coming toward her, with a grin as broad as all outdoors, a steaming cup held out to her. "Have a cup of hot chocolate?"

Why, oh why, was life so unfair? Why couldn't she be ten years younger and able to—*Stop it!* she scolded herself. *Life has no consciousness, so it can't be either fair or unfair. It's random, and some days you get the short stick.* "Thanks," she said, and wrapped her hands around the hot cup to warm them up. But she kept her eyes averted. She didn't want to show him too much.

That would be the most stupid thing she'd ever done. So she stared down into the chocolate depths in the cup in her hands. "More than thanks, in fact. This has been an incredible afternoon. I have truly enjoyed myself." She raised her eyes, but not to him. She nodded to the row of silent figures. "I have become acquainted with snowmen."

Chapter Seven

Monday morning at the Hartley Public Library. Liz set her book bag down beside her desk. She loved her job, but Monday mornings were not fun. Monday morning meant that Attila would be at the reference desk with her. What joy, she thought sarcastically. Well, maybe today would be different. Maybe Attila would remember that they were there to serve the public, not the other way around. Yeah, and maybe pigs would fly.

Liz pulled out her chair and sat down. She let her gaze drift all around her work cubicle. Books on her desk, on the shelf, a cooking magazine she'd looked at on Friday during her afternoon break. It was all neat and organized. It was familiar to her. This is who she was. She was a professional librarian. She had a career in libraries. She'd worked hard to get through graduate school, then had worked at the library in the town where she'd grown up. Then she came here, to Hartley. The town was different. The snow was certainly different. But the library, other than Attila, was enough of the same to allow her to fit in right away. Library patrons asked the same kinds of questions no matter where they lived. What is the capitol of Hungary? Who won the Olympic bronze medal in ice dancing in Japan? How many chromosomes are in a goat? Where are your books on potty training? And the reference books were the same. The *World Almanac,* the encyclopedias, *Granger's Index to Poetry, Chase's Annual Events.*

Liz was a librarian. She'd grown up surrounded by books. She'd devoured books all her life. Books were as much a part of her as breathing. This was who she was. This was who she would always be.

Then why did she feel so different?

"Well, well, well."

Liz glanced over her shoulder. "Hi, Kendra."

Kendra's eyes twinkled. "So, tell us all about it."

"All about what?"

"Your dates with Romeo. We can't stand it. I almost called you last night when Janine told me, but she said it was probably too late."

"My dates with Romeo?"

"Gee, Liz, for someone as smart as you are, you don't seem to be too bright today. Yes, your dates with Romeo. You were seen sledding at Kedrick Park on

Saturday afternoon, and, according to my sources, he had his hand on your elbow."

"According to your—Kendra, he was holding on to my elbow so I didn't slip!" Liz chuckled at her friend. "And I don't exactly call sledding a date."

"Well, what about building snowmen yesterday? You're seen with Romeo—we're talking Romeo here, not some ordinary mortal—two days in a row and you say these were not dates?" She plastered her hand on her heart. "I'm crushed. Here I thought you were in the middle of the Romance of the Century."

Liz grimaced. "How did you hear about it, anyway?"

"Joshua Martini's mom told Kaitlyn's mother, and Kaitlyn's mother told Janine, and she called me. The grapevine is alive and well in Hartley, Ohio. For social news it's even better than the *Hartley Herald*. Of course, that's not saying much."

"Then get right back on the grapevine and spread the word that there's nothing—I repeat, nothing—going on between Alex Hogan and me. You got it?"

"Now, why is it," Kendra asked the ceiling, "that whenever a woman starts seeing a man, and it starts to turn into the Big Something, that woman tells—no, *insists*—the woman *insists* there's nothing going on? Have you ever noticed this phenomenon, Liz? I bet it has its root in some prehistoric caveman behavior patterns. It's probably genetically encoded in our brains. I wonder if Jean Auel has ever looked into this."

Liz broke out laughing. "And the friends always

124

insist there's something going on when there isn't. This is another strange phenomenon."

"You can deny it all you want, but the clerks are going wild over this one. They're so jealous, it looks like St. Pat's Day out at the desk."

"Tell them there is nothing to worry about. I'm not involved with Romeo. I'm old enough to be his mother." Well, that was a slight exaggeration, but it sounded good. "We're just friends. I hadn't gone sledding in ages; since college, in fact. And I'd never made a snowman before. I grew up in Arizona, remember? So he invited me along. Besides, he found Julia, so naturally he has an interest in her."

Kendra's eyes narrowed in speculation.

Liz tried again. "Honest. I wouldn't lie to you."

Kendra's shoulders sagged. "Rats! We thought this would be the romance to end all romances, and we'd get to watch it unfold." She shrugged. "It was going to keep us going all winter long."

At lunch, Liz was in the break room heating up leftover broccoli chowder in the microwave. Carol, the other librarian, came in and flopped in the chair by the window. She put her hands over her face. "Honestly, Liz. I was just on the reference desk with Attila. You know how he likes to think he's a real librarian. How did he ever get the job of director, anyway?"

"Maybe he knows someone important," Liz suggested. She opened the microwave door and reached in to stir her chowder. It wasn't hot enough yet. She set the dinger for another few seconds.

"Maybe." Carol didn't sound convinced. "We know he didn't sleep his way to the top." She shuddered dramatically. "What a horrible thought."

"Maybe he read all the books on how to go on an interview and get hired." The microwave dinged. Liz took out her chowder and carried it over to the table. "Evidently the board was impressed."

"Impressed by a Darth Vader wannabe? I bet he dressed all in black and the Force was with him."

"The board doesn't care about his black clothes. They care about the fact that he appears to be doing a good job running the library."

"That's because," Carol pointed out, "we run the library while he holes up in his lair."

Alex turned his truck into the Kmart parking lot, making a quick stop before returning to the bus lot and starting on his afternoon run. He had to buy a baby card for Sharon and Dave.

There were cards for every possible occasion. Birthday cards for various ages of celebrants, for various relationships of celebrants. Get-well cards, sorry-you're-moving-we'll-miss-you cards, congratulations-on-your-new-job and congratulations-on-your-retirement. Finally, Alex found the welcome-new-baby cards. He looked them over. He didn't want something cloyingly sweet. But neither did he want a cartoon that described the trials of new parenthood. He wanted a simple congratulations-and-welcome-to-the-world kind of card. That shouldn't be difficult to find, should it? Frowning, he checked the cards one by one. Finally he found one that would do.

Standing in the checkout line, he noticed a young woman two lines over. In her cart a little boy, about two, was playing with a toy car. The woman was visibly pregnant. She looked radiant.

That's what I want, he thought. *I want children. I want a wife who wants children. That shouldn't be difficult.* Choosing a wife is not like choosing a greeting card; you don't settle for one that will do. So far, Alex Hogan hadn't settled.

"I want a book on Morse code," the child announced.

"What do you want to know about Morse code?" Liz asked him. It was four o'clock, and the library was thick with after-school kids doing their homework. At least, *some* of them were doing their homework. Some of the kids were there to allegedly help their friends do their homework. Most of the time, if they were girls, they merely giggled. If they were boys, they leaned back in their chairs and tried to look cool.

"I want to know about Morse code."

"We have lots of different books about Morse code," Liz said calmly. "What kind of book do you need? Do you want to know what it's used for? Or do you want a book to help you learn Morse code? Or do you want to know how and why it was invented?"

The child looked confused. Liz helped him out. "What grade are you in?"

"Third." The child scraped at a piece of tape on his notebook.

"Is this for a school report? Or is it for your own reading?"

"I hafta do a book report on Morse code."

Liz grinned. "Okay. I think we have the kind of book you need over here." Liz led the way through the maze of shelving and finally arrived at the right place. "Here; look at this book. It has a little bit of everything about Morse code. Do you think this is the kind of book your teacher wanted you to read?"

The child took the book gingerly, holding it as if he was sure it was going to explode. But he nodded, grateful to have a book at last. "Thanks," he muttered.

"Any time," Liz answered with a smile. The smile was wasted on the child; he didn't look up to see it. But the smile was habit. Liz liked people. Liz liked helping people find their answers in books. "If you need something else," she told the child, "let me know."

"Okay."

Third-grader, Liz thought as she wound her way back to the desk. Let's see; the child was probably eight years old. If the adoption had worked out, she'd have had a daughter who was about eight years old now.

She'd still be in Arizona, married to Richard. And her mother would've had to have found something else to be the great disappointment of her life.

"You want to know who invented skis?" Liz asked another student. The inventions report was happening at the middle schools. Kids were coming in to find information about the origins of toothbrushes and teabags and Post-it Notes.

"I need a diagram that shows all of a cow's stomachs."

"I need a book about Leonardo DiCaprio."

"Where are the Avi books?"

"How's it going?"

Liz looked up to see Kathryn standing there. "The parking lot is packed," her friend continued. "And you just about need a bulldozer to get through this crowd."

"Monday afternoons at the library," Liz answered. "Traditionally the busiest day of the week. Are you here officially, or did you just want to harass your local librarian?" There was an actual lull in questions at the moment, so Liz could chat. She knew, however, that any lull was subject to immediate change.

"Want to know what time you get off work and if you have any plans."

"Five, and no. What do you have in mind?"

"Dinner at Chile Verde so you can bring me up to speed on the latest, and so that I can bring you up to speed on the latest in my life."

Liz blinked. "There's a latest in your life? A latest that I don't know about?"

Kathryn looked smug. "I'll tell you over Mexican and a margarita. But only if you tell me yours."

"Deal. I'll meet you there a little after five."

Kathryn wiggled her fingers as she meshed back into the crowd.

"I need stuff about the McCarthy Era."

The lull was over.

Liz and Kathryn scooted into the warmth of Chile Verde. "Whew!" Liz muttered. "It's so cold out there!"

"You still haven't adjusted to Hartley winters," Kathryn laughed.

The hostess led them to a table by the fireplace. Liz stood for a moment, rubbing her hands in front of the heat. "Much better," she told Kathryn.

They ordered drinks—iced tea for Liz, a house frozen margarita for Kathryn. Then, munching on a chip dipped in excellent salsa, Liz scanned the menu.

"Whatever you order," Kathryn warned, "save room for the chocolate torte. Have you tried it yet? It's incredible. And it doesn't have any calories if you eat it with a friend."

Liz snorted. "Yeah, right."

"It's true," Kathryn countered, her eyes on the menu. "Sally Foster told me. She says that's why she never eats chocolate alone. Okay. I feel like hot tonight." She turned to the server, who'd appeared with their drinks and a request for their order. "I'd like the Santa Fe Shrimp, please."

Liz closed her menu and handed it to the server with a smile. "I'd like two chicken enchiladas with sour cream, guacamole, and rice and beans."

"You always get enchiladas," Kathryn pointed out when the server had disappeared. "Why don't you branch out and try something different?"

"It feels like an enchiladas night," Liz said with a chuckle. "Besides, the enchiladas are excellent. And take that from someone who grew up in the Southwest."

"And never saw snow in the flesh until three years ago," Kathryn added. "Which reminds me," she added, a mischievous expression on her face, "of the reason we're here tonight. Tell me about Alex. I know you were over at his house all Sunday afternoon. Spill it."

Liz frowned. "How did Alex come into it?"

"You left Arizona, and Richard, which leads to Alex," Kathryn said smugly. "You now live where there's snow, which leads to snowmen, which leads to Alex."

"All roads lead to Alex?" Liz asked dryly.

"Yup," was the cheerful reply.

Liz studied the ice in her glass of tea. "He came over on Sunday morning to shovel my driveway. I made him popovers and he invited me to make snowmen. I'd never done that before." She looked up at her friend. "Kathryn, it was amazing. All these people showed up and helped. It was like some great big community effort. Just to make snowmen. I've never seen snowmen like that before. Some of them had breasts and skirts. And there were snow kids. Then Alex came out with hot chocolate for everyone, and then people started singing Christmas carols, for Pete's sake."

"What's wrong with Christmas carols? Or singing, for that matter? I like singing."

"You're a music teacher," Liz pointed out. "You have to like singing."

"But even if I weren't a music teacher, I'd still like singing."

Liz picked up the paper straw–wrapper and absently began to twist it around her little finger. "It was just so Norman Rockwell."

"What's wrong with Norman?"

"Nothing's wrong with Norman," Liz tried to explain. "It's wrong with me. After everyone left, Alex and I took the Styrofoam cups into the house. His house is amazing. It's huge. There are probably five bedrooms and a couple of bathrooms and a huge living room with a fireplace that's bigger than mine. The kitchen isn't terrific; but then, I'm a snob about kitchens. And you go out through a door in the living room and you're in his workshop. Have you ever seen his work?

Kathryn shook her head. "Just heard about it from Sally."

"Alex makes the most amazing chairs." She shook her head, trying to find the words to explain how those chairs affected her. "He makes rocking chairs and cradles. There's this smell of wood that is so pure and fresh, it's unworldly. He had lots of woodshavings on the floor from a chair he was finishing. And he has tools. All lined up according to type."

"Do they have little call numbers on them?" Kathryn teased.

Liz chuckled. "No. But they are in perfect order. Alex said his family has been giving him tools for his birthdays and Christmases forever. He's kept every one. They're all hanging on his walls. And there are all these chair backs hanging on pegs on the walls. Some have been carved, some haven't; some are scrolled, some plain. But they were all going to be rocking chairs." She stared for a moment at the paper straw-wrapper in her hands. "Rocking chairs and cradles," she repeated quietly.

"What's wrong with rocking chairs and cradles?"

"It's not wrong with them. It's wrong with me."

"Then what's wrong with you?"

Liz gave up on the now shredded bit of paper. "I like him," she said softly.

Kathryn snorted. "We *all* like Alex. He's one of the most universally liked people I know."

"I like him a lot."

Kathryn's eyes widened in sudden understanding.

"Your dinners, ladies." It was the server. "These plates are very hot," he cautioned as he set them on the table.

"Thank you," Liz told him absently.

"If there's anything else you need, don't hesitate to ask," the server told them with a professionally friendly smile. "Enjoy your dinner."

"So you finally admit it," Kathryn said smugly when the server was out of earshot.

"Yes, I admit it. But only to you. Only because you're my best friend. Only because . . . "

"Because . . . " her friend prompted.

"Because it's so awful. It's so wretchedly unfair."

"Hold it." Kathryn pointed her fork at Liz. "Aren't you the one who always tells me that life has no consciousness, so it can't be either fair or unfair? Don't you always say that things just are the way they are?"

Liz nodded, feeling morose.

"So how is it unfair that you like Alex?"

Liz took a bite of enchilada. A small bite, because it was still steaming. "In case you hadn't noticed, I'm older than he is."

"So? What's your point?"

"According to Sally, I'm ten years older than he is."

"Ten years is good. It means you're in your prime and he's in his. You know the old joke about how we used to say women should find a man older and more mature, but now we know that men don't mature. So we should get 'em young and train 'em right." She scooped up a bite of rice and beans and shrimp. Her eyes closed in rapture. "This is so good. I think we should canonize the person who dreamed this stuff up."

"Kathryn, be serious."

"I am serious. I wonder if they give out sainthoods for cooking."

Liz chuckled in spite of herself. "I doubt it."

"Back to the great unfairness. You're sounding like your mother, you know."

Liz groaned. "This is no time for insults."

"It's true. Alex is a terrific guy; you're a terrific woman. He has a dog. You're a cat person. But he likes cats, too, and you told me Burl and Julia didn't have a problem with each other. You're a librarian. He drives a school bus and makes things that rock. You're ten years older than he is." She scooped up another bite and chewed it thoughtfully. "I don't see what you're concerned about. Of course, I deal with young kids all day, so I'm not used to big-people problems. Now, if you two were squabbling over ball-and-jacks at recess, or throwing rocks into the parking lot, then I'd know what to do. But, Liz, I don't see a problem here. I think you should get to know him better, and see what develops." She gave a salacious leer. 'Besides, you'll be the envy of every unattached female in Hartley."

"I can't do that."

"Why not? Seems perfectly reasonable to me."

"His goal in life," she said carefully, "is to have children. Plural."

Kathryn stopped midscoop and deliberately put down her fork. She stared at Liz, her eyes brimming with sympathy. "That sucks," she said softly. Then, after heaving a deep sigh, she scooped up another bite of shrimp and chewed thoughtfully. "Well," she said at last, "as you said, you're older than he is. We're not talking about a forever kind of thing. The two of you can have a good time for a year or so. It's better than being alone."

"I don't think Alex is looking for a good-time kind of thing." *And,* Liz thought to herself somberly as she spooned sour cream onto her enchilada, *I don't want a good-time kind of thing, either. I want forever.*

Alex sanded the wood of the cradle until it was smooth and silky as a newborn baby's cheek. His arm felt like rubber. He flexed it, shaking out the stiffness. Next would come a coat of stain, then more sanding, then sealant, then more sanding, more varnish, more sanding. Putting the wood together was easy. The sanding was the hard part. Yet it was also contemplative work. He'd once read that monks worked with their hands to better let their minds turn to God. His mind, however, was turned toward Indiana and his baby sister.

Dave had called from the hospital. "We're here, Alex. Sharon wanted you to know. We'll call you when it happens." He sounded terrified and giddy at the same time. Almost as bad as when they were seniors in high school and Dave had finally gotten up the courage to ask sophomore Sharon for a date. Alex kept telling him she'd go out with him, but Dave had been a wreck. Just like he was now, waiting for their little *El Niño* to be born.

Alex had been in the workshop ever since the call came. Burl was snoring under the workbench. The phone was at hand.

Sometimes Alex felt out of place. In a world that expected men to rise to the top of corporate ladders, all he wanted was to raise a family. In a world that valued competition, he was more interested in community. "Archaic, eh, boy?" he said to Burl. Burl's answer was an extra-loud snore and a deeper settling into sleep.

He glanced at the antique cuckoo clock on the wall. Five minutes till nine. Sharon had been at the hospital for three hours. He turned back to the cradle.

Liz gathered up Julia and her book and headed to bed. "We're going to read," she announced. Julia, tired after chasing the feather-on-a-string for half an hour, didn't protest. Liz punched her pillows into a backrest shape and slid under her covers. She reached for her book— that biography of Julia Child—and opened up to her bookmark. Julia, her Julia, the cat Julia, stomped around on the bed for a few minutes. Then the kitty stalked over to Liz and clambered up on her lap, on top of the book, where she curled up and turned on her engine.

"Are the babies sleeping?" Liz asked, putting her hand on Julia's belly.

Julia purred. She raised her chin, an obvious hint. Liz obliged, checking out the gash on her chin. It seemed to be better every day. Who in their right mind would kick a cat? A kitten? Maybe they weren't in their right mind. She robbed Julia's chin, and her head—all the places Julia liked. How familiar the little cat was now. And she wasn't as unattractive as she'd been. Or maybe it was just because she was Liz's cat now. Suddenly, Liz realized that she didn't miss Skillet anymore. Oh, she'd loved Skillet, and always would. But that empty place was filled now. Julia, who was very much alive, had insistently shoved her way into Liz's heart. Not as a replacement for Skillet, but as an addition to her.

"You're safe now, Julia," she murmured to the purring cat. "No one is ever going to kick you again. Not you, and not your babies. And you'll never be hungry—well, you're always hungry, but you'll never be starving. And you'll always be safe. We're all right. Just the two of us. You and me. And the kittens."

She would remain friendly to Alex Hogan if she saw him again. But she wouldn't think of him while she was answering reference questions. She wouldn't check the meeting room schedule to see if there were any class visits when he might be driving the bus.

It wasn't until she turned off the light that she realized she'd forgotten to ask Kathryn what her news was.

Chapter Eight

"You're awfully cheerful this morning," the bus supervisor said, a smile wide across her worn face. "You look like hell, but you're sure cheerful."

"I was up most of the night," he admitted, shoving his hand through his hair.

"Did Sharon have her baby?" one of the other drivers wanted to know.

Instantly, as if *baby* was a magic word, there was a cluster of women surrounding him. They all knew about Sharon, of course. They took great pride in mothering him. Most of them had children either grown or in high school. They often tried to introduce him to what they considered eligible young women. He sometimes felt like their mascot.

He pulled a small piece of paper from his pocket and checked it. "She had a girl," he announced. "Seven pounds, three ounces, and nineteen inches long. In the middle of the night." He'd written it down—the women had told him what they wanted to know.

"What's her name?"

"How is Sharon feeling?"

"When will you go to see her?"

The questions came one on top of each other. These women knew him well. "They haven't named her yet, Sharon was feeling fine in the middle of the night when she called, and this weekend. In that order," he said with a grin.

There was a collective sigh. For a moment the hush was magical.

"So when are *you* going to make us honorary aunts?" one of them asked.

"Oh, hush, Lenore," another one put in. "He has to get married first."

"Not today, you don't," another pointed out.

"Alex does," the one named Lenore insisted. The rest nodded in agreement, patting him on the shoulder on the way out to their buses.

Their voices grew thoughtful as he overheard them tell each other bits about their own experiences with childbirth. It seemed to bind them together in some way he couldn't understand. He was an outsider.

That afternoon, when he was cleaning out his bus, Lenore knocked on the door. "Yoo hoo!" she called. She held out a pink paper-wrapped box, tied with a pink ribbon bow. "It's for Sharon and the baby," she said. "From all of us."

Alex was stunned. "Thanks," he managed to get out as he reached for the box. "This is so nice of you."

"New mothers need all the help they can get," she said with a grin. "Trust me; I know."

New mothers, he thought, finishing up with his bus. Unbidden, an image of Liz as a new mother insinuated itself into his mind. He liked Liz, liked her a lot. She was many of the things he wanted in a wife, besides being able to cook like a dream. She liked pets, she was intelligent, she was kind—which was different from being nice. She was thoughtful. And she was older than he was. He didn't know how much older, but there was this thing called a biological clock. He stared out the window at the clouds in the sky. He could almost hear faint ticking.

Tuesday was a repeat of Monday for Liz, except that Attila spent the day in his office—his liar, Cecily called it—presumably doing paperwork. "Why," Cecily said to Liz during their lunch break, "is he a librarian if he seems to hate libraries so much?"

"I don't think he hates libraries," Liz answered. Her lunch today was a bagel and cream cheese, along with a green salad. "He just doesn't like the people who come in. He doesn't like them messing up the shelves. He should work at the Library of Congress, where patrons don't go into the stacks."

"He should have been a drill sergeant. Did you see his latest missive? It says staff is to park at the very back of the parking lot."

Liz frowned. "That's where we always park."

"But now," Cecily said, flinging her hands up in disgust, "there's a written policy about it. If I didn't have a new car to pay off I'd tell him to shove it. Isn't there a book called *How to Work for a Jerk*, or something like that?"

"If there isn't one, you should write it."

"We should." Suddenly, Cecily's face brightened. "I know. We can all write it together. We can self-publish it and sell it. It can be a fundraiser for the library. We'll make a fortune."

"You look very pleased with yourself," Liz commented.

"It's a great idea. I think the rest of the staff will love it."

"The rest of the staff is too afraid of getting fired."

"Oh, don't be a killjoy." But it was said without rancor.

"Who's killing joy?" Kendra stuck her head in. "Someone is committing murder in the staff room?"

"I had a great idea and Liz says it won't work. I called her a killjoy."

"Watch it," Kendra warned. "We like to keep on her good side, so she brings us truly scrumptious things to eat. Hey, Liz, can I put in a request for that chocolate fudge stuff?"

* * *

Kathryn showed up after school again, but this time Liz wasn't scheduled on the reference desk, so she had a couple of minutes to talk. "About last night . . . " she began.

"Don't tell me you've changed your mind about liking Alex?"

Liz grimaced. "No, not that. But I forgot to ask you what your big news was. Is."

Kathryn struck a pose. "You are looking at the music director for the Hartley Community Theater's production of *The Sound of Music.*"

"Oh, Kath, that's wonderful. You'll have a terrific time." Besides, she thought, it would get Kathryn's mind off Paul, her significant jerk. "I'll come on opening night and sit in the front row."

Kathryn shrugged. "It's not like we're Broadway or anything. Most of these people haven't had any formal training, but they're enthusiastic."

That night, on the way home from work, Liz stopped off at Abernathy's to buy the ingredients for Kendra's "chocolate fudge stuff." She bought enough for a double batch. One to take to work, and one to eat all by herself, next to the fireplace, her cat on her lap, her book in hand. *Well, Liz,* she told herself as she stood in the checkout line, *you were married once, so I guess that makes you technically ineligible to be called a spinster or an old maid. But that's what it sounds like to me. How depressing.*

At least Julia was happy to see her, Liz thought when she shoved the door open with her foot and maneuvered the grocery bags into the kitchen. She set the first load of bags on the counter. "Hello, Julia, my sweet kitty. How was your day?" She scooped up the cat and rubbed her chin on the cat's head. Julia wiggled to get down. Julia ran to her bowl and yelled.

"Oh, so you're only glad to see me because I feed you?" She laughed as she scooped kitty food into the bowl. "You need to be a patient kitty and let me get out the can opener. I bought you some more yummy canned kitty food to mix in with this dry stuff. I get chocolate; you get canned cat food." Julia fully approved of this division of the spoils.

Liz made three more trips to the car for groceries. She'd done herself proud at Abernathy's, she thought as she surveyed the bags before her. She was going to spend the week baking for the library staff.

Alex spent the next night working on the cradle for his new niece. By Wednesday night it was ready to go to Indiana. He stuck a great big pink bow on it. "Whaddya think, Burl?"

Burl was interested in the ribbon.

"Don't drool on it."

Burl settled on his haunches and sent him a look full of reproach.

Thursday, after he left the bus lot, he drove his truck to the library. He needed some CDs to listen to on his trip. He slowly drove around the parking lot until he saw her car. She was at work. He wondered if he'd see her. He wanted to see her. No, he didn't. For a moment he sat in indecision. Then he turned off the engine and got out of his truck. He needed the CDs, and he could at least find out how Julia was. After all, he was going to take one of the kittens. He had an interest in the mother's well-being.

"Ohmigod!" Liz heard Kendra squeal softly. She looked over at the checkout desk to see Kendra motioning to the other young clerk. "It's Romeo."

The two clerks went through the pheromone routine again. Honestly, Liz thought, they acted as if they'd never seen a man before. *Now remember,* she cautioned herself, *this is a platonic friendship. You know how to do that; you've done it before.* So she rose from the information desk to meet him.

"Hello, Alex." She kept her voice professional, almost impersonal. Since there was no possibility of anything ever happening between them, it would be best if no one ever knew about her feelings for Alex. No one but Kathryn, she amended. The clerks would all pity her, and she wouldn't be able to stand it. She'd never live it down.

"Hello, Liz." His voice was a mirror image of hers. For an instant, she let her gaze meet his. But that instant was enough to send her insides fluttering. His eyes looked tired, she thought. He was smiling, but without

145

the joyful abandon she'd seen on Sunday afternoon. The joyful abandon that she'd fallen in love with.

"How's Julia?"

Interesting that he was keeping their conversation on the same surficial level. It was as though he'd come to the same realization that she had. They could be friends but nothing more. For a moment, she felt a pang of regret. Regret for what could have been, what should have been. Then she turned away from regret. *Let's rejoice in what we have,* she told herself, *instead of pining after what we want.* "Julia's fine. She's still eating like a horse. The cut on her chin isn't noticeable anymore. I'm taking her in to see Dr. March on Saturday."

"Is something wrong?"

Liz laughed, a bit embarrassed. "It's just me. I want to make sure everything is progressing as it should, that she and the kittens are healthy. I'm being an overanxious mother, I guess."

"I don't think so. She's a kitten herself. Let me know if there's anything I can do," he told her.

"I will," she answered, knowing she wouldn't. They stood for a moment in silence. Then Liz retreated into her librarian persona. She felt safe there. She was also aware that the clerks were not-so-surreptitiously watching them. "Can I help you find something?"

He sighed. "I came in to look through your CDs. But I know where they are."

"Well, if you can't find what you want, let me know. I'll see what I can do."

146

"I will," he said, and she knew he wouldn't.

They stood for a moment longer, their silence saying more than their words. Then Liz said softly, "Nice seeing you, Alex."

"Same here."

Then the phone rang and Liz had to answer it. "I hafta have," said the thin young voice on the line, "five books about the effect of classical music on radish seeds." When she looked up, Alex was gone.

That evening, Liz was putting on her coat when one of the clerks scurried into the back room to find her. "What did he say?"

There was no need to ask who the *he* was. "He wanted to know how Julia's doing," Liz answered.

"Is that all?"

"You sound disappointed."

The clerk shrugged her shoulders dejectedly. "We wanted it to be something more romantic," she admitted.

"Life is not a romance novel," Liz said mildly. "In reality there's often no happily-ever-after ending." She wasn't sure whether she was talking to the clerk, or to herself.

Alex drove straight home from the bus lot on Friday afternoon. He put the bow-festooned cradle, now protected by several layers of worn quilts, in the back of his truck. He slung his duffel bag in alongside it, and set the present from the other bus drivers on top. He added dishes and a canister of food for Burl. "Let's go, big guy." Burl was ready and willing. Burl loved going for rides.

As he pulled out of his driveway, he glanced at the snowmen. They were melting, losing their shape, turning into tall blobs. "Life is ephemeral," he told Burl, "which is why it's so special. Listen to me, waxing philosophical." Beside him, on the seat, Burl didn't answer. He was busy looking out the window. Dogs lived in the moment. No future, no past. Sometimes, Alex thought, that was a good idea. It probably kept them sane.

On the way over, he and Burl listened to Erik Satie and Sebelius. They sang along with early Dan Fogelberg—at least Alex sang. Burl watched intently out the window. Finally, at nine o'clock, Alex pulled into Sharon and Dave's driveway. Burl, recognizing where they were, thumped his tail on the seat and panted more loudly than usual.

Almost before he had the engine turned off, the front door opened and his little sister rushed down the sidewalk to him. He caught her up in a big hug. "Why aren't you inside?" he demanded, loosening his grip on her to clip on Burl's leash.

"Because I had to see you!" was her answer. Then she looked over his shoulder. "Hello, Burl."

Burl clambered out of the truck to lean against her.

"How do you feel?" he asked.

148

"Wonderful. I never thought I'd feel this good after having a baby."

"You won't feel so wonderful if we don't get you back inside." He kept his arm around her as he and Burl walked her up to the door. "Where's Dave?"

"Hello, Alex," his brother-in-law and close friend greeted him from inside the door. "Meet your niece." She was wrapped snugly in layers of baby blanket, in the crook of his arm. All Alex could see of her was her red and wrinkled little face, with her eyes closed and miniature eyelashes. She was tiny and pure and new. Then Dave held her out to him. He took this miracle in his arms, holding her carefully. She weighed less than a minute. "Hello, there, little *El Niño*," he whispered to her.

"Alexis, meet your uncle."

For a moment Alex felt the world stop. He stared at his brother-in-law. Then his throat got lumpy and the world started again.

"We named her after you," Sharon put in unnecessarily.

"You're Sharon's favorite brother and you're my best friend," Dave explained.

"I hope you don't mind," Sharon added.

For a moment, Alex was afraid his voice wouldn't work. "I'm Sharon's only brother," he managed.

"That's beside the point."

He looked down at baby Alexis, asleep in his arms. It

was the next best thing to holding his own baby. He could hold her forever.

The next morning he woke early. He stretched out in the double bed. He tried to go back to sleep, but he heard footsteps on the stairs, and Sharon murmuring to the baby. Evidently the baby was awake.

Yawning, he climbed out of bed and into his jeans. He stepped over Burl, who was still snoring softly, on the rug at the foot of the bed. Then, barefooted and barechested, he made his way downstairs to the kitchen. He heard a soft voice. It was his sister singing to Alexis as she nursed. They were by the window, enthroned in the rocking chair he'd given Sharon and Dave as a wedding gift. Little baby grunting noises accompanied Sharon's soft singing. They were Madonna and child.

"Good morning," he said softly, not wanting to disturb the peace of the moment.

She looked up and her eyes widened. "Woo, woo. And you wonder why women get tongue-tied when they see you coming," she teased. "It's a good thing you don't wander around half-nekkid all the time. You'd cause regular pileups on the streets of Hartley. They'd declare you a public menace."

He rolled his eyes. "Knock it off," he said with affection.

"Will not. I'm your sister. I'm allowed to tease you." She shifted Alexis onto her shoulder, where she gently patted and rubbed the newborn-sized back. Alexis let out a newborn-sized but very satisfying belch.

"Here, Alex, come sing to the baby while I make breakfast." Sharon started to stand and Alex rushed to help her.

"You're supposed to rest," he scolded. "I'll make breakfast."

"You don't know where I keep things. Besides, you won't have many chances to hold her while she's tiny."

Alex gazed into the unfocused eyes of the tiny baby on Sharon's shoulder and was eternally lost. He held his arms out for the baby. She flailed her little arms and screwed up her face. He gently rocked her in his arms for a few moments until she settled down. An entire person in such a tiny package. It was amazing. It was miraculous. He drank in the feeling of holding her, committing it to memory so he wouldn't forget. He watched, enchanted, as her little mouth opened into a yawn and her tiny eyes slowly slid closed.

"So," his sister said, measuring coffee into the maker and clicking it on. "What about this woman? What's happening?" She opened the refrigerator and poured some orange juice.

"Nothing." He concentrated on the baby sleeping in his arms.

"Why not?"

"She's . . . ."

"Watch it, buster. If you say she's too old, I'll slug you. This is where we women stick together like glue." She set a glass of juice on the table where he could reach it. "I know you want to get married and turn 'em out like Volkswagens. You've always loved kids. Remember when Shelby and I used to bring the Kittner kids over here to baby-sit? You always knew how to talk to them. Incidentally, Kenny Kittner is in high school now. That makes me feel old."

Alex heard Burl clump downstairs. "In here, Burl," he called, quietly so he wouldn't startle the baby. "Follow the smell of coffee." The dog ambled into the kitchen and nosed his way over to the counter. Sharon gave him a quick hug and opened the back door to let him out. After a minute she let him in again. Burl stood by the door for a moment, looking around the kitchen. Then he moseyed over to Alex. "Sharon . . . " Alex nodded toward Burl.

Sharon looked unconcerned. "Burl is family; it's not as if he was some stray off the street. Besides, the sooner he gets to know her, the sooner he'll realize she's one of us. Just don't let him drool on her too much."

So Alex held the baby on his lap where Burl could meet her. After some serious sniffing, through which Alexis remained blissfully asleep, Burl sat down and stared at her, looking suitably impressed.

"She looks like Shelby," Alex commented, studying his niece.

"Think so?" Sharon buttered a piece of toast. "Mom says she looks like you when you were a baby." She set the toast on the table by his juice, "Now, tell your little sister. Other than her age, what's wrong with this woman?"

Chapter Nine

"Liz, she looks fine," Dr. March said, slinging her stethoscope around her neck. "She looks much healthier than she did last week."

"She's cleaner."

The vet laughed. "She doesn't have that starved waif look."

"Not the way she eats."

Julia practically preened on the examination table, winding from one to the other. "She's milking it for all she can get," Dr. March said with amusement, rubbing Julia behind the ears.

"She's not subtle," Liz agreed.

At the receptionist's desk, Liz stopped to show Julia off.

"She's sure a friendly cat," Suzette said as Julia

demanded that her head be rubbed. "Not afraid of strangers, is she?"

"Say, Liz," Jessie said, coming through the door that separated the reception area from the clinic, "I hear you learned to make snowmen."

Liz groaned. "Does the whole town know?"

"Nah. Just the people on the grapevine. But you know how news spreads sort of logarithmically, so by now I'd say about ninety percent of the population of Hartley is aware that you spent Sunday afternoon with Alex Hogan."

"Then, for the record, yes, I learned to build snowmen."

"You never made a snowman before?" Suzette asked.

"I grew up in Arizona," Liz explained. "Not a lot of snow out there."

"Why did you come here?" she asked, astonishment coloring her tone.

"I wanted to learn to build snowmen. Julia, dear kitty, it's time to go home now. Say good-bye." She waved the cat's paw before settling her in the cat carrier.

Jessie walked her to the door. "Say, Jess," Liz said, "why does everyone in this town have an obsessive interest in what I do?"

Jessie waggled her eyebrows. "It's not you, m'dear," she said in a faux Victorian-matron manner. "It's the school-bus driver. We all have an obsessive interest in him." She dropped the persona. "We like the people we like to be happy."

"Happiness police?"

"That's right," was the cheerful reply. "Happy 'R' Us, Inc."

"Don't get your hopes up on this one," she said firmly, opening her car door and sliding the cat carrier in. "Alex and I are only friends."

"I've heard that one before."

"But this time it's true. I'm older than he is."

"Albert Einstein's first wife was older than he was."

Liz shook her head at Jessie. "Nice try, but it won't work."

She pulled into her garage and sat there for a moment. "We're home, Julia," she said with a sigh.

From inside the cat carrier, Julia yelled.

Liz gave Julia the last of the canned food for a snack. It was time to make a trek to Abernathy's. Then she picked up the phone and dialed Kathryn.

"Kathryn, I'm depressed. Come help."

"Help you be depressed? I'll be right over."

She was.

Kathryn scooped Julia up and settled down in a kitchen chair. "So talk to me."

Liz poured steeped tea into mugs and got out a plate for cookies.

"Forget the plate," Kathryn ordered. "Just bring the whole cookie jar."

Liz brought the cookie jar.

"I don't think this is all about Alex," Liz began. She sat down, and Julia clambered over onto her lap.

Kathryn was silent, but studying her. Engine revving, Julia butted her head into Liz's hand.

"I mean, Alex is very nice, and very good-looking, but anything other than friendship between the two of us is out of the question and I know it." Julia curled up on her lap.

"If it's not about Alex, then what is it about?"

"I'm forty."

"Most of us are, at some point in our lives. Unless we die young, leaving a good-looking corpse."

Liz sighed in exasperation. "You're not there yet."

"But I will be in three months. Tell me, what's it like? Does your body really start falling apart? Do you suddenly see this hill and automatically start to roll down it?"

"It's not funny. I look around at all the other people I know who are my age. They have marriages and families and washers and dryers. They have minivans to take the kids to hockey practice. The whole bit."

"Last time I looked, you had a washer and dryer," Kathryn pointed out. "And you're conveniently forgetting that lots of people who are the Big Four Oh, have also experienced the Big D."

"But they have lives."

"So do you. You just want theirs."

"You're determined not to let me wallow, aren't you?"

"Friends don't let friends wallow. Unless they're all pigs."

Liz groaned. "Don't get started on pigs."

"Why not? I like pigs. They're very intelligent. I cried buckets when I saw *Babe*. So did you, as I recall. That scene where he says, in that choked voice, that he wants his mom. It gets you every time. That's one instance where the movie was actually as good as the book. Must have been some sort of accident." She stuck her hand into the cookie jar. "Some people, when they're depressed, go to the mall and buy all sorts of clothes they can't afford." She took a big bite of cookie and crunched thoughtfully. "My sister," she said through a mouthful of crumbs, "buys practically bolts of material that she'll never get around to sewing. Other people go get their hair cut. It's an individual sort of thing." She took another bite. "Now you, when you get depressed, you bake cookies. Not lasagna or pot roast. Nothing substantial like that. You bake cookies. Why should that be?"

"Are you complaining?" Liz asked as Kathryn reached into the jar again.

"Not at all. Just wondering why. What part did cookies play in your childhood?"

"You've been reading too many self-help books."

"Self-Help for Dummies," Kathryn agreed. "Seriously, though, Liz, remember who taught you to make cookies?"

"My grandmother."

"Remember how we used to go to her bakery after school and she'd let us decorate sugar cookies? And she didn't mind when we ate the broken ones. Good memories, aren't they?"

"Very good."

"That's probably why you bake cookies. They bring back memories of being safe and loved. I bet your mother never baked cookies in her life."

Liz grimaced at the thought of her mother in the kitchen. "She made the pot roast."

"I remember that pot roast from our childhood. Thirty-five years is a long time to be best friends."

Liz shuddered. "Just think—we were best friends for five years before Alex Hogan was even born. Now, that's enough to make me run away screaming even if it weren't for the baby issue. By the way, my mother called last week to tell me that Richard and his wife are expecting *numero* four."

"I bet she really turned the screws, didn't she?" There was no love lost between Kathryn and Liz's mother. There never had been.

"She said maybe if I'd gone to better doctors . . . "

Kathryn made a rude noise. "I know she's your mother and all that, but she's still a gorgon. Is that your cat purring, or is it a low-flying plane? Sheesh! She's a noisy cat."

Liz wiggled a finger under Julia's chin. "I think my mother's unhappy."

"That's her problem, not yours. You can't take responsibility for her unhappiness. All the books say so."

Liz waved the cookie in her hand. "Remember when we were in fifth grade and . . . "

"And Freddy Underwood paid his little sister twenty-five cents to eat his spider collection?" Kathryn roared with laughter. "Oh, Liz, I'm so glad you decided to move to Hartley."

"I'm so glad you talked me into it."

"I just hated the thought of you still living there and constantly running into Saint Richard the Perfect and his perpetually pregnant wife."

Liz shook her head. "Richard's a nice guy."

"You keep saying that. He just dumped you for something that wasn't your fault. I don't call that nice. What ever happened to that part about sickness and health?"

Liz sighed. "He *is* nice. He was—is—the kind of guy who *should* have children. Just like Alex. Richard is a terrific father, and Alex will be too, someday. The world needs more men like that." She shrugged. "Unfortunately, my body didn't cooperate when it had the chance."

"You're saying you *really* don't have any bitter feelings toward him?" Kathryn's eyes had narrowed. "Why do I *not* believe you?"

Liz smiled wanly at her friend. "I *really* don't. But, more than the age issue, that's why I can't be anything other than friends with Alex, no matter how I feel about

Thrill to the most sensual, adventure-filled Romances on the market today...

FROM  LOVE SPELL BOOKS

As a home subscriber to the Love Spell Romance Book Club, you'll enjoy the best in today's BRAND-NEW Time Travel, Futuristic, Legendary Lovers, Perfect Heroes and other genre romance fiction. For five years, Love Spell has brought you the award-winning, high-quality authors you know and love to read. Each Love Spell romance will sweep you away to a world of high adventure...and intimate romance. Discover for yourself all the passion and excitement millions of readers thrill to each and every month.

Save $5.00 Each Time You Buy!

Every other month, the Love Spell Romance Book Club brings you four brand-new titles from Love Spell Books. EACH PACKAGE WILL SAVE YOU AT LEAST $5.00 FROM THE BOOK-STORE PRICE! And you'll never miss a new title with our convenient home delivery service.

Here's how we do it: Each package will carry a FREE 10-DAY EXAMINATION privilege. At the end of that time, if you decide to keep your books, simply pay the low invoice price of $17.96, no shipping or handling charges added. HOME DELIVERY IS ALWAYS FREE. With today's top romance novels selling for $5.99 and higher, our price SAVES YOU AT LEAST $5.00 with each shipment.

AND YOUR FIRST TWO-BOOK SHIP-MENT IS TOTALLY FREE!

IT'S A BARGAIN YOU CAN'T BEAT! A SUPER $11.48 Value!

Love Spell  A Division of Dorchester Publishing Co., Inc.

Get Two Books Totally
FREE —
An $11.48 Value!

▼ Tear Here and Mail Your FREE Book Card Today! ▼

it. It's not out of some great big noble thing. It's more selfish than that. I don't want to go through all that mess again. The insistence that it doesn't matter, when it really does, and so it eats away at the relationship, until there's nothing left. Kathryn, I really believe it hurt Richard as much as it did me. If Alex and I develop a romantic relationship he'll never have children of his own. He wants that. He deserves that. And some unborn baby deserves him as a father. And I can't be part of that picture, no matter how much I want to be. Unless and until I meet a good man who does not want kids, it's gonna be just me and Julia."

"You and Alex could always"—Kathryn paused thoughtfully as she bit into another cookie—"adopt."

The word slammed into Liz like a freight train. It was one thing for her to think of what was in the past. But it was a whole other thing when the word was used for the future. Offered as a possibility. It took her a whole minute to be able to get the words out. "I won't go through that again."

Kathryn nodded knowingly. "I didn't think you would. But I wanted to make sure you knew your options." She planted her chin in her hand. "You know, it really burns me. I mean, look at all the scientific breakthroughs. We have put men on the moon, and the post office has finally come up with stick-on stamps— now *there's* a serious boon to mankind. Too bad medical science wasn't able to come through for you."

Liz shook her head. "Today there are things that can

be done. But they came too late for me." She'd resigned herself to it a long time ago. "We're being depressing. Tell you what: Let's make something really fattening for dinner and then go to the movies."

"*Titanic* is back in town at the dollar theater," Kathryn said glumly. "We can go see it on the big screen and cry copious amounts of tears. It'll be real cathartic."

"Why *did* you leave town?" Cindy Hall asked him, her eyelashes fluttering overtly. She had always been about as subtle as a Mack truck. She looked exactly the same as she had ten years ago, when Sharon and Shelby insisted she had a crush on him. She still wore too much makeup and skirts that were too short. But now she was divorced with a young boy and hunting for husband number two. She was also still Sharon's friend, which was why she'd shown up on the spur of the moment. While she'd cooed over little Alexis, she was also obviously trying to coo over him, too.

"College, remember?" Alex tried not to be short with her.

"Oh, yes, Somewhere in Ohio, wasn't it?" She sidled closer to him, close enough that she could rest her hand on his arm. Her perfume assaulted him.

"Excuse me, Cindy. I thought I heard Burl barking outside," he lied. But he made it to the back door and into the yard before he burst into laughter.

Dave, from the patio, threw a Frisbee for Burl. From the drool drops on the cement and the pawprintsmashed snow, it looked as if they'd been at it for a while. Burl cheerfully loped off after the Frisbee. "What's so funny?" Dave asked.

"Cindy Hall."

"Still lusting after you, is she? Well, don't take it personally. She lusts after anything under the age of fifty that's male and single. She wants a father for her boy."

"That seems like a reasonable goal."

"But"—Dave took the Frisbee from Burl and threw it again—"the kind of men who are attracted to her type of female charms would probably not be very good father figures."

"Probably right."

"Sharon has told her so dozens of times, but Cindy doesn't get it. Sharon says it's because Cindy was the cheerleader-prom-queen-beauty-pageant-winner type. She thinks the only thing anyone will ever be interested in is her looks."

"That's sad."

"Yeah, it is. Because when she's not on the prowl, she's actually a nice lady. Maybe if you got to know her, the two of you could . . . you know?"

"Yes, I do know, and no, I don't think so."

"Just a thought," his friend said. "Here you go, Burl."

Alex didn't have his jacket and it was chilly. Hands in his pockets, he leaned against the back of the house and watched his dog go after the Frisbee.

"Sharon tells me you've met some woman."

Alex groaned. "I asked her not to tell the family."

"I'm not family, I'm her husband. I'm also your best friend. That's enough, Burl, old guy. My arm is giving out." Dave sank down on the concrete bench. Resigned, Burl put his head on Dave's knee, Frisbee hanging out of his mouth and little clumps of snow sticking all over his coat. "So, tell me about this woman of yours."

"You sound like Sharon"

"Yeah, well, after living with someone for a few years, I think you do begin to sound alike."

They kept a companionable silence for a few moments, broken only by Burl's panting. Then Alex said, "I like this woman a lot, but she's older than I am."

"Significantly older?"

"I think so."

Dave scratched his head and leaned back to squint up at the sky. "Is it truly the age thing that's got you bothered?"

Alex stubbed his toe at the cement. "I think so, but don't tell Sharon. She's threatened me with bodily harm."

"You always were looking for the perfect woman. Trust me, buddy, she doesn't exist."

Alex raised his eyebrow.

"We've been best buddies since we first bashed each other over the head with trucks in our sandboxes. Remember those old sandboxes? I wonder what happened to them," he mused. "I'll have to get one for Alexis."

"Not for a couple of years," Alex pointed out. "She has to be old enough to eat the sand first."

"Hmm. I guess you're right. Anyway, Alex, you've always been looking for the perfect woman. In high school you had this standard of perfection. You even kept a list of all the qualities you wanted in a girlfriend. Remember that list?"

"I don't—" Alex began.

But Dave hurried on. "If the girls you went out with didn't have all those qualities—which they couldn't, because it was perfection, after all—you broke up with them. Gently, of course, because you never wanted to hurt anyone. In college it was the same thing. You could never find the perfect one. Buddy, maybe it's because you're looking for something that doesn't exist."

"You're sounding like Sharon again," Alex tried to joke. Dave had hit the hammer right on the head, as he always did. Dave knew him too well.

"Maybe that's because Sharon and I've discussed this time and time again. Well, she talks, I listen, and she calls it a discussion. She's your sister. She loves you. She wants you to be happy."

"I am happy."

"Yeah, and I have a bridge," Dave said with a chuckle. "When Sharon says *happy,* she means the happily-ever-after kind of happy. She thinks that you should be married and have a dozen kids."

"I do, too."

Dave rubbed his chin. "It must be genetic, this idealistic belief in the all-American family."

"If we didn't have any ideals, we'd be pitiful." Alex hugged his arms. It was chilly outside, but he didn't want to go back in and face Cindy Hall's perky and suggestive smile. He'd rather be cold.

"What's pitiful," said Dave sternly, "is seeing you hungering after a family so bad and yet not doing anything about it because you're afraid."

"I'm not afraid."

"You are, too. Take this woman—what's her name? Liz? You're afraid to get to know Liz better because you actually might fall in love with her, and if she *is* too old to have children, you'll be a mess. By the way, Sharon says women in their forties have children all the time. Even in their fifties. But you know how she exaggerates." He stuck his hands in his pockets and leaned against the back of his house.

They were quiet for a few moments, in a companionable way.

"Say, Alex . . . " Dave said.

"What?"

"You still got that list of yours?"

Alex snapped his fingers at Burl. The big dog ambled over to see what was up. "Yeah," he admitted.

Dave hooted. "Sharon won. She bet me you still did."

"What were the stakes?"

"A month of doing the grocery shopping. Your sister hates the grocery store with a passion. Since you still have that list of yours, I've got something else for you to put on it. The ideal woman loves to go to the grocery store."

"Liz says she loves to grocery shop," Alex said thoughtfully.

Just then the back door opened, and Sharon stuck her head out. "What're you guys up to?"

"Playing Frisbee with Burl," Dave said. "Where's the baby?"

"Cindy's gushing over her."

"By the way, Sharon," Dave said in a casual voice, "since I'll be doing the grocery shopping for the next month, is there anything you need this afternoon?"

Sharon looked from one of them to the other in question. Then her face cleared in understanding. "My brother the list maker." She shook her head at him. "Do that woman in Hartley a big favor and rip up that list into tiny little pieces." She disappeared into the house for a moment, then popped back out, a small bright yellow box in her hands. She tossed it to him.

"Marshmallow Easter chicks?" he asked.

"I buy them up after Easter and keep them in the freezer for snacks. They'll keep for years. They're really good when they're petrified. Go ahead," she urged, her voice growing more serious, even challenging. "Open it up. You'll find lovely little chickies. They're wonderfully sweet and they look so pretty with all the colored sugar. But you know what, big brother? They are mostly air. There is no substance to them at all. And after you've had too many of them, they'll make you sick to your stomach. And I'm not just talking about Easter candy."

Alex grinned at his sister. "Are you calling me shallow?"

Sharon flapped her hand at him. "You know I don't think that you're shallow. In fact, sometimes you're so deep that you're obnoxious. I just want to make sure you remember what's important. I don't want you to *be* shallow."

Funny thing was, Alex thought, what Sharon was telling him was nothing he hadn't told himself.

The headlights of the oncoming cars made a rhythm as he drove home on Sunday evening. Was she the one? So many things seemed perfect. Her thoughtfulness, her willingness to try new things, and ah, yes, her cooking. He liked the way she talked about Julia. You could tell a lot about a person from the way they talked about their cats or dogs. And from the way she talked about Julia, he knew she'd be a fine mother. But how could he be positive? He wanted to find a wife. The *right* wife. He wanted to grow old with her and dandle their children and even grandchildren on his knee. He wanted to wake every morning with her at his side and kiss her every night. "I'm beginning to sound like a sentimental country and western song," he told Burl, sitting on the seat beside him. Burl gave him a quick glance, then returned to staring out the window at the countryside flying by.

Well, he thought, he'd simply have to get to know her better—spend time with her. He'd have to woo her, court her. Subtly at first, then with more enthusiasm. He'd never thought of librarians as people of great passion; he'd always thought them more staid and in control. But he knew passion and reckless abandon was lurking somewhere in Liz, and he intended to release them.

He would move slowly and subtly, so that he could be sure. It would take time, but working with wood had taught him about the need for care and patience. Not that he was very good at patience, but he knew about it. Speaking of working with wood—Liz had a lovely house, but one thing that was definitely missing was a rocking chair. That would have to be fixed.

"You sure look thrilled," Cecily said. "And on a Monday morning, no less. Or is it Friday and no one told me?"

"It's Monday all day," Liz answered her as she took out her key to open the staff door.

"Then, pray tell, what are you so thrilled about? More snowmen?"

Liz groaned as she held the heavy door open for Cecily. "When are you all going to stop assuming there's something going on when there most certainly isn't? I'm thrilled because I think I felt the kittens." She followed Cecily into the library and set down her book bag.

"That's wonderful! When are they due?"

169

"In four or five weeks." She unbuttoned her coat and slid it off.

"We ought to keep one here, to be a library cat. You know, like in that movie *Puss in Books*. That guy said there were library cats all over the country. Why shouldn't Hartley Public join the enlightened libraries of the world?" Cecily handed her a hanger.

Liz chuckled. "Can you imagine Attila's face when we tell him we want a library cat?"

"He'll turn a putrid shade of psychedelic purple."

"Who'll turn purple?" Kendra was coming in the door and wanted to know.

Cecily giggled. "Attila will turn purple when we tell him we want to keep one of Julia's kittens to be our library cat."

"We're gonna do that?" the clerk breathed. "Cool!"

"No," Liz said firmly. "We're not going to do that. Cecily was just thinking wishfully."

"Gee," Kendra said, looking around the staff room. "We probably could keep a kitten back here. There are lots of places to hide it when Attila comes through."

"No," Liz repeated. "No, no, no."

"We'd take perfectly good care of the kitten," Kendra insisted.

"I'm sure you would, but not in the library."

The clerk's shoulders sagged. "It was worth a try."

"Not a very good one," Liz told her with a laugh.

* * *

At five o'clock, Liz congratulated herself for not thinking about Alex all day. Of course, Monday afternoons were always busy. A fifth-grader had come in looking for books on fish. When asked, he'd told them that his teacher had assigned a fish report today, which meant that a whole classful of kids would come to the library looking for five books on their particular kind of fish. Yeah, right. This afternoon a middle-schooler had mentioned the invention report was due on Wednesday. So on Monday and Tuesday night, every procrastinator in middle school would be at the library looking up information about the inventor of dental floss, or the purse, or MTV.

Well, Liz thought, shouldering her book bag, she could forget about inventions and fish and presidents and famous people who came from Ohio. She was going home. Home to Julia, where she was going to feel the kittens all evening and not think about Alex.

But there was someone leaning against her car. Someone in a dark green parka, someone whose golden hair gleamed in the parking lot light.

"Hello, Alex," she said, feeling a grin burst through her like a flame.

"Hello, Liz the librarian." His voice was soft as a summer breeze and just as welcome.

Then she was standing next to him, her face tipped back slightly. He reached out to take her book bag. "Let me hold this while you open your car door," he said.

171

"It's heavy," she warned.

"I know. I think you have a secret desire to be a bricklayer, so you cart bricks around all day in case you need to whip one out to build a wall."

She chuckled. "No bricks. Only books."

"Heavy books. Like encyclopedias?"

"No. Just books."

He peered into the bag. "What do you do with all of them?"

"I read them."

"Some heavy reading."

Liz pulled the back door open, then reached for her bag. "Thanks," she said.

He toed a small clump of old ice. She waited, watching, wondering. Forget about the fairness issue. She wanted to be friends with Alex. Since that was all she could have, well then, she'd treasure it.

"I thought," he said, hesitantly, "that since you cooked lunch and popovers for me, I'd like to take you out to dinner."

Her eyes widened. That was the last thing she'd expected him to say. "Tonight?" she said before she could stop herself.

"Tonight, or any other night."

She thought. "I have to get home to Julia. I know. You can come to my house for supper." She smiled her biggest, most inviting smile. "It's not an imposition. I told you, I love cooking for other people. Besides, I think I felt the kittens this morning. I sort of want to be there."

172

He studied her for a moment under the parking lot light.

"Why did you wait outside in the cold?" she asked. "You could've come into the library."

Was it her imagination, or did Alex Hogan really blush? "Whenever I go in, the young women at the checkout desk watch me." He stubbed his toe at the ice again. "It makes me uncomfortable."

"Oh, dear," Liz murmured. She'd have to talk to the clerks. "They don't mean anything by it," she tried to explain.

"I know."

"I'm sorry. I'll talk to them. But, back to supper. Please come home with me and let me cook for you."

He smiled, a slow smile, a smile that began somewhere inside and crept over his face until it shone. "When you put it like that, I'd be a cad to refuse."

Where, oh where, was Kathryn when she needed her? Liz thought as Kathryn's phone rang and rang and rang. Finally the answering machine picked up. Liz waited through the message, then said, "Hi. It's me. Just wanted to let you know, before you hear it on the grapevine, that Alex came over for supper—it was pleasant, just-friends kind of stuff. We felt the kittens move. Call me when you have a chance."

Then she remembered *The Sound of Music*. Kathryn was at tryouts. Listening to the would-be stars of Hartley sing the songs. Kathryn would be busy with the show for the next couple of months. *Liz, old girl, you're on your own.* Julia landed on her lap. "Hello, kitty." The cat shoved her head at Liz.

"Well, Julia, what did you think of dinner? You sure made a fool of yourself over Alex. Still, I know how you feel."

Tuesday after lunch, while Liz was at the reference desk, Alex called. "Can I take you to dinner tomorrow night?"

"Oh, I'd like that," she said, purposely not saying his name. "But I work on Wednesday evenings. I know. Do you like manicotti?"

"Love it."

"I'll make it for you on Thursday night."

"Lady, you make it hard to refuse."

"Good. Julia and I will see you then."

"But only if you promise to let me take you out to dinner some other time."

Liz smiled at the thought. "It's a deal."

A few minutes later the phone rang again. "Hartley Public Library. This is the reference desk. How may I help you?"

"I have a reference question," said a familiar voice.

"Alex?" she said in a whisper, so the clerks wouldn't overhear.

"I have a reference question. There's an old saying. I wonder if you could look it up for me and tell me where it comes from."

174

"I'll try."

"The way to a man's heart is through his stomach."

Liz burst out laughing.

"I'm serious, Liz the librarian," Alex protested. "I want to know who said it."

"Okay." She squelched her chuckles. "Let me get this straight. You want to know the origin of the saying 'The way to a man's heart is through his stomach.' Is that right? This might take a few minutes. Do you want to hold on? Or shall I call you back?"

"Tell you what. Take your time, and let me know on Thursday night. I'll be expecting an answer." She could hear the grin in his voice. It did tickly things to her insides.

"I'll look it up and let you know on Thursday," she promised.

"You certainly look all starry-eyed." It was Cecily, coming out to the reference desk, a stack of book review magazines in her arms. "What's up?"

Liz glanced at her friend quickly. "Just a funny reference question."

"Do tell." She set the magazines down with a thump. "We need some humor around here." When Liz told her, Cecily grinned. "Most quotes are from either the Bible or Shakespeare. Hi," she said to the woman who'd come up to the reference desk. "Can I help you?"

"My son is doing a report on Benjamin Franklin. Can you show me where the books are?" the woman asked, and Cecily was off to the shelves, the woman in tow.

* * *

Wednesday night, Alex began working on a rocking chair for Liz. He chose maple. It was a warm, rich wood. A maple rocker gleaming in firelight was a sight to behold. Liz would like maple.

Wednesday night, as Liz knew it would be, was busy with the invention report. Who invented paper? Where did they go to school? Were they married? Who invented popcorn? Why did they invent it? On and on and on.

Toward the end of the evening, Carol, the other librarian working that night, sank down low in her chair. "Don't teachers realize that some of the answers to these questions simply don't exist?"

"I assume that is a purely rhetorical question," Liz remarked. "Hello there," she greeted the young person coming up to the desk. "How can I help you?" The child was obviously not in middle school, so she felt safe from inventions.

"Where are the shark attack books?"

"You want books about shark attacks?" Liz asked.

"Yeah. With lotsa pictures." The child obviously relished the thought of blood and gore.

"Julia, I'd like you to meet manicotti," Liz said to her cat. She was making the manicotti tonight, so on Thursday evening, when she got home from work, all she'd have to do would be to pop it in the oven.

176

Julia, from her perch on the counter, looked suitably impressed. Julia was always willing to try new food.

Liz covered the baking dish with foil and slid it in the refrigerator. Then her eye caught a bag of coconut. "Do you see what I see?" she asked her cat. Julia didn't answer. Julia merely regarded her solemnly with her large golden eyes.

"I think I'll make something special for tomorrow's dessert. Something perfectly decadent." She opened her cupboards and brought out a bag of chocolate chips, a can of condensed milk and a box of graham cracker crumbs. She set them on the counter next to the bag of coconut and a jar of pecan pieces. "Yes, indeed. Perfectly decadent," she murmured as she melted a stick of butter.

Thursday evening was a long time coming, but finally it was here, and Alex was in her kitchen. Looking, as always, as if he belonged there. "Julia Child says to make your salad dressing fresh, and to make sure the greens are dry so the dressing adheres." She whisked the vinegar and lemon juice. She added a pinch of freshly ground black pepper and basil, and some chopped garlic. Then she added the olive oil a drop at a time, whisking all the while. "There," she announced at last. She poured the dressing in a cut-glass cruet and set it on the table.

"It looks like a lot of trouble."

"Ah, but wait till you taste it. Remember? Eating should be a sensual activity." Oh, dear. She didn't mean her voice to sound so . . . so . . . come hither. Maybe he didn't notice it. But the twinkle in his eyes that sent a heat rushing through her insides told her that he had, indeed, noticed it.

Get a grip, she told herself sternly. *You're not playing brinksmanship—trying to see how close you can get to the brink without actually going over. So calm down.* Just then, the oven dinger dinged, reminding her of dinner.

She set the pan of manicotti on the trivet on the table. "Julia helped me make this."

"Julia Child or feline?"

"Feline. She likes to help me cook."

"She's just fascinated by food because she's always hungry," he said teasingly.

"She is that." Liz glanced around the kitchen. "Where is she? Julia?"

There was a *mrrow,* and Julia's head popped up from Alex's lap.

"There you are. Julia, come over here; you need to leave Alex alone so he can eat."

"She's fine," he protested.

She eyed him carefully. "Well, all right," she relented. "But don't let her up on the table. She's a champion mooch. She'll eat anything that doesn't eat her first, and even that's debatable."

Alex fixed his gaze on the pan of manicotti. "Don't worry. I won't let her spoil her appetite."

Liz chuckled. "That's impossible."

"She's eating for at least four, remember?"

"I never forget."

"And one of them is mine."

They chatted on through dinner, about the cheeses in the manicotti, about the salad and the salad dressing. Even about the steamed broccoli. Now there was a safe topic of conversation, Liz thought. Broccoli. It was as if they'd both come to the same conclusion: that they would be good friends. *This is not a bad thing*, she told herself as she watched him scoop another serving of dinner. *We all need friends.*

"Save some room for dessert."

"Dessert? Do I hear the magic word?"

She chuckled. He looked like a child on Christmas morning. "Yes, and it's decadent and should probably be outlawed."

"I can't wait."

"You have to finish your dinner first."

"Are you going to make comments about starving children in India?"

Liz burst out laughing. "No, that was my mother."

"My mother, too." Their gazes locked, held, then broke. Liz busied herself with bringing dessert plates to the table. Then the decadence, cut into little pieces and artfully arranged on a doilied fancy plate.

He looked at the plate. "They're so small."

She shook her head. "Bigger is not always better. Size doesn't matter. It's the whole sensual experience that counts."

"Women have been telling us guys that for years."

He burst into great gusts of laughter. He couldn't help it. She'd said it so innocently; then, when she'd realized what she'd said, she'd turned a brilliant magenta. But he couldn't leave her standing in the middle of her kitchen, looking embarrassed, the plate in her hands.

He set Julia down. And in one motion he was at her side, the plate on the table and his arms around her. She felt good in his arms; soft and comfortable. She made him feel good. He felt at home. More at home than he'd ever felt before. He pressed his cheek against her hair, inhaling the faint scent of something floral. *Careful, buddy,* he cautioned himself. *Don't push too hard. In fact, don't push at all. Don't be in a hurry.* But he was in a hurry. He wanted to sweep this woman off her feet and into her bed. Or his bed. Didn't matter whose bed, as long as it was soft and had a lot of pillows.

He made himself release her but kept his hands on her shoulders so she couldn't turn away. "You're still blushing."

"I'm mortified," she admitted, not meeting his gaze.

"Don't be. Can't you see the humor in it?"

"Not really." She was still avoiding his gaze.

180

He was going to have to do something to put her at ease. His arm around her shoulders, he gently shoved her into her seat. "It looks very good," he said seriously. He picked up the fancy silver serving thing and slid it under a bite-sized piece of the dessert. "What is this?"

"It has various names. It's one of those recipes that have become almost legendarily clichéd."

He held it up so he could see it closely. It looked like nothing he'd ever seen before. "Here you go." He set it on her plate, then another on his. He kept an eye on her as he popped his bite in his mouth. Delicious. "You're right," he said at last. "It's so good, it's decadent. I can see how too much of this would be overwhelming."

She nodded as she wordlessly took a bite of hers.

He couldn't bear to see her like this, embarrassed. He had to make things wonderful for her. She deserved all the wonderful he could give her. And he could give her a lot. He *would* give her a lot. It was time to forget about slow and subtle. It was time to give her wonderful.

"Liz," he said, and waited for her to look up. "I think we need to talk."

"All right," she said carefully. Then she got up and moved over to the stove.

"What are you doing?"

"Making tea." She poured water from a steaming tea kettle into a blue-and-white teapot, then spooned in tea leaves. When had she turned the kettle on? He must have missed it. He let her putter for a few more moments, until at last she brought the teapot and teacups to the table. She sat down carefully, pulling Julia onto her lap. She folded her hands on the table in front of her.

"Let's talk," she said.

Chapter Ten

He sat there, staring intently at her, longingly, as if he didn't know what to say. Well, she'd put him out of his misery. "Nice weather we're having, isn't it?"

A frown furrowed his forehead. "What?"

"I said, we're having nice weather. You know, sort of as an icebreaker. No pun intended. Sometimes when people want to start a conversation but don't know how to do it, they begin by talking about the weather."

He grinned slightly. "Yes, we did have lovely weather today. It's been warming up."

"I hear there's another cold front due to come across the state tomorrow."

For a moment he didn't answer, just continued staring, as if he were some hungry peasant and she a bakery shop. So she picked up the tiny silver strainer and poured tea. It made her feel very Victorian. She wasn't

183

sure she liked that feeling. She didn't think she'd get along with corsets.

He reached out and took her hands, holding them firmly, but not so tightly that she couldn't get away. If she wanted to. She didn't. Slowly, she moved her gaze up to meet his. His eyes were piercing, alive, intense. So this, she thought abstractly, is what it means to be mesmerized.

"We need to talk about what's between us," he said.

"And what is that?"

He shrugged. "I think that we feel an attraction for each other." He paused. His gaze dropped to the table, to their hands, hers still clasped in his. "At least I feel an attraction for you, and I think you feel the same."

"Yes," she said softly. "I do." She gently slid her hands from the shelter of his. "But that doesn't mean we have to do anything about it. People are more than a mass of raging emotions. Besides, I'm ten years older than you are." There. She'd thrown down the gauntlet.

He traced the design on the tablecloth with the point of his knife. "Ten years," he said thoughtfully. "That's quite an age difference."

She felt her face grow hot. She hated to blush. "You don't have to make it sound so definite." She hoped she didn't sound defensive.

He grinned. It was a slight grin. "Isn't it?"

She had to grin back. An equally slight grin. "I guess it is. There's nothing we can do about it, though, is there? We can't ignore my age and hope it will go away." She spread her hands out on the table in front of her. If she said it before he did, she would save face. "So I guess we should just be friends. Good friends." She glanced quickly at him. He was watching her, studying her, considering. Alex Hogan certainly wasn't one to make snap decisions.

"Is that what you want?" he said at last.

No, she cried out silently. *It's not what I want, but it's what I think I can have.* "Yes." There was another silence. She looked up to see that he'd shuttered his eyes, closing off a part of himself. She'd probably done the same thing without realizing it.

Alex raised his cup of tea. "Then here's to the beginning of a glorious friendship between Liz the librarian—"

"And Alex the school-bus driver," she finished for him, raising her own cup.

After a swallow, he set down his cup and shoved the plate of decadence toward her. "And now for something completely sensual," he said, a teasing glint in his eye. She thought she'd seen a quick stab of pain, but she must have been mistaken. "Even," he added, "if it is small."

This time she couldn't resist laughing.

"Oh, Kathryn, it was so . . . oh . . . I don't know. Liberating, I guess. Yes. It was liberating."

"Liberated at last?" Kathryn's voice was teasing. "One usually thinks of liberation coming after a release from prison, or after one takes off a bra that's too tight.

Or, in my mother's case, her girdle. Remember girdles? Thank goodness we missed them. So why do you feel liberated?"

"Because I'm free to be friends with Alex. We've agreed that even though we might be attracted to each other, we'd rather be friends."

There was a short pause. Then Kathryn said, "That's probably a good thing. That way neither of you will get too involved. By the way, did you tell him? That you can't have bambinos?"

Liz paused to scoop Julia up onto her bed. Pregnant kitties shouldn't jump very high. Of course, Julia pounced and leaped all over the place. She didn't know the meaning of the words sitting still. "No. It never came up. And it probably won't. It's not something I go around telling people."

"You mean you don't wear a great big scarlet *B* for barren?"

Liz chuckled. "You mean *H* for hysterectomy. No, silly. Besides, Hartley is a small town, and you know how those kinds of things get around. The grapevine would have a great day with this one. You're the only person who knows. Except my gynecologist, of course. A lack of a uterus is sort of hard to miss."

"Hmmm."

"What 'hmmm'?"

"Look, Liz, I'm your best friend, and I love you like a sister. But sometimes you're not very smart. I think

186

you should be up front with Alex. As long as you're putting things on the table, why not this, too?"

Julia clambered up on Liz's lap and turned on the charm. "It's just a very personal thing."

"Because it makes you feel less of a woman." It was a statement, not a question. Kathryn had been her friend for a very long time.

Liz tickled Julia's chin. "Not exactly," she said slowly.

"Then what, exactly?"

"I feel left out. As if everyone except me got a ticket to a special party. As if everyone except me knows this little secret. You know how women talk about having babies? They tell all the gory details of their experiences in childbirth, and it's as if it's their initiation into some exclusive club. I'm not a part of that. I never can be."

"I don't have children," her friend pointed out.

"But you could, if you wanted to."

"Liz," Kathryn's voice was patient, "I teach elementary school, remember? Believe me when I say that there are times that most mothers would envy you."

Liz smiled. "You are such a comfort," she said sarcastically.

"Yeah, well, it's late, and this comfort has to go to beddy-bye. We get up at the crack of dawn, you know. Gotta be at school when the little darlings arrive."

"Good night, friend."

"Good night, ladies, good night," Kathryn sang.

Liz replaced the receiver and pulled up the covers. She reached for the book on her night table. "I haven't gotten much reading done since I met Alex Hogan," she told Julia. The cat sprawled on the other pillow, closed her eyes and purred louder. "Or since you came to live with me. I seem to spend my time cooking, or doing things with Alex, or playing chase-the-feather with you." Since Julia obviously wasn't going to answer, Liz opened her book. The biography of Julia Child. "Did you know that Julia Child didn't know how to cook until she was in her midthirties?" she asked her cat. Julia opened her eyes at the sound of a page turning. The feline Julia was more impressed by the bookmark sticking out of the book. Julia pounced.

"Oh, my!" Liz looked at her cat. "Julia, it's Thursday night. I missed 'Mystery.' This is the first time in years that I've missed 'Mystery.' "

"I forgot to ask you," his voice said over the phone. "Did you find out who said 'The way to a man's heart is through his stomach'?" It was Friday afternoon. Traditionally, at the library, the slowest hours of the week.

"I forgot to tell you," she answered, smiling into the telephone. "Let me find the piece of paper." She rummaged in her book bag for her note. "According to several sources I consulted," she said, listing the titles of the books in her best librarian voice, "that saying is attributed to a woman named Fanny Fern, which was a pseudonym for Sara Payson Willis Parton. She wrote that line in a work called *Fern Leaves,* which was published in 1853. However, there are several other quotes from the same period of time that are similar. Is that the exact information you needed?"

"That is exactly what I wanted to know. I have another question for you. Do you know of any librarians who are free this evening?"

Her smile grew into a grin. "There are four librarians here today. Shall I ask them?"

"No, that won't be necessary. I think one librarian is enough. You, for instance. Are you free this evening?"

"As a matter of fact, I am. What did you have in mind?"

"How about dinner and a movie?"

This was a date! Liz thought. Alex was asking her out on a date. She hadn't been on a date for more years than she wanted to remember. Still, she squelched the quickening of her pulse. It wasn't a real date. This was just two friends doing something together. "Sounds wonderful."

Saturday it was a trip to Columbus to the art museum, where they moseyed in quiet contemplation past miles of paintings. Then to the conservatory, where they moseyed in warm, fragrant, humid air past miles of flowers. Sunday was bitterly cold, with a raw north wind. They rented videos and watched them in front of a respectable fire in the fireplace. They also watched Julia try in vain to catch Burl's tail. Liz didn't know

which one she enjoyed watching more. When the fire
had burned down to crimson coals, they roasted marshmallows and ended up with sticky fingers.

When Julia finally gave up on Burl's tail and crawled
up on Alex's lap, he picked her up and held her to his
chest. She turned up her engine. She knew she had a
good thing.

"Can you feel the kittens?" Liz asked as she was
rewinding the video.

"I'm not sure. What do they feel like?"

Liz frowned. "Like little lumps. Pretty soon they'll
be even more active. People say sometimes it's like
feeling a prizefight going on."

"I wonder what she'll think of that. Julia, you have
no idea what you're in for."

Liz shoved another marshmallow on the long fork.
"Do you want another one?" she asked him. When he
nodded, she slid on a second marshmallow. "I only
hope Julia knows what to do with them. Jessie says
every time she's ever had a litter of puppies she stays
home for the first week and watches them breathe. Sally
says the same thing about kittens. But I can't take the
week off work." She opened the fire screen and balanced the fork on a smoldering log. "Sally and Jessie
have both promised to come over and play midwife.
I've never midwifed a litter of kittens before. My cats
have always been spayed." She sent him a rueful grin.
"I guess Julia and I both have a new experience coming

up." She slowly rotated the marshmallow over the coals.

"You sound uncertain about it."

"I've been reading books about birthing kittens. Some of them say that sometimes mother cats don't know what to do with the babies and kill them. She's so young, a kitten herself." She checked the marshmallows. Not quite done. She slid them back over the coals. "Maybe I'm worrying for nothing."

Alex reached over with his socked foot and tapped her ankle. "Have you talked to Melissa March?"

"She says not to worry, that Julia will undoubtedly be fine, but that if I notice any signs of odd behavior, I should call her."

"I think that's good advice. Especially the part about not worrying."

Liz checked the marshmallows. This time they were a perfect all-over golden brown. Tongue sticking between her teeth in concentration, she carefully slid the first one off the fork. "You have to be careful that the whole thing comes off, not just the outer brown part. Ta da!" She held it out to him.

"How do you get them so perfect?" he asked in amazement. "Mine always burn."

"You always stick them too close to the fire. You're too impatient."

He grinned at her unrepentantly. "I've been told that before."

"Maybe you should listen. The best things in life take time." She popped her own marshmallow into her mouth. It was wonderful.

"We did this backwards."

"You mean you eat them before you roast them?"

She frowned at him. "No. We ate dessert first."

"What do you suggest?"

"I have baked potato soup in the Crock-Pot. And I made it with lots of bacon. Just for you."

"So that's what's been smelling so delicious. In case you hadn't noticed, all through 'Brother Cadfael' I was drooling like Burl."

"Then I'll bring soup out. No, don't get up. You'll disturb Julia, and Burl will probably want to go out. Let's let them sleep." She glanced at the videos on top of the table. "Do you want another 'Brother C,' or *The Shawshank Redemption?*"

"*Shawshank,*" he answered. "My sister Sharon recommended it. I didn't know who Tim Robbins was. She told me to watch this movie."

He heard the sound of a fork against a bowl. "What are you doing?" he called into the kitchen.

"Making biscuits. Can't have soup without biscuits. They'll be done in a jiffy."

He chuckled. "Fanny Fern was right," he called to her. Liz was amazing. She thought nothing of making food at the drop of a hat. Excellent food. "My jeans have gotten tighter since I met you. It's all those

192

popovers and biscuits and manicotti and small yet sensual bits of decadence."

She appeared in the doorway, dough-covered fork in her hand. "Do you want me to stop cooking for you?"

"No!"

Her eyes twinkled. "That was a definite answer."

"I love it that you cook."

"I'm glad you love it," she said with a grin. She disappeared into the kitchen. He heard the oven door open, a pan being slid onto a rack, and the door close. Nice, homey sounds. He closed his eyes and settled deeper into the couch. With Julia's purring rumble against his chest and Burl snoring at his feet, the warmth from the fire and from Liz, he was so comfortable and content, he could stay here, without moving, forever.

Yeah. Forever. That sounded like a good idea.

"Yoo hoo!"

"Hi, Kath," Liz called back. "I'm getting my sweats on. I'll only be a minute." She pulled her sweatshirt over her head. She picked up her shoes and padded into the living room to where Kathryn was playing feather-on-a-string with Julia. The feather was losing.

"This cat is manic."

"I wish I had her energy." Liz slipped her door key into her pants pocket. "Ready?"

"I'm so glad it warmed up today," Kathryn said as they headed down the sidewalk. "Walking in the cold isn't fun."

Liz slanted a look at her friend. "You call this not cold?"

"You're just a hothouse flower."

"You grew up in the heat, too."

"But I got out of the heat and came up here a long time ago. My blood is used to the cold. You wait, when you've been here a few more years, you won't even notice the cold."

"Sure," Liz said. "Like I really believe that."

They turned right at the corner. "So tell me everything that's going on in your life," Liz said.

"You don't want to be bored."

"Bored is for friends. You know all the boring details of my platonic relationship with Alex. It's your turn to spill it."

Kathryn spilled it all the way to the high school, where they left the sidewalk and headed across the field to the track. Ten times around was their usual quota. The track wasn't as interesting as doing their walking on the street. But the track was lit by the lights of the all-night gas station on the other side of the fence. It was easier to see the track than the street. They could talk and talk and not have to pay attention to jagged sidewalks in the dark.

By the first time around, Liz was caught up on the cast and crew for *The Sound of Music*. Sylvie Novino, who was three months pregnant, was playing the oldest Von Trapp daughter, which was no surprise, since everyone knew that she loved Rodgers and Hammerstein, and she still looked like a teenager. They just hoped she wasn't showing much by the performance date. The woman who was playing Maria was, of all things, a former nun. Now she taught fifth grade. Liz knew her from the library. Of course, she knew many of the cast members. Not well, but at least by name. Hartley was a small town that felt like a small town. Everyone knew everyone. That was one of the things she liked about it. And also one of the things that could be the most annoying. The reading on the anonymity gauge was nil.

"If I could sing worth beans, I'd probably have tried out," she told Kathryn. "It sounds like fun."

"It is fun. It's community theater."

Liz was curious. "Why would you rather be music director than one of the players?"

"I decided it was time to do something completely different. Besides, the extra rehearsals give me an excuse to put some distance between me and Paul."

They walked a few yards in silence. "You were supposed to spill it all," Liz reminded her friend.

"You want to see my guts?"

"Sure. I've seen your guts before, and I've no doubt I'll see 'em again. This is what friends do—look at each other's guts and say, 'Yup, they're ugly,' and help each other go on from there."

They walked a few more yards in silence. Then Kathryn sighed loudly. "He's not what I thought he was." She shoved her hands in her pockets. "He's old-fashioned. You know, the kind of man who thinks women should stay at home and raise babies. I have absolutely no intention of having babies. Ever." Kathryn shot her a glance. "I know it's a sore subject with you, so I never wanted to bring it up."

"I'm a big girl. I can take it."

"He's such a product of his own time. He's forty-nine. He has all the traditional beliefs we grew up with. And out of."

"We had to. We had to support ourselves."

"I don't think I can go back to the kind of life he wants to give me. You know, the little-wife kind of thing. I've come too far, baby."

"Can you two talk about it?"

"You know, Liz, I don't even think it's worth it anymore." She unpocketed her hands and held them out in front of her. "Since I've been on the production side of the musical, I've gotten to know lots more men. Including Carl Petersen. Do you know him? He's the high school shop teacher. He's doing the sets." She looked up at the sky. "But I am *not* going to talk about him, so don't bother asking. When there's something to tell, I'll tell all." She shot Liz an accusing glance. "Unlike some people I know."

Liz merely chuckled. Kathryn was given to flights of the dramatic. "I'll be patient. Unlike some people I know," she retorted in Kathryn's exact tones.

Kathryn frowned. "Seems like the younger they are, the more they're what we want them to be." She stopped walking and put her hand on Liz's arm. "Is that why you like Alex so much?"

Liz pursed her lips in thought. "I like Alex because he doesn't try to change me."

"Maybe I ought to find a younger man and have my own fling. I could sure use some fun. Time is not exactly flying."

"I'm not having a fling," Liz said quietly. Firmly.

"Well, what do you call it, then?"

"We're good friends."

Kathryn raised her eyebrows skeptically. "What about sex?"

"It isn't an issue."

"Well, what about when it *is* an issue? Unless he's gay, it's bound to come up. No pun intended."

"Alex Hogan is not gay," Liz stated firmly. "And sex is not going to be an issue. We're friends. It's a great thing to be." She started walking again.

But was it? she thought later that night as she slid beneath the covers. Alone. As she'd been for over ten years. Alone. Granted, Julia was there, purring up a storm. But a cat wasn't the same thing as a man. She punched her pillow into a more comfortable shape. It didn't do any good. She was still as restless as she'd ever been.

With a sigh, Liz got out of bed and shoved her arms into her thick terry-cloth bathrobe. She pulled her slippers on against the cold of the night floor, then wandered out into the kitchen. Maybe some hot chocolate would help her relax. She doubted it would. Still, chocolate was always worth a try. She poured a cup of milk and set it to heat gently in the microwave.

The thing was, she thought, as she stared out into the dark night, she'd always been alone. Even when she was married to Richard. Odd how you could live with someone and still be alone, still be lonely. When the timer dinged, she pulled out her hot milk and stirred in chocolate syrup. She set the spoon in the sink, where it looked forlorn and lost. Carol, the other reference librarian, often commented that she got heartily sick and tired of her husband and children leaving their dirty dishes in the sink instead of putting them in the dishwasher. "How much longer could it take to open the stupid dishwasher?" she'd ask anyone who'd listen.

Right now Liz thought she'd give anything to have someone else leave his dishes in the sink. *Be honest,* she chided herself. *Not just anyone. Alex. You'd give anything to have Alex leave his dishes in your sink. You'd give anything to have Alex here so he had dirty dishes to leave.* It was such a lovely fantasy, which was the real reason she hadn't told Alex she couldn't have children. As long as he didn't know, she could pretend that someday things might work out for them. She wasn't willing to give up the fantasy. Not yet. Not when being around Alex made her feel more alive than she had in a long time.

She carried her cup of hot chocolate back to her bedroom, where she scuffed off her slippers and slid out of her robe. Julia, coiled on the other pillow, didn't look up. For once, Julia was quiet. She was a quiet sleeper, unlike Burl, who snored and snuffled and snorted in his sleep. Alex had said it was something he'd had to get used to when Burl came to live with him—the noise at night.

Alex. Suddenly, Liz had to talk to him, hear his voice. She glanced at the clock. Ten o'clock. Was that too late to call? She knew Alex got up practically in the middle of the night to get to his bus on time. But she also knew he sometimes watched the 10 o'clock news. She decided to risk it. She reached for the phone.

"Hello." His voice wasn't the voice of a man suddenly awakened.

She was suddenly shy. "It's me," she got out, feeling herself blush.

"Hello, Me," he teased.

"I, um, I just wanted to say hello. And thank you for being my friend." Then she heard what she'd said and she rolled her eyes. "Gee, that sounded pretty Hallmark."

"Are you all right?"

"I'm fine."

"You sound strange."

"I'm fine," she insisted. "I was talking to Kathryn this evening. We went walking, and spent a couple of hours talking. It made me realize that I value your friendship."

"I'm glad," he said. "I value your friendship, too." She could hear the sound of puzzlement in his voice.

"I'm sorry if I woke you."

"You didn't. I'm waiting for Burl to come in. Then I'm going to bed."

She'd peeked into his bedroom once. It was peaceful, in a utilitarian sort of way. A simple chair and table. And a big bed heaped high with covers and pillows. Oh, dear, she thought, better not think of Alex in his bed. But it was like pink elephants. Once she'd told herself not to think of Alex in his bed, the vision stuck. And what a vision it was. Liz closed her eyes to capture it more fully.

"Liz? Are you still there?"

Her eyes popped open. "Yes. I'm still here."

"I value your friendship also. And your cooking," he added. "I can't forget your cooking."

She wanted to cook for him forever and ever. But over the phone, she heard him open his door. Evidently Burl was coming in.

"Well, good night," she said softly.

"Are you sure you're okay?" he asked again.

"Very sure. It's late, and I know you need to get up early, but I just wanted to thank you for being my friend."

"You're welcome."

"Good night, Alex."

"Good night, John Boy."

Liz chuckled as she hung up the phone and drew her covers more closely under her chin. Then she had to rearrange her nightgown, which had become all twisted. She wondered if Alex wore pajamas. Somehow, she didn't think so. He wasn't the pajamas type. He was an in-the-buff kind of guy. She'd hugged him a couple of times, so she knew there wasn't an ounce of extra anything on his body anywhere. Jessie was right—he did fit the breed standard of perfection for the human male. And right now, at this very moment, that piece of perfection was naked and settling into his bed, perhaps languorously stretching those long legs. Those long, naked legs.

"Oh, why did I have to think of Alex *au naturel?*" she moaned. "Now I'll never get to sleep!"

Her eyes felt gritty the next morning as she put water on for tea. "And a great big congratulations to Kari, here," the morning weather forecaster said with a great big smile as he motioned to the woman anchor. "She and her husband are expecting another little bundle of joy."

Kari's smile wasn't as great and big. Probably morning sickness, Liz thought sourly as she snapped off the television. The whole world was fertile, fecund and blossoming. Even Julia was beginning to show. *Liz, you're being a child,* she chided herself. *You can't have one, so you decide to act like one. That's really adult of you.*

Liz mashed canned cat food into Julia's dry chow. Julia watched her like a hawk, trying to paw at the bowl. "There you go, little one," she crooned as she set down the bowl. Julia gobbled her food hunched over her bowl, the sides of her belly bulging slightly. The kittens were growing.

It was another of those pink elephant things, Liz mused as she stirred her tea and watched her cat inhale food. Any other time she'd not have paid the slightest attention to Miss Morning Show Kari's announcement. But now, because it was a sore subject with her at the moment, Hartley's entire pregnant population persisted in parading past her. Intellectually, she knew fate was not thumbing its nose at her, but it hurt, nonetheless.

The visibly pregnant woman made her way to the reference desk. Liz gave her a professional smile. She hoped it wasn't an actual grimace.

"Can you please show me where the books on Lamaze are?"

"Of course. Do you have a specific title in mind? Or do you want to browse the section?"

"Let me browse." The woman's smile was radiant. It was the kind of smile that invited the whole world to join in.

Liz didn't. Not even a twitch of her lips. Instead, she put one trusty-librarian-made-for-walking shoe in front of the other as she led the woman to the 618's. "The information on pregnancy and labor and delivery are here, on these three shelves. If you don't find exactly what you're looking for, let us know." She had to get away from those shelves. No, what she really had to do was get a hold of herself. *Grow up, Liz,* she scolded herself. *Taking it out on every pregnant woman who comes into the library will do no good. It'll only make you more miserable.* She realized she wasn't being very noble. She didn't like that in herself. "There are also some videos in the AV section," she made herself say as penance. "If you're interested, I'll be happy to show you where they are."

The woman smiled her smile again. This time, Liz managed to smile back. "I'd rather have books today, but thanks." She placed her hand on her belly. It was one of those pregnant-woman gestures that Liz suspected was unconscious. After all, Liz told herself, if you had a baby growing inside you, you'd probably go around all day patting it, too.

Chapter Eleven

That afternoon, Liz found herself at the reference desk with Carol, and decided to poke around the baby question. The way one poked a bruise to see if it still hurt. "When you got married," she asked during a lull, "did your husband want children?"

Carol looked thoughtful for a moment. Then she nodded. "I think it was some sort of elitist thing at first. He said that if all the thinking people—the people who were concerned with the fate of the earth—all stopped having children, the world would be in worse shape than it was already. He went to Berkeley, you know. So he said it was our responsibility, our obligation, as intelligent people to have children." She chuckled to herself. "That was, until he saw Megan being born." Her face grew a beatific smile. "Then he turned into the prototype of the doting father. When the other two were born he just had more children to dote on."

"What about now?" Liz wanted to know.

"Now? When he's had a few glasses of wine, he'll wax philosophical and say children are the completion of his life. And he brings me flowers every year on their birthdays. The big dope still can't put his dirty dishes in the dishwasher, but he brings me flowers on my kids' birthdays. So I keep him. Say, why this sudden interest in the little monsterlets?"

But Liz was saved from answering by a flustered woman who rushed up to the reference desk. "My son has to do a report on prehistoric mammals in Ohio. Can you show me where the books are?" Another short-lived lull was over.

"What does Attila think this is? The sixties?" Furious, Kendra rattled the piece of paper in front of Liz's nose.

"Hold it still. I can't read it when you're waving it around like that."

"There's one in your mailbox, too. We all got one. This time he's gone too far, Liz."

Liz hurried across the staff room to the row of mailboxes. Sure enough, there was a new missive from Attila. " *'It has come to my attention,'* " she read out loud, " *'that hemlines are rising at a disproportional rate.'* " Liz looked up at Kendra and grinned. "Disproportional to what?" she asked.

"Keep reading," Kendra growled.

" *'This must stop. A library is not a disco.'* Disco? Disco in Hartley? *'Beginning tomorrow morning, any staff member who wears a skirt that is more than two inches above the knee will be sent home to change. This will be considered unpaid leave.'* "

"Two inches!" Kendra was outraged. "Do you believe this? He's treating us as if we're children. It's insulting. That's what it is. I'll bet he's going to get out a ruler and make us kneel down and measure our damn skirts. I know," she added with a wicked gleam in her eye, "we'll sabotage all his rulers. He doesn't know what six inches is, anyway."

With an amused grin, Liz sank down in the one remaining comfortable chair. She decided to try some of the techniques she'd learned at those seminars on dealing with difficult patrons. "You sound upset," she observed.

"I am upset! So are all the other clerks."

"Upset about what?" It was Cecily, with a basket of storytime supplies on her arm.

"Attila's newest missive," Kendra grumbled. "We've had it."

"Ah." Cecily nodded wisely in understanding. "You mean you're all revolting?"

"It's outrageous!" the young clerk asserted, evidently missing the pun.

Liz tried to smother her laughter.

"It might seem like nothing to you, Liz, but all your skirts are long anyway. We're younger. We want to wear short skirts. And then we get stuck with a boss who has a small-town sixties kind of sensibility. Don't you see how unfair this is?" she wailed plaintively. "Will you go talk to him for us? Please?"

Liz shook her head. "I'm not getting into this one," she said.

"C'mon, Liz," Cecily urged. "Where's your team spirit?"

"My team spirit is defined by edible goodies," Liz said firmly. "You're on your own with this one." She grinned. "But if it'll help, I'll bring in something truly scrumptious next week."

One of the other clerks stuck her head in the staff room. "Phone for you, Liz, on the public line." She waggled her eyebrows. "It's a guy."

Kendra and Cecily pounced. "I bet it's Romeo!" Kendra hissed.

"Shhh!" Cecily hissed, making hushing motions "Let's listen."

Liz picked up the phone and turned her back on the two younger women. They were right; it was Romeo.

"Say, Liz, I was wondering if you'd help me out."

"Sure. What do you need?"

"I need a big favor." She thought she heard a teasing glint in his voice.

"How big is big?" she asked, smiling. "Bigger than

207

six inches?" Behind her, she could hear Kendra and Cecily begin to giggle. She looked over her shoulder and rolled her eyes at them.

"This one is really big."

"That big?" she asked with a knowing grin at her friends. "Gee. I know I told you size doesn't matter, but I don't know if I can handle one as big as that." Her friends dissolved into hilarity.

"I need you to come with me this weekend. My family is having a big get-together for my parent's anniversary, and I want you to be there."

Liz was puzzled. "Me?"

Alex cleared his throat. "My sister has this friend who has been trying to . . . well, she makes it very uncomfortable for me. She's nice and all that, but I'm not interested in her, and she . . . I thought if I brought you, you could . . . "

"So you want me to play your girlfriend."

"Yeah," he said, relief in his voice. "Just for the weekend. I'll make it up to you."

'You'll make it up to me?" she asked, watching Kendra and Cecily closely. "How?"

"I'll think of something."

"Will you promise I'll like it?" Her friends were practically drooling. She stuck out her tongue at them.

"Promise. We'll leave on Friday after you get off work and'll be back Sunday late afternoon."

Liz thought. "I'll see if Kathryn can take care of Julia." Then she decided to give Kendra and Cecily one more thrill. "If I'm going to be playing your girlfriend, will we be sharing a bedroom?" Her friends gasped.

There was a long pause before he answered. "Would you like that?" His voice was suddenly soft and warm, sending little spiking tingles up and down and all over her insides. "Would that make you happy?"

Visions of Alex danced in her head. Yes, she wanted to shout, quoting James Joyce. Yes, it would. Yes. Yes. "I just wanted to know, um, how, um, realistically do you want me to pretend to be your girlfriend?"

"As realistically as you want." His voice sounded like melted chocolate, smooth and silky.

Kendra and Cecily were clutching each other, excitedly intent on what she'd say next. "That real?"

"I know it's asking a lot of you," he said, "but I really want this woman to get the idea that I'm not up for grabs."

"Well, then." Liz grinned at her friends as she spoke into the phone. "Let's give her a show. Consider yourself grabbed."

Kathryn was, of course, very agreeable to checking in on Julia several times during the weekend. "Especially if you leave lots of goodies for the babysitter," she said. "Chocolate goodies." She patted her thighs as she reached for another cookie.

Liz laughed as she moved the cookie jar out of Kathryn's reach. "I think I can manage that. I have to make something to take anyway, you know; a thank-you gift for Alex's sister and mother."

Kathryn closed her eyes and munched her last cookie in bliss. Suddenly, her eyes popped open. "Doesn't it make you nervous?"

"What?"

"Pretending to be his girlfriend. You're so much older than he is. Aren't you afraid someone will think you're his mother or something?"

"That's my best friend," Liz said sarcastically. "Always the first to point out that the emperor has no clothes."

"I keep telling you, that's what friends are for. Besides," her friend persisted, "I know you don't look your age, and sometimes you don't even act it, but aren't you afraid someone will think about the word *gigolo*? Or maybe they'll think you're sex-starved or something." She pointed a finger. "Maybe they'll think he's after your money."

"I don't have any money." Liz didn't even want to think about the sex-starved comment.

"I know that, but they don't." Kathryn leaned forward against the table. "Doesn't it bother you?"

Liz thought. "No," she said at last.

Kathryn frowned. "Why not?"

"Because it isn't real, that's why. It's just an act. To get Alex off the hook with this friend of his sister's. Alex and I are friends. You just finished telling me that friends help friends who are in a jam."

"Or a pickle, or any other food phrase you want to bring into it to distract me with. But what if it were real?

What if you really were his girlfriend, going to meet his family for the first time. His parents are probably what—only fifteen years older than you are. Wouldn't it bother you then?" She stretched to reach the cookie jar. "Get these things away from me, please," she said through a mouthful of cookie.

Liz shoved away from the table to set the cookie jar back on the counter. She swiped the counter for stray crumbs, then straightened the stack of books she'd brought home.

"Wouldn't it?" her friend persisted.

"I don't know," she said at last.

"Well, this is advice time. If I were you, and the most gorgeous guy I'd ever known asked me to pretend to be his girlfriend and I was ten years older than he was and was in love with him, I'd sure want to know if it bothered me." She ran out of breath.

"But you see, Kathryn, you're *not* me, and this *is* just pretend, and it's not ever going to ever be anything but that." Liz took another swipe at the counter. "I'm certainly not going to worry about something that's a moot point. It's a complete waste of time."

"Then why do you insist on wiping a spotless counter? And why do I hear a little smidgen of regret in your voice?"

"The trouble with best friends," Liz said into the air, "is that they think they know everything about you. And they think they have the right to stick their noses into business that is not theirs."

"And they also," Kathryn stated smugly, "take care of your cat when you decide to go gallivanting around the countryside posing as girlfriends to gorgeous men."

Liz leaned against the counter. "I guess you're right."

"Of course I'm right," came the smug reply. "Speaking of said cat, where is she?"

"Sleeping. Oh, that reminds me . . ." Liz said, before Kathryn could return to her original subject. "I'll leave you lots of cat food, and Dr. March's phone numbers. I'll have to remember to let her know I'm leaving town and that you'll be taking care of Julia. Oh, and I'll have to get the phone number for Alex's sister, too, in case of an emergency."

Kathryn waved her hand. "Relax. Taking care of a cat for a weekend isn't like doing brain surgery. I have cats, remember?"

"But she's pregnant."

"Well, she's not going to have her kittens this weekend. I've had pregnant cats before. Trust me; she'll be fine. I'll check on her twice a day, and if there's even the remotest hint of a problem, I'll call Dr. March. Don't be an overprotective mother."

Liz chuckled. "I am."

"She's coming," Alex told his sister that night on the phone. He braced himself for Sharon's excited screech. He was glad he had.

"How wonderful. We'll all get to meet her."

"We'll be there around ten-thirty. You sure it's no problem to put us up? I can call Mom."

Sharon made a rude noise. "Mom has a house full of people already. Remember, Shelby's offspring will be wreaking havoc over there. Besides, it'll be easier for Liz if she eases into the family gradually, if you know what I mean. Mom may be tactful, but Shelby doesn't know the meaning of the word *subtle*. You don't want your overbearing sister to scare her off."

"You're not all that subtle yourself, kiddo."

"Ah, but I can be."

"Make sure you are."

"Will do. See you Friday."

Alex sank down into the couch. Burl took this as a definite invitation. Burl wasn't subtle either.

"I'm taking her to meet the family, big guy."

Burl thumped his tail against the couch and tried to haul more of himself onto Alex's lap.

"She's going to pretend to be my girlfriend."

Burl heaved a long and windy sigh.

Alex stared out the window into the winter night. There was nothing, as far as he could see. Only black. Only night. He needed to shake Liz out of the just-friends thing she'd somehow gotten emblazoned in her brain. He wondered if asking Liz to pretend to be his girlfriend was such a good idea after all. "It seemed like the thing to do at the time," he told Burl. "I hope she doesn't think it's insulting."

Burl grunted and stretched.

"Maybe," he said to the black dog, who was half on his lap, "maybe I should explain that I don't mean any disrespect at all. I know she'll get along with my family, and I know everyone will love Liz. Maybe then, if we don't all overwhelm her, it won't have to be pretend." He absently ruffled the fur on Burl's head. "Maybe it will even be this weekend." Suddenly he felt optimistic.

"You're sure off in la-la land," Cecily remarked the next afternoon at the reference desk. She dropped the *Physicians' Desk Reference* on the desk. It landed with a heavy thud. "You haven't budged from that dreamy-eyed stare for the past five minutes. I've timed you."

"You don't budge from stares. You're mixing your metaphors."

"I'm not mixing them, and you're right; you don't. At least you didn't until now. So what gives?" She waggled her eyebrows and twirled an imaginary mustache. "Dreaming of the great performance to come?"

Liz grinned at her friend. "You read too many children's books."

"You don't read enough children's books," Cecily answered perkily.

"They pickle your brain," Liz teased.

"No, that's all the cookbooks you read. I've never

known anyone who could read a cookbook like any normal person reads a novel."

"Great plots in cookbooks."

"But then you bring us food, so I guess we forgive that little idiosyncrasy. So, are you looking forward to the great getaway? You're leaving Friday after work, right?"

"As if you didn't know," Liz said with a grin. "You all know more about this whole trip than I do."

Cecily shrugged. "It's just better than a soap opera. Can I help you?" she asked the suit-and-tied child who came to a deliberate stop before her.

"Will you please show me your books on arcane knowledge?" the solemn child asked.

Better than a soap opera? Was that supposed to be a compliment? Liz wondered.

"No," she told Julia that night. "You can't climb in there. This is a suitcase. It's for putting clothes in, not kitties." But Julia thought otherwise. Julia thought it was a great place to hide. It even had ribbons to play with.

Liz scooped her kitty out of the suitcase and hugged her under her chin. "I'm going to miss you, you rascal." Julia wiggled to get down. "I wonder if Alex's sister has any critters. Other than a baby." A baby. "I asked him if it would be too much for her, with a new baby, to have us staying there," she told her cat. Her cat ignored her. She carefully folded a pair of slacks into the suit-case. "Alex said his mother's house would be full of his other sister and her kids." She slipped a sweater off its hanger and put the sleeves together. "So it looks like I'll be staying with a baby. I can't seem to get away from them. Babies and pregnant women. And pregnant kitties."

Julia gave up on the suitcase ribbons. She tromped across the bed to the pillow, where she threw herself down and began to wash her spotless belly. Her begin-ning-to-bulge belly.

"That's right," Liz muttered. "Rub it in."

But Julia had stopped washing. She was suddenly immobile. Listening intently.

The doorbell rang.

'I hope it's not too late," he said.

It would never be too late for a visit from Alex, she thought. "Come in."

The gleam in his eye made him look younger, and somehow even more attractive. It was a gleam of mis-chief, of a secret, of utter delight. But still he stood on the step, the gleam growing brighter.

"You don't want to come in?"

"Can you come out and play?"

It was the last thing she'd expected him to say. "Now? At this hour?"

"Best time for a snowball fight. Why, I've had regu-lar snowball battles on nights such as this."

"You're crazy."

"Yes, ma'am, I am. But then, why are you laughing?"

Liz shook her head in amazement. "Because I've—because you're—because I don't believe you're serious."

"Serious is my middle name. You never had a snowy childhood. I intend to correct that oversight. So, put on your coat and get yourself out here."

Snowy childhood? Come to think of it, she hadn't had much of a childhood at all, always trying to make her mother proud of her, trying to live up to expectations that she now realized were unrealistic. Now here was Alex, who never asked her to be anything other than what she was, who always listened and encouraged, inviting her to be a child again. "I'll be right out."

In a whirl she pulled on socks and shoes, shoved her arms into her coat sleeves and was out the door. "Alex?" Where was he? She looked around. There were three or four snowballs on the front steps, but no Alex.

Suddenly, a snowball sailed out from behind a bush and splated at her feet. Without thinking, she picked up one of the porch snowballs and hurled it toward the bush.

"Come on, librarian lady," his voice taunted her from behind the bush. "You can aim better than that!" The war was on.

They battled through her yard and out into the deserted street. They ducked behind trees and bushes and Alex's truck in her driveway. Liz's mittens quickly became caked with tiny bits of clumped snow, and her nose grew numb. If she'd paid the slightest attention to her feet, she'd have noticed that they felt like solid ice, but she was having too good a time to bother with such details.

Where was he hiding now? Liz peeked around the side of the house and scanned her yard. She didn't see him anywhere. She listened intently, but there was no sound. The night was pure silence. She reached down and scooped up a handful of snow and packed it quickly and quietly, always on the lookout, always ready to heave it the instant she caught sight of him. Where was he?

Suddenly, an arm whipped around her waist, and with a howl of victory, Alex pulled her over and she landed on top of him in the snow.

"I won, librarian lady."

Liz, giggling, tried to sit up, but he pulled her back. "I hope you're not expecting some sort of reward," she giggled.

"I have the only reward I want."

"What's that?" She rolled over in the snow to find him dangerously close. Closer than he'd ever been, close enough to kiss. "What's that?" she asked again.

"This weekend you're pretending to be my utterly devoted girlfriend." His voice was a mere whisper, a whisper in the silence of the night. "I am sure you will give a stellar performance. A performance worthy of an Oscar."

A shiver that had nothing to do with the temperature

slithered around and up and down Liz's insides. "I hope you enjoy it," she whispered back, her gaze locked with his.

"I know I will."

He was going to kiss her, she thought. He was really going to kiss her. She could see it in his eyes, and in the way he tilted his head, so that his lips were but a whisper away from hers. She could feel it in the slight tensing of his body. He was going to kiss her. The shiver slithered again. She licked her lips in anticipation.

"Do you know what I'm going to do now?" he asked, his voice dark and promising.

"No," she lied.

The twinkle returned to his eyes. He sat up abruptly and began to brush snow off his jacket. "I'm going to go home. Lady, you have no business keeping me up at all hours of the night." He grinned and pulled her up, brushing her off, too.

"Me keep you up?" she asked in mock outrage. "And just who bullied whom into a snowball fight?"

"Bullied?"

"Yes, bullied. I was minding my own business when you came to my door and bullied me into coming out to play with you." She scowled playfully at him.

"Well, it's all your fault." He shook his finger under her nose.

"Why is it my fault?"

"Because how was I supposed to let you go on living

219

without ever having a snowball fight in the middle of the night? Answer me that."

Liz planted her hands on her hips. "Are you saying my childhood was deprived?"

"Yes, I am," Alex drawled. "And I'm here to correct it." Alex shoved his hand into his jeans pocket and pulled out his car keys. "You, librarian lady, are going to have a terrific time with me this weekend. You will return to Hartley a new person. No one will recognize you." He reached out a forefinger and ran it down her cheek. The touch was gentle. The touch was tender. "You're cold," he whispered. "You need to crawl into a nice warm bed. Come on, let's go."

Yes, Liz thought dreamily, her eyes almost closing on their own as she allowed Alex to lead her up the steps to her front door. She would love nothing more at this moment than to crawl into a nice warm bed. With Alex Hogan. He held the front door open for her and ushered her in.

She stood for a moment, poised in the doorway, gazing into his eyes. Unspoken questions flying back and forth. But then his lips brushed her cheek, and before she could reach out to him, he was in his truck. And she was standing in her doorway, in the night. Alone.

The next day at work, Liz wound her way through the miles of shelves to the 636.8s, the number Mr. Dewey had reserved for cat books. She quickly scanned the shelves until she found the book she was looking for. It was a book about breeding cats. Then she went in search of the clerk who was in charge of the newspapers. When she went home that evening, she had the cat book in her book bag and a stack of old *Wall Street Journal*'s in the trunk of her car.

Pulling into her driveway, Liz saw Kathryn's car was parked in front of the garage. What was Kathryn doing here? Liz wondered. She frowned in thought. It wasn't their usual walking night. Getting out of the car, she saw Kathryn on her porch. Something flat and square was in her hands.

"I have a good-luck present for you," Kathryn called out.

"I need good luck?" Liz pulled her book bag out of the car with one hand and with the other, scooped up the newspapers. She bumped the car door shut with her hip.

"When going to meet a man's family, a good-luck gift is always appropriate."

"Have you been reading Miss Manners again?" Liz teased. *"Manners 101?* Or *Manners for the Complete Philistine?"*

"Ha, ha. Very funny," Kathryn retorted. "Hurry up and unlock the door. I've been waiting in the cold all alone. I have play practice tonight, so I don't have much time."

Liz rolled her eyes as she inserted her key in the lock. "Bossy, bossy, bossy. It's a good thing we're friends." She shoved the door open and ushered Kathryn inside.

"What are the newspapers for?"

"Birthing kittens."

"Great use for the *Wall Street Journal*." Kathryn took the stack from her. "Where do you want these?"

"Oh, right there in a pile by the door, I guess."

Kathryn deposited the papers with a thump. "I really can't stay," she said, holding out the package. "But I want you to open this." She sounded excited.

Liz dropped her coat over the back of a chair and took the cheerfully wrapped box. "I don't suppose you'll tell me what's in it?" she asked.

Kathryn raised her eyebrows. "That would be defeating the whole purpose of wrapping it," she said.

Liz narrowed her eyes as she stared at her friend. "I can't tell if this is a joke or not."

Kathryn looked innocent. "This is not a joke," she announced. "You, my best friend, are going into battle. I can't let you go naked."

"I'd hardly call it battle," Liz protested. But she unwrapped the box anyway. The name on the box was that of Hartley's premier department store. Kathryn never shopped there—she always said that store was much too grand for the likes of them. Liz sent her friend a puzzled glance. Her friend shrugged. Liz opened the box and peeled back the pale pink tissue paper.

"Oh." The sound escaped her lips. She lifted it out. The silk felt warm and alive in her hands. She held it up. "I can't wear this," she protested. But her voice was soft. "It's too beautiful."

"Yeah. It's lovely," Kathryn agreed. "And it matches the nightgown."

"What nightgown?"

"The one still in the box."

Liz draped the dressing gown over her arm and peered into the box. Sure enough, nestled innocently in the tissue paper was a matching nightgown. Kathryn held it up for her. It was simple and elegant, without looking slinky and cheap. The kind of thing Liz would feel comfortable wearing, if she dared.

"I can't wear this," she said again.

"I cut the tags off and threw them away, so you can't return it," Kathryn said smugly. "So if you're not going to wear it, you better call the Salvation Army right now and ask them to come and get it. Which is a shame, because it's exactly your size, which I happen to know because you and I have worn the same size for years."

Liz stared dumbly at her friend. "Why?" she finally asked.

Kathryn shrugged again as she slithered the silk gown back into its box. "I told you: I couldn't let you go into battle naked."

"I wasn't planning on going naked."

"But you would have gone with your great big terry-cloth bathrobe that you've had since the Richard years, and your old cotton knit nightgown, and your bed socks." Kathryn scowled. "It would hardly've been a

223

romantic sight. At least you've outgrown curlers, and you don't do cold cream."

Liz shook her head. "You've never seemed very positive about my relationship with Alex."

Kathryn looked out the window. "I guess," she said, "I was jealous. Here you were, my best friend, falling in love with a terrific guy. It's magic, when you're first falling in love." She was silent for a moment. Then she took a deep breath and continued. "My relationship with Paul was ending. Actually, it was over. But I was afraid to admit it. Even to you. Even to myself." She smiled. An apologetic smile. "When you see someone else, even your best friend, find something that you want—something you want more than anything—well, it doesn't bring out the best in you."

Liz carefully folded the silk robe back into the box. "Have you told Paul that it's over?"

Kathryn nodded.

"When?"

"Last night." Kathryn's voice sounded just plain worn out.

"How did he take it?" Liz asked.

"I think he was relieved. I think deep down he knew that things weren't right between us. Then again, he's a man. They're not very perceptive." She attempted to make her voice sound more cheerful. Liz was not fooled.

"How do *you* feel?" she asked.

Kathryn didn't answer right away. Liz sat quietly, giving her friend time.

"Empty," Kathryn said at last. "I feel empty." She grimaced. "I need some cookies. Homemade cookies. Those chocolate crinkle cookies your grandmother used to make every Christmas."

"Comfort food?"

Her best friend nodded. "Yeah."

"I'll make you some," she promised.

"Thanks." Kathryn pushed herself up from the table and shoved her arms into the sleeves of her coat. "I gotta go," she said forlornly. "Play practice. I've gotta go coach a bunch of kids singing about their favorite things." She hummed a few bars of the Rodgers and Hammerstein song. For such a cheerful song, it was rather wan humming.

Liz saw Kathryn to the door and switched on the outside light against the dark of the driveway. Then she waved as her best friend drove away into the night. Alone.

Chapter Twelve

Friday was a perfect winter day, crisp, cold, and clean. Just like a toothpaste commercial, Alex thought as he pulled up into the bus lane in front of Montrose Elementary School. He opened the bus door.

" 'Bye, Mr. Hogan," they said as they passed him.

"See you this afternoon," he answered as the kids hustled off the bus and merged into the swarming mass pouring into the school.

He waved to the teacher on duty. This morning it was Kathryn Leslie, Liz's friend. The one who was going to take care of Julia while Liz spent the weekend pretending to be his girlfriend. Kathryn waved back with a broad grin. He felt himself blush and wondered how much Kathryn knew.

A few minutes later, he was heading back to the bus

lot. The streets of Hartley looked like an advertisement for small-town America. It was a good thing Hartley was out of the way, or they'd be overrun with people fleeing the cities. Back at the lot, he set the brake and hauled himself out of the driver's seat to check the aisles. He found a backpack full of books. Either some child was highly forgetful or there was a homework assignment left undone; "I accidentally left my backpack on the bus," was still one terrific excuse. This way the child would have the whole weekend to complete the assignment. Alex grinned while he shook his head. Kids were still kids. Thank goodness.

As he headed toward the bus office, Lenore was coming out. "Alex," she hailed him, "I have something to show you. Inside." She followed him into the office. "Look," she said, pointing.

It was a thank-you note from Sharon tacked up on the bulletin board. And the next to it were three photographs of Alex holding the baby. She looked so tiny, so fragile, so new.

"She's beautiful," Lenore said sincerely. "Of course," she teased, "we expected nothing less of your niece." Lenore had helped train him. They were very good friends. She was one of the people who could get away with making cracks about his looks.

"Knock it off," he said without rancor. And without looking away from the photographs. "She is beautiful, isn't she?" he agreed.

Just then, the door opened, bringing in another bus driver. "Oh, goodie," the newcomer exclaimed over Alex's shoulder. "Baby pictures."

"Sharon sent them along with a thank-you card," Lenore explained.

While the two women were chatting about babies, Alex finished his office business and hustled outside into the clear air. He stood still and took a few deep breaths, thinking of little Alexis and the terrible trio—Shelby's kids. Thinking how a child turned two people from a couple into a family. Speaking of families—he had to hustle himself home and load up his truck. He was going to go visit his family. With Liz.

Behind him, he heard the office door open. He didn't turn around.

"Don't worry, Alex," Lenore's voice accompanied a couple of comforting pats on his back. "You'll have your own kids someday." And she strode off to her car without another word. Without even turning around.

Was he that transparent? Alex wondered. Did everyone know how much he longed for a family? Did Liz know? Of course she knew that he wanted a family, but did she know how much? Did she know he wanted a family with her? She was stuck on this friends-only thing. Her age might make it possible only to have two children, not the half a dozen he'd always wanted, but those two children would be cherished.

Speaking of family, he had a lot of things to do before his afternoon bus route. Because as soon as Liz

228

the librarian got off work, she and he, along with Burl, were heading out on their journey. A journey that might just prove to be the biggest adventure of their lives.

"Now, I've left the can opener on the counter," Liz told Kathryn that afternoon.

Kathryn's teasing voice came over the phone. "I know how to find my way around your kitchen."

"I put Alex's sister's phone number on the refrigerator. And Dr. March's phone numbers—the clinic number as well as her home phone. And when I took Julia in this afternoon, I told her that I was going out of town and that if there was a problem, you'd be calling."

"Why did you take her in? Is she okay?"

"I took her in on my lunch hour. I just wanted to make sure she was okay before I left her."

Kathryn groaned. "You're obsessive."

"I'm responsible."

"You're obsessive."

"She's a kitten who's going to have kittens. I'd be an irresponsible pet owner if I didn't take her in for prenatal care."

"You're obsessive."

"You just like saying that word. It's one of those words you learn in teacher school." She heard Kathryn snort. "But I have to go now," she said. "I have to be out on the information desk in five minutes. Then I'm leaving at six-thirty. So you'll be over tonight to check on her?"

"And in the morning. And then tomorrow night. And Sunday morning. Liz, just go. Have a good time. Don't worry. She'll be fine."

"Yeah," Liz agreed. "I know she will. I guess I'm just nervous."

"Nervous about leaving Julia? Or nervous about meeting Alex's family? Or nervous about playing the girlfriend?" Kathryn was shrewd.

"All three." Then she thought. Her best friend deserved honesty. "Not really. Only the second two."

"You want to talk about it?"

"I really can't. I really have to get out to the desk." Besides, there were clerks in the room. She didn't want her reservations to become part of the continuing saga of Liz and Alex. They all knew that this was the big weekend—and they all had an inordinate interest in it.

"You said you had to be out there in five minutes. This gives you five minutes to spill your guts. C'mon. You'll feel much better."

"Sorry. I can't do it right now."

"You mean there are busy ears listening?"

"Yes."

"Well, go kick Attila out of his office and use his phone."

"I don't think so."

Kathryn sighed. "Tell him you're having a personal crisis and—"

"That's not possible."

Kathryn sighed. "I know. Your boss has aspirations

230

to be the next Genghis Khan. He went to dictator school and now he thinks the world exists in order to give him a job."

"He's not all that bad."

"Yeah, well, it'll do you great gobs of good to get away from him for the weekend. Now don't be nervous; you'll do fine. Just wear that silk stuff proudly, and if they serve spaghetti, remember, whatever you do, cut it, don't twirl it."

Don't be nervous, Liz thought dryly as she headed out to the reference desk. *Sure, you're going to spend the weekend with Alex's family, and they just might tar and feather you for robbing the cradle, but don't be nervous. Yeah. Right.*

Don't be nervous, Alex told himself as he hefted the last of the rocking chairs into the back of his truck. Of course, they didn't look like rocking chairs right now. They were all shrouded in thick blankets to keep them from becoming damaged. Three of them were going to a small shop in Indiana, and the fourth was a present for his parents. *So, you're bringing a woman home to meet your family. Just because this is the first time you've brought a woman home since college doesn't mean there's a reason to be nervous. The family will adore Liz. She'll charm them to pieces without even trying. And Liz will love them. Even Shelby's brood, who, being typical rowdy preschoolers, can be trying at times. So there is nothing at all to be nervous about.*

231

Alex strapped the chairs to the sides of the truck so they wouldn't shift during the drive. Then he shoved his duffel bag between them, along with a bag of Burl's food. He lowered the back of the truck and made sure it caught on the latch.

He made one more check around his house, to make sure everything that was supposed to be off was off. That the thermostat was lowered. That the timer for the lights was set. He took a look in his workshop. There was the chair he was making for Liz. The pieces were all there, shaped and sanded, ready to be bonded together. Then would come the finishing steps, the staining and sanding, more staining and more sanding, ending in a chair that would shine and gleam. Oddly enough, that was where he and Liz were in their relationship. All the pieces were there, and they seemed to fit; they just needed to be put together and finished. What was the human equivalent of wood glue? he wondered. He reached out to touch the spindles that would make up the back of the rocking chair. He itched to take up the pieces and put them together right now. Working with wood was calming, and at this moment in time he needed that calm, that feeling of certitude. But there was no time to work on the chair. He had to pick up Liz and be on their way.

"Ready, big boy?" Alex opened up the passenger side door.

Burl clambered in. He was always ready to go on a

journey. Burl had no reservations at all. "But then, you aren't bringing a woman home," Alex told him.

Burl panted agreeably.

Alex closed the door and strode around the truck, automatically checking the tires. Still plenty of good tread. Then he got to the driver's door. He stopped. This was it. He was really going to do this. He was going to drive over to Liz's house, put her suitcase in the back of his truck, put her in the front seat, and together they were going to spend the weekend with his family. He was, in effect, announcing to his family that he was seriously interested in Liz. Even if it was just pretend. He hoped his sisters didn't embarrass him too badly. He took a deep breath. He opened the door and climbed in.

"Let's go," he said to Burl.

Burl grunted.

Her seat belt fastened with a metallic clunk. It was a sound of finality. As if reading her mood, Burl thumped his tail at her. "You're a nice dog," she told him. Burl grinned a doggy grin. It was warm in the truck, so she unbuttoned her coat and shrugged out of the sleeves. She didn't want to arrive all hot and sweaty. It wouldn't make a good impression.

Then Alex was in the driver's seat. He was starting the engine. "Are you nervous?" he asked.

She looked back at her house, where the living room light would stay on until Kathryn turned it off later that evening. Julia was silhouetted in the window. "Nervous?" she asked. "No. Not at all." But she lied.

"Good." He sounded hearty. Too hearty, she thought. "There's nothing to be nervous about." So he was nervous, also. Somehow the thought brought her a strange sort of comfort.

"You said you'd be in charge of tunes for the trip. What did you bring?"

He reached down and handed her a box of CDs. "Take your pick," he invited.

She tipped the box so she could see the titles by the light of the streetlamps. He had a rather eclectic taste in music. Classical, Motown, early rock, New Age. She pulled out the Beach Boys. Then she put it back. She didn't want him to think she was an old fogey. "What do you usually listen to?"

"You're wimping out," he accused with a smile. "Come on. Make a decision. Whatever one you choose will be fine. I love them all."

She closed her eyes and reached for one. It was the Beach Boys.

"Thinking of summer?" he asked as he slid the disc into the player.

"Right now it seems like a good idea."

The music filled the truck. Alex threw his head back and sang joyously about girls cruising to hamburger stands and forgetting about libraries and having fun, fun, fun.

Suddenly, she felt tremendously happy and hopeful.

Fun, fun, fun. *That's what we're going to have,* she thought. She began to sing along, too.

Somehow the trip seemed shorter than he knew it to be. He knew that it was because of Liz. She asked him all about driving the school bus, and about working with wood. She told him about her boss; the staff called him Attila, she said. They talked about Julia, and Burl. They talked about music they both knew, and books they'd both read. Movies they'd both seen. And food.

On the border between Ohio and Indiana she'd pulled out a tin of cookies. She'd made four batches, she said. One for their trip, another for Sharon, a third for his mother, and a fourth for Kathryn Leslie, who was taking care of Julia. "My grandmother used to make these every Christmas," she told him. "A batch for me and a batch for Kathryn." And he remembered that she'd told him she and Kathryn had grown up together in Arizona.

Burl stared at the cookies. He drooled. He couldn't have any because they were chocolate. "Chocolate is a no-no for dogs," Alex told Burl. He reached in the back seat and rifled through a bag. "Here you go, old guy. Dog cookies, just for you." Burl was thrilled.

When they got off the interstate, Liz said, "Does your sister know that I'm just pretending to be your girlfriend?"

Alex looked over his shoulder before he merged into the left lane. "No."

"Don't you think she should know?"

"Sharon doesn't know how to keep a secret," he said. "She has the best intentions in the world, but her face gives everything away. I thought that if she knew, she'd feel the need to tell her best friend. Everyone in town is one of her best friends."

"So you told her that we were going out together?"

"I told her that we were seriously involved."

"Seriously involved?"

He thought for a moment. "Do you think that was the wrong thing to do?"

"No, not necessarily," she said. But her voice sounded hesitant.

"Good, because we're almost there."

Then they were pulling into Dave and Sharon's driveway. Burl thumped his tail on the seat and woofed.

This was it, Liz thought to herself. She could play the part of Alex's girlfriend with reckless abandon. Well, maybe not reckless, though certainly she would love to have the opportunity for some abandon. In fact, abandon with Alex would be fun. Little slivers of anticipation shot up her spine. But then she was out of the truck and Alex, his arm firmly around her shoulders, was introducing her to Dave and Sharon. The baby was asleep, they said. Burl wound himself around everyone's legs, tossing his tail around cheerfully.

"I'm so glad to meet you," Sharon said, giving her a quick hug. "Alex has told me lots about you."

236

What lots? Liz wondered. But she was delighted with Sharon's open friendliness.

"Hey, Alex," Sharon said over her shoulder as she led Liz up the sidewalk, "I'm going to take Liz into the house. Just put everything in the living room and we'll sort it all out."

Stepping into Sharon's house was like entering a familiar world. It was comfortable, inviting, the kind of home that welcomed everyone.

"It's sort of old-fashioned, I know," Sharon said. "But it's the house we grew up in. When the three of us were all married and gone, Mom and Dad decided they didn't need a house this big. So they moved into a smaller house across town, and Dave and I moved here." She pointed vaguely. "Dave grew up one street over. His parents still live there. His mom and our mom met when they were pregnant, so Dave and Alex sort of didn't have a chance. They had to be best friends. But you probably know all of this."

Then Alex was there. And he casually drew her close, his arm around her shoulders. As if it was the most natural thing in the world. Liz stilled. Then, as if she'd done it hundreds of times in real life instead of only in her dreams, she slipped her arm around his waist.

"Picture time," Dave announced.

"Oh, no," Alex groaned. "Dave has this camera fetish," he whispered loudly to Liz.

"I heard that." Dave had a camera aimed and ready. "Smile at the birdie and say cheese."

Liz obeyed. "Cheese."

But Alex, at the last second, planted a great big smacking kiss on her cheek.

Sharon clapped her hands excitedly. "That should be a good one! Liz, you looked so surprised!"

"Good night," Liz said and shut the door. She looked around. So this was the room where Alex had grown up. On the dresser was a framed photograph. She bent closer to look at it more carefully. It was a younger Alex and Dave, wearing graduation robes and mile-wide grins, mugging for the camera. She'd recognize them anywhere. There were bookshelves on the wall opposite the bed. She moved closer so she could read the titles. Some early Heinlein stood next to Poe, who stood next to *The Field Guide to North American Insects.* Then there were several other geography type titles. At the end of one the bookshelves was another framed photograph. Young Alex, probably twelve or thirteen, holding a scruffy-looking cat. Alex had a typical Alex grin on his face. The cat looked tolerant. Liz felt herself smiling.

There was a soft knock on her door. It was Alex.

"Do you have everything you need?" he asked.

Now *there* was a million-dollar question, Liz thought. "Tell me about this cat." She pointed to the cat in the photograph.

"That's Pirate. He showed up on our back porch one day. I liked him immediately. Sharon and Shelby didn't want to keep him. They wanted a fluffy kitten to dress up in doll clothes. You can't see it in that picture, but he had lost his eye and was full of scars. That's why we named him Pirate. Once he'd gone to the vet's and gotten cleaned up and rid of his fleas, he became one of the family. We had him for eight or nine years before he died of old age. Pirate was a great cat."

Until she had seen this room, Alex's childhood had never been so immediate and so fascinating. Suddenly, she wanted to know about his childhood. She wanted to know the things he'd done, the places he'd gone to school, all about his friends. "Cats can be great friends for kids," she said.

"Cats and dogs," he agreed. "And speaking of dogs, I need to bring Burl in for the night before he starts to bark. But I wanted to make sure you were okay."

"I'm fine," she said with a smile. "I'll see you in the morning."

He reached out and briefly, gently, touched her cheek. "Sleep well," he whispered.

"You, too."

Then he was gone. She heard his cheerful, bouncing step on the stairs. Bits of Alex were all over his room, keeping her company, bringing him close to her.

She undressed and folded her clothes carefully onto a chair. She slithered the silk nightgown over her head. It felt sensual, and as decadent and sinful as chocolate *pot de crémè*. There was no one to see her, so she let herself, just this once, pretend. After all, the whole weekend was pretend. Wasn't it? She slid her arms into the matching dressing gown, enjoying the feeling of the silk on her skin. She smoothed the gown. Wait. There was a lump. She stuck her hand in the pocket. What in the world—? She pulled it out to look at whatever it was.

"Kathryn, you idiot," she whispered, amused at her best friend's unsubtle hint. "What am I going to do with a condom? And a ribbed one. Fluorescent pink." What could she do with it? She couldn't throw it away. What if someone found it in the trash basket? Oh, how embarrassing. How obnoxious. She had to bury it deep in her suitcase. In that inside zippered pocket. But wait; she should wrap it up in something first. To make sure no one would see it. Wrap it in what? Her eye caught a box of tissues on the bedside table. That would do. She carefully wrapped the foil packet in tissue, then zippered it into the pocket. Surely no one would find it there. When she got home and did her laundry she'd find it again and would throw it away properly—so there was no chance of being caught with the thing. Oh, what was Kathryn thinking? *Nothing,* she reminded herself, *that you haven't thought yourself.* Only Kathryn was smart enough, or optimistic enough, to do something about it. But fluorescent pink? Ribbed?

The condom properly hidden, Liz sat down on the bed. It was covered by a quilt—handmade, Liz guessed. Sharon had put several folded blankets on a chair in case she got cold in the night. It was thoughtful of her. But then, Sharon seemed like a thoughtful person.

She stared at the bed for a moment. Alex's bed, she thought as she slid under the covers. She was in Alex's bed. Without Alex. Something about that seemed wrong. She stretched out, trying to gather up all the bits of Alex that were in this bed, in this room, to hold them close, to bring Alex closer. To luxuriate in the knowledge that she was in Alex's bed. That she slept on Alex's pillow. She closed her eyes and imagined that the warmth from the covers was warmth from his body.

The clock on the mantel struck one. This was not a comfortable couch, Alex told himself once more as he punched the pillow into what he hoped would be a more comfortable shape. He'd always thought it was. Maybe the couch was uncomfortable because he wanted to be upstairs. Upstairs in his old bed. With Liz.

Burl, on the floor at his side, let out a series of soft snores. Burl thought the living room was quite nice. Burl thought everywhere was nice. Burl was not discriminating. Burl did not have an almost overwhelming desire to be with Liz.

Chapter Thirteen

A baby was crying. Liz jerked her eyes open. No, it wasn't a dream; there really was a baby. Then she remembered. She was at Sharon and Dave's house. The baby was real. After a few short moments the squalling stopped.

She tried to go back to sleep, but her mind was too full. There were too many things to think about. She didn't want to think about them, so she pulled on her clothes and wandered downstairs.

She found Sharon in the kitchen making coffee, the baby in her arms.

"This is Alexis," Sharon said. "She didn't get to meet you last night." She held out the baby. "Will you hold her while I finish making coffee? Dave went out to get fresh doughnuts and Alex is still snoring on the couch in the living room."

Liz carefully took the baby, feeling the tiny body, so fragile, so new. She settled into the rocking chair, little Alexis cradled in her arms. The baby fit her arms perfectly, awakening a giant baby hunger. She began to rock, slowly, holding the baby close to her heart. She drank in the feeling of a baby in her arms. Memorizing the clean baby smell, the feel of a terry-cloth jumpsuit, the bulk of diapers on a rounded baby bottom. The pain of her barren state seared her soul. Hot tears filled her eyes. She fought them back. "Hello, sweeting," she whispered at last to this miracle. "I'm Liz."

The baby's gaze wandered randomly until she found Liz's face. Then, without breaking her stare, she waved a fist around and stuck it in her mouth. She sucked her knuckles.

"Do those knuckles taste good?" Liz asked. "Like pizza? Or chocolate?"

"Or popovers?" It was Alex, leaning against the door jamb, shirtless, shoeless, wearing nothing but sweatpants on his long legs. The gold of his skin looked smooth; the gold of his hair was sleep rumpled. But his smile, oh his smile. If there were angels in heaven, Liz thought, they looked exactly like Alex Hogan. His gaze was dark as it caught hers and held it with a gentle touch. Suddenly, she didn't want to pretend anymore. She wanted to touch him, taste him, and have it be real.

I want this, Liz screamed silently, begging, pleading. *I want this man. I want a life with this man. And a child. I want to love him, and be loved by him in return.* Yet, even as she pleaded and begged, she knew that there could never be a happy ending. She could never give Alex what he wanted.

"Good morning, brother mine." Sharon's voice barely broke into Liz's consciousness, but it was enough to drop her back into reality with a sound thump. This was not a game anymore, but she had promised Alex she would play. How ironic it was. She could touch him all she wanted, and he would never know that it wasn't pretend. If this was all she'd ever have, then she wanted all the abandon she could get.

"Good morning, Alex," Liz murmured with a smile.

"I see you met little *El Niño,*" Alex said as he crossed the kitchen to let Burl out. On his way back from the door, he bent down and kissed Liz on the cheek. "Good morning," he whispered warmly. "I hope you slept better than I did."

She reached out her free hand and ran it up Alex's arm and around his neck, drawing him nearer. He was wonderfully warm and comfortable. She closed her eyes to better savor the feeling of his silky smooth skin. She could get used to this very quickly. "I slept wonderfully, thank you," she whispered. He rested his cheek against hers for a moment.

"Okay, you two, knock it off in front of my daughter," Sharon scolded playfully. "We keep it G-rated around here." She set two mugs of steaming coffee on the table. "And speaking of G-ratings, Alex, go clothe your gorgeous self before Dave gets back with the doughnuts. No one can eat breakfast with your nekkid chest staring them in the face."

Alex cheerfully slung his arm around her neck. "Are you presuming to boss me around?" he kidded.

"Watch it, buster. I have hot coffee in my hand and I'm not afraid to spill it."

Alex released his sister and dropped a kiss on her cheek. "Just for you," he said as he ducked through the doorway.

Sharon snorted. "He has no idea what the sight of his bare chest does to women," she said.

Liz sighed. She knew what that sight did to her. "Yeah," she finally said.

Sharon tucked one leg under her as she sat down. "Do you want me to take the baby?"

Liz looked down at the baby. She was asleep. "No," she said softly. "Let me hold her a little longer. She's beautiful. She looks a little bit like Alex."

"You should've seen all the girls at our high school whenever Alex walked by. Even when he was fully clothed. And when he was running on the track team, in those little shorts . . . *wow*. You think Burl drools? Trust me, a Newfoundland is nothing compared to teenage girls lusting over my brother. It was disgusting. He, of course, was oblivious."

"That's part of his charm, though, don't you think? That he is so unaware of the effect he has on women."

Then Liz remembered what Alex had said about the library clerks making him feel uncomfortable. "At least, if he's aware of it, he doesn't exploit it."

"He's too nice for that."

Liz took a sip of her coffee. "Yes, he is." She cocked her head. Somehow she felt that Sharon could be an ally, someone she could trust. "Sometimes I wonder if he's too perfect. Jessie, who works for our vet in Hartley, says he is a perfect example of the breed standard for the human male." She didn't add Jessie's comment that Alex was the kind of man who most definitely should be bred. Sharon was, after all, the man's sister. "Sometimes I worry that I don't see any negative qualities in him. Maybe I'm not paying attention; maybe I'm not seeing things I should be seeing. Maybe there are danger signs all over the place and I'm so smitten I'm blind to them." She watched the baby in her arms make little sucking noises in her sleep.

Sharon leaned back and sipped her coffee thoughtfully. "I don't think so," she said at last. "Alex isn't perfect, not by any means. For one thing, he can sometimes be very impatient. That's his most obvious imperfection." She drummed her fingers on the table in thought. "He also knows what he wants, which can be a good thing, but it can also make him a little too inflexible. But there's nothing about Alex that you'd ever have to worry about. He's loyal, faithful, courteous, nice. And in tight jeans, he has a terrific butt." She grinned cheekily.

Liz blushed.

"C'mon," Sharon goaded. "Don't tell me you haven't noticed."

"Noticed what?" Alex came into the room and dragged a kitchen chair over next to Liz, where he turned it around and straddled it backwards.

"Your terrific butt," Sharon said unrepentantly.

Liz couldn't meet his gaze. She just couldn't. She knew she was blushing. She concentrated on the baby instead. But she peeked at them through her lashes.

"Sharon," Alex said plaintively, "you're embarrassing Liz. Remember we had a little talk about subtle?"

Sharon glanced under the table at Alex's legs. "Those jeans don't look very subtle."

"That's because Liz feeds me so well."

Sharon beamed. "Feeding you is good. But you should probably get a larger size pants if you want to do the baggy look."

Liz gave up all pretense of not watching them. It was like trying to keep track of a Ping-Pong game. "Do you always talk to each other like this?"

"Like what?" they said at the same time.

"Like you're . . . like you're . . . You tease each other," she said at last.

"Sure do." Alex nodded. "She's my sister. I have teasing rights."

"Do you have brothers or sisters?" Sharon wanted to know.

Liz shook her head. "I'm an only child."

Sharon's face crumpled in sympathy. "How awful."

"You didn't think so when you were in high school," Alex taunted.

"Yeah, well, you weren't so hot back then yourself."

Just then, from the backyard, Burl erupted into a flurry of excited barks. Alex hurried to bring him in.

"Dave's home with the doughnuts."

Alex couldn't keep his gaze from straying toward Liz. Finally, he gave up and allowed himself to watch her, revel in her, enjoy her. After all, they were pretending to be involved. When he'd seen her sitting in the rocking chair holding the baby, he'd felt the whole world go *clunk.* He'd never been as sure of anything as he was sure that he wanted Liz. He wanted Liz rocking his baby—their baby—in a chair he'd made.

The party was at Alex's parents' house. As they were loading up all the things Sharon needed to take, Liz was amazed at the amount of paraphernalia that went with a new baby, Dave pulled her aside. "Listen," he said. "This family, it's like *Little House on the Prairie* or something. You think that it can't possibly be real, that no family could be that apple pie. Not a single dysfunctional member of the bunch. But, trust me, I've known these people all my life and it *is* real. They're the most genuine, most squeaky clean people I know."

Liz nodded. "I was beginning to get that impression."

Dave gave her a quick smile. "I'm glad. I think

248

you're good for Alex. By the way, Alex says you like to go grocery shopping."

Liz wrinkled her forehead in confusion. "I love grocery shopping."

Dave shook his head. "Amazing," he said. "Amazing. Stick around, Liz. Maybe some of it will rub off on Sharon."

"What will?" Sharon asked, coming out of the house carrying a very well wrapped bundle of baby.

"Your single imperfection, my dear," Dave said with a grin. "You hate grocery shopping. She breaks out into hives if she has to go to the store," he added to Liz in the kind of loud whisper meant to be overheard.

Sharon merely laughed. "That's why I have you, my love. I can give you a list and you go away and come back with everything I need. Oh, Alex," Sharon called to her brother, who was loading a covered tray of goodies into the truck. "Shelby just phoned. The trio of terror want to make sure you bring Burl. I told them there would be too much commotion at Grandma and Grandpa's house and they could see Burl tomorrow morning. Shelby's kids," Sharon explained to Liz. "They're lifelong members of Burl's fan club." And she was off to bundle baby Alexis into her infant car seat.

"This is the scenic route through town," Alex explained. He wanted to show her where he'd grown up. "That's my old elementary school," he pointed out.

"It was only half that size when I went there. The junior high school is around the corner."

"Looks like a school to me."

"The trees were smaller then, too. When I was growing up, this was the outskirts of town. Now it's in the middle of things." He turned down another tree-lined street. "This is the furniture store where I worked when I was in high school."

"Where you learned to make chairs?"

"And tables and cabinets and other things. They still sell some of my things." He jerked his head to the back of the truck. "This is where I dropped off those chairs while you were in the shower this morning."

"What made you decide on rocking chairs?"

"I like the way they look, all the curved lines. I like the way they feel when they move." He leaned forward to see her better and waggled an eyebrow at her. He chuckled when she blushed. "I like the way they make people feel comfortable and relaxed. My mother once said she didn't know how women raised babies without a rocking chair." He turned another corner. "And this is my old high school."

"Is that the track where you ran in itty-bitty shorts and all the girls drooled?"

Alex groaned. "You've been listening to Sharon."

"She said those girls drooled more than Burl."

"My baby sister has always had this problem with exaggeration."

"I don't know. I probably would've. Drooled."

He shot her a look. She was sitting peacefully in his truck, watching the trees go by. Looking totally innocent. Too innocent.

"So how do you think we're doing so far?" she asked, still looking out the window.

"Doing?"

"You know. Pretending to be madly, passionately in love with each other."

"I think we're doing fine." Then he glanced at her again. There was something about the way her head was tilted, about the way she wasn't looking at him. He felt himself begin to smile. "Do you think we need some, uh, practice?"

"What do you think?" she asked, her voice casual. Too casual.

"When two people are madly in love with each other, they kiss in a way that lets other people know they've done it a lot," he told her, keeping his voice light. "We haven't done it a lot."

"We haven't done it at all," she said serenely.

"Good point." He thought for a moment. "It would hardly do for our cover to be blown by such a silly thing as not having practiced kissing, now wouldn't it?"

"Sure would."

Alex quickly glanced in the rearview mirror, then swerved over into the left lane. He turned a corner more sharply than usual.

"What are you doing?"

"We're going to get us some practice." He made

another turn, and soon he saw what he wanted. He pulled into a parking lot and stopped the truck.

"Where are we?"

He didn't answer. He climbed out of the truck and strode around to let Liz out. "Liz the librarian, this is the town park, suitably deserted for our purposes."

"What are our purposes?" she asked, a slight smile on her face, a slight tinge of red on her cheeks, a definite sparkle in her eyes. He caught his breath.

"Trust me," he said. He took her by the hand and led her, at a fast walk, down to the edge of the trees. Where was that old trail? He scanned the line of trees. There it was. "Down here."

"You're leading me down a garden path?" she teased.

"Not a garden," he answered with a chuckle. "We're going into the woods." A few more yards and they were there.

"Oh," she said in surprise. "A gazebo. In the middle of the woods."

He led her up the wooden steps into the very center, where he stopped. He turned to look at her. "Not just your average gazebo." He was fascinated by the way her eyes grew dark and wide. "You are beautiful," he whispered. Because she was. He drank in the sight of her, the scent of her, the feel of her cheeks against the palms of his hands. His hands were calloused and rough. Her cheeks were silky smooth. He thrilled to the feel of her touch as her arms encircled him, drawing him closer to her. Then he could wait no longer to taste her. He swiftly bent his head, and her lips met his.

They became as entwined as the vines on the gazebo, and just as irrevocably, as their lips and tongues explored and teased and learned each other. Alex discovered a spot below Liz's ear that made her shiver with delight. Liz set Alex aflutter with a drift of butterfly kisses across his cheek. Alex streamed his fingers through Liz's hair, lifting the silken stuff to let it sift down in a rich cloud.

"Oh, Liz," he groaned at last. He oh-so-regretfully pulled his mouth from hers. "We have to stop." He was out of breath. "Or I won't be able to."

"All right," she said, and her voice was trembling and out of breath, too.

He pulled her close, wrapping his arms around her, tucking her head under his chin. Together they stood until their hearts slowed and their breathing became more regular.

"Why isn't this your average gazebo?" she said at last.

He smiled against her hair. "When I was in high school, it was a notorious make-out place."

She chuckled softly into his chest. "I suppose you're very familiar with it, then?"

He shook his head. "I never came here."

"Where did you take them?" she asked curiously. Then, "I'm sorry. I don't mean to embarrass you. It's really none of my business."

"There weren't many girls I wanted to bring here and make out with. You're the first in a long time."

He felt her still; then she pulled away so she could look him in the eye. For a long moment they gazed at each other. "That's sweet," she finally whispered.

"It's true." And it was.

She got a teasing glint in her eye. "Do you think we practiced enough to fool even the most discriminating observer?"

He grinned back at her, noting the tinge of blush on her cheeks, the full just-kissed look of her lips, the tousled appearance of her hair. She was irresistible. "I think we could fool anyone. But just in case, I think we should keep practicing." And he proceeded to do just that.

"Won't we be late?" she asked between kisses.

"We'll tell everyone," he murmured against her lips, "I was showing you the sights."

Chapter Fourteen

Cars crammed the cul-de-sac where the senior Hogans lived. Alex pulled his truck into the crowded driveway. "I'm going to stop here while I unload and get you inside, and then I'll move the truck over to the next block," he explained as he set the brake. "Wait here a moment."

"What can I help you carry in?" Liz asked as he ducked out of the truck. Now she was nervous. Nervous about meeting Alex's parents. And at a party, where there would be loads of people who all knew each other. Having a job to do, even something as simple as carrying in a goodie tray, would make it easier.

He opened her door and gave her a hand to help her out. "Not a thing," he said cheerfully.

Suddenly, two preschoolers were hurtling themselves across the front lawn. "Uncle Alex, Uncle Alex!" they screamed.

At the edge of the driveway, Alex bent down and joyously scooped them both up in his arms and whirled them around. "Hello, you monsters!" he told them as he finally set them down.

"Liz," Alex said, beckoning to her, "I would like you to meet two of the terrific trio. This is Justin who is four, and this is Jennifer, who is three."

"Hello," Justin said, but Jennifer stuck her finger in her mouth and looked at Liz curiously.

"Hello there," Liz said. "I'm very glad to meet you. Your Uncle Alex has told me lots of things about you."

"What kind of things?" Justin wanted to know.

"That you both love Burl."

"Burl," Jennifer agreed, nodding her head.

That was easy, Liz thought as they all made their way up to the front door.

Alex's mother, Rita, was warm, with a comfortable shape. She pulled Liz into a welcoming hug. "I'm so very glad to meet you, dear," she said. But that was all she had time for before they were joined by someone who had to be Shelby. Alex plucked a round-looking toddler from the young woman's arms and gave him a smacking kiss on the cheek. "This is Joshua James. And this ravishing young woman, who is his mother, is my sister, Shelby. Shelby's husband, Arthur, is somewhere around. Shelby, this is Liz."

"We are so very happy to meet you, Liz!" Shelby

exclaimed. "Arthur's in the family room, watching the pre-game stuff. IU basketball," she said confidentially to Liz, her eyes, so like Alex's, twinkling. "It's practically a religion in this town."

Liz barely had time to catch her breath before she was swept away into another round of introductions. Finally, she gave up trying to remember people's names. There were just too many. People of all ages were there to help celebrate the anniversary of Alex's parents. Everyone knew Alex, and everyone was thrilled to see him. And everyone told her what a wonderful guy he was. Until Liz felt a prickle at the back of her neck. She turned around.

Glaring at her from across the room, next to the buffet table, stood a young woman in a flashy dress, a cup of punch in her hand. The expression on her face was not a happy one. So this was Sharon's friend. The one who had designs on Alex. The one she was protecting Alex from by pretending to be his girlfriend.

Until now, Liz realized, it had been a game, for fun. She hadn't considered that there was a live human being at the other end of the charade. A live human being who was very unhappy. It didn't matter, she thought, that the woman in the flashy dress wasn't right for Alex. Alex wasn't into glitter and glitz. Alex was into snowmen and sleds. But still, the woman hurt.

Liz glanced away from the woman and turned to scan the myriad of chatting and laughing people until she saw him, in a cluster of guests. He truly looked like a Greek god, she thought. Part of it was his looks, sure, but the other part was the way he held himself. His calm assurance, his way of greeting people with a smile that was all the more special because it was so genuine. Then her gaze caught his. And held. And his smile lit the room. A smile that was for her. She wanted to do some television commercial thing and fly into his arms, but there were too many people in the way, and besides, she didn't know how to fly. There was also a very unhappy woman across the room. Oh, rats! If she didn't at last try to be friendly to the woman, Liz thought, she'd probably spend the rest of her life regretting it. One of those moments that, once lost, would never come again. Sheesh! She was beginning to sound like one of Kathryn's self-help books.

She steeled her shoulders. *C'mon, Liz. Disarm this woman with your friendliness and charm.* Yeah, right. The woman didn't seem to be interested in charm at the moment. She seemed interested in skewering Liz with her glare.

Liz wound her way through the throng as if innocently heading for the punch bowl. Then she was there. She picked up a cup, ladled out her punch and took a sip. It was excellent. Not too much of any one thing, but a perfect blend of flavors. She'd have to ask Sharon what was in it. Well, she told herself, here goes nothing. She turned to the woman in the flashy dress. A woman who, from the looks of her, owned stock in the makeup business. "Hello," she said in a bright, friendly voice. "I don't think we've met. My name is Liz Hadley."

"I'm Cindy." The words were spoken grudgingly, and only because politeness demanded them.

"Are you from here?" Liz continued.

"Yes. I'm a longtime friend of the family." The implication was that Liz was an outsider.

Outsider or not, she was determined. "It's a lovely town. At least, what I've seen of it is. It must be beautiful in the summer, when all the trees are out. I grew up in Arizona, where there aren't a lot of big old trees like this." She decided to pretend that Cindy didn't have an attitude. After all, more bees could be caught with honey than with vinegar.

Cindy made a polite noise of agreement.

"And snow. I'd never seen much snow before."

Another noise.

Well, Liz thought, remembering her reference training, *it's time to ask an open-ended question.* "What kinds of flowers do people grow here? Hartley is famous for herbs."

"All kinds, I guess. Tulips and daffodils in the spring. Roses and stuff all summer long. I'm not into gardening. I tried it once, but my son thought the digging part was fun, so he tried to dig up everything."

"How old is your son?"

"He's eight. He's out in the backyard, playing with the other kids." She nodded toward the picture window overlooking a huge backyard.

Liz looked out to where a dozen or so kids were doing kid stuff. "Which one is he?"

Cindy pointed. There was pride in her voice as she said, "The one with the blue jacket. His name is Clint."

Clint was a cute kid, Liz thought, and he was playing well with the others.

"He looks like a wonderful child. You must be very proud of him. I don't have any children. I imagine it's a difficult thing to raise kids in today's world."

Cindy nodded. "Not nearly as easy as raising cats."

Liz smiled to herself. Here was their point of agreement. "I love cats," she said. "I've had cats all my life. Do you have cats?"

Cindy nodded. "I have a black-and-white named Lucky and a Siamese named Susie."

"I have a formerly stray mackerel-striped cat named Julia. I found her a few weeks ago." Liz decided not to bring Alex into it. Not when things were actually going well. "I took her in for shots and my vet told me she's pregnant. So we're expecting a litter in the near future. I've never had a litter of kittens."

"We had kittens two years ago," Cindy offered. "Lucky got out and"—she shot Liz a rueful grin—"got lucky. Now she's spayed."

Liz chuckled. "Did she eat a lot when she was pregnant? Julia eats like a wolf."

After that, there was no shortage of conversation between the two of them. People who love their cats, Liz thought, can talk for hours about them. They can become positively obnoxious about them, and only another cat person would understand. Well, Cindy and Liz were both cat people. They understood. And so they shared cat stories.

"She seems to have made friends with Cindy Hall," Sharon leaned over the back of the couch and whispered in his ear. "That must've taken a minor miracle."

"Miracle," Dave said from next to him on the couch. "There's a miracle! Whoa! Look at that guy go!" Then, without taking his eyes off the television, he leaned toward his wife. "Not now, Sharon, we're beating the shorts off Ohio State." He scooped another handful of potato chips out of the bowl on his lap and passed it over to Arthur.

Alex chuckled at Dave's enthusiasm. "Miracle, eh?" he whispered to his sister.

The several men who were gathered in the family room around the television for the ritual known as IU basketball cheered furiously as their team scored another basket.

"They've been huddled together for the past twenty minutes," Sharon whispered back. "After I checked on the baby, I went over to get some punch, and I heard them talking about birthweights and placentas. This could be a good thing."

Dave and Arthur both shushed her. She stuck her tongue out at them.

Alex chewed on this for a moment. Birthweights and

261

placentas? Liz was talking about birth? With Cindy Hall? That didn't make sense. He never thought of Cindy as the kind of person who would be interested in discussing such things. It hardly went with the femme fatale image.

Another cheer erupted as IU scored yet another basket. Followed shortly by a groan as OSU stole the ball and took it down the court. Alex let his mind wander from the game into the other room. Liz talking about babies. This he had to see.

"Can't stand it, eh, Ohio boy?" Dave teased as Alex stood up.

"You got it, Indy boy." Alex grinned as he punched Dave playfully on the arm. "I gotta get outa here."

But on the way to the punch bowl and Liz, he was waylaid by his mother. He slung his arm around her and gave her a great big kiss on her cheek. "Happy, Mom?"

"To have all my children and grandchildren under one roof, even for such a short time? Yes, I am!" She beamed at him. "You know how rare this is."

"Oh, Mom, don't turn the screws."

"I wish you lived closer, dear."

Alex hugged her again. "I know. But I love Hartley."

"And now there's someone who lives there who is special in your life."

"Liz."

"She's lovely, dear. She's also the first woman you've brought home in a very long time. Since . . .

when was it? College?" His mother's gaze sought his. "I was beginning to despair for you."

"I like Liz, Mom. I like her a lot."

"I'm sure you do."

But he didn't hear unqualified acceptance in her voice. She was holding back about something. "Liz is special," he tried to explain.

"Special in what way?"

"I think she may be the one."

His mother was silent for a moment, her lips pursed in thought. "Sharon said she's older than you are."

"Ten years."

"Ten years can be a long time."

Alex shrugged. "If it was ten years the other way, would you say the same thing?"

His mother stilled for a moment. "I don't know." Her voice sounded troubled.

"I don't know either. I've thought about it, and I still don't know."

"Does the age difference bother you?"

Alex thought. "Not really. It's pretty much immaterial." He grinned ruefully at her. "It's a good thing, too. Because there's nothing we can do about it."

"Just be careful, dear. Think things through very seriously. Don't be afraid to talk to us about it. Remember, your dad and I are always here for you."

He hugged her again. "I know."

Her mother nodded over toward the punch bowl,

where Liz and Cindy Hall were still deep in conversation. "She does seem to have made friends with Cindy Hall. That speaks quite well of her."

"She's a fine woman."

"She must be, if you like her."

"When you get to know her, you'll agree."

"I'm sure I will."

Wild whoops and exuberant cheers erupted from the family room. IU had obviously scored another basket.

Finally, when all the guests were gone, and IU had won the basketball game, the Hogan men trooped outside to listen to the engine of Shelby and Arthur's van. It had made clunking noises all the way over today. Liz found Sharon in the kitchen, stacking dishes in the dishwasher. "Is there something I can do to help?" she asked.

Shelby stuck her head around the counter that separated the family room from the kitchen. "I have something that will be the biggest help in the world," she said, with a grin that Liz had seen on Alex. "Joshua James and Alexis are both sound asleep upstairs, in one of the bedrooms."

So Liz was set on the family room couch with the older two of the trio of terror and a stack of books.

"The Snowy Day." Liz began the first book. But she was interrupted by Justin, who had to snuggle closer, then Jennifer, until both of them were almost on her lap.

264

"The Snowy Day," she began again. Jennifer gave a little sigh.

By the time she'd finished *The Snowy Day* and *Ginger Jumps,* Jennifer was breathing heavily. Justin, however, pulled another book from the stack. *"Diggers* by Margaret Wise Brown," she read.

"It's about lotsa machines," Justin said wisely.

"Then it sounds like a great book," Liz agreed.

"It's one of his favorites," Shelby put in from across the room. "He can practically recite it."

And, indeed, as Liz read the book, Justin chanted parts along with her. When she finished that book, Justin reached for another.

"That's probably enough, Justin," his mother said. "You don't want to tire Liz out."

"It's not a problem," Liz told her. "I like reading to them." And she did. She looked down at Justin, who was deciding between an Arthur book and a book by Eric Carle. Then at Jennifer, fingers in her mouth, who was slumped over against her in sleep. Liz glanced over into the kitchen and caught Shelby's gaze. "It's not a problem, truly," she repeated.

"If you let him, he'll have you reading to him for hours." Shelby laughed.

Three books later, Jennifer was still sleeping soundly, her head on Liz's lap. Justin was still listening attentively, his entire being focused on the book. The door to the garage opened and the men trooped in.

Justin looked up briefly, then back to the book again. Evidently, the little boy had his priorities set. Liz kept on reading. Then Alex came up behind her to look over her shoulder. She kept on reading. Alex kissed her neck. She ignored him and continued with Justin's book. Alex nibbled her earlobe. She shivered, her eyes closed at the delicious sensation.

"Read the next page, Liz," the child told her. "Read the next page."

Liz read the next page.

Alex slid his fingers up around the back of her neck and streamed them through her hair, while his lips trailed kisses down her cheek. Liz bent her head toward the book. "I'm reading to your nephew," she whispered to Alex.

"Well, then, will you read to me tonight?" he whispered back suggestively.

"Do you have a stack of picture books, too?"

"Sure do. I have some great bedtime stories."

But that night, back at Sharon and Dave's house, Alex didn't bring out a stack of books. Instead, when Sharon and Dave went upstairs to bed, he led Liz into the living room.

"Won't they wonder what's going on?" she asked him.

"Nah. They expect us to spend half the night necking. They'd wonder what was going on if we didn't."

"We can't have them wonder, now can we?" she asked, teasing him. "That would blow our cover." Then she truly saw the look in his eyes, and she couldn't say anything more. Bedtime stories indeed! Alex did things with his hands and her body that made her shiver and softly moan. Things she hadn't felt for a very long time, things she wanted more of. She needed more of. She needed Alex. And she needed to show him how much she needed him. His groans told Liz that he needed her as well. But not here, not now. Soon, their bodies seemed to proclaim. Soon.

Driving back to Hartley on Sunday, Liz was filled with impressions of Alex's family. Dave was right—the Hogans were so squeaky clean, it was almost unreal. Alex was like something out of a fairy tale. Like every childhood fantasy she'd ever had. She found herself staring at him as he drove. She liked the way his hands held the steering wheel, confidently. She liked the way his lips were twitching into a slight smile.

"You're staring at me."

"Yes, I am."

"Why?"

Because she loved the sight of him, loved the way his hair curled against the collar of his parka. Loved the way his eyes lit up when he quickly glanced over at her. Loved the sound of his voice, especially when he teased her. But she couldn't tell him that.

"Why?" he persisted.

"Because you're much more interesting to look at than the interstate. This is not the scenic part of Ohio."

"We'll have to go there this summer."

"Go where?"

"The scenic parts of Ohio." And this time, when he glanced over at her, it was with eyes that were very warm. So warm they made her shiver.

He climbed out of the truck and around to open the door for her. "I'll get your things," he told her. "You go see Julia."

Julia! How could she have forgotten her pregnant kitty? Liz bounded up the front steps and shoved her key in the lock. "Julia," she called as she opened the door. "Julia, kitty, kitty, kitty."

In an instant, Julia was there, *mrrow*ing at her, winding around her legs, sounding like a locomotive. Liz scooped her up and held her close.

"How is she?" Alex was there, her bags in hand. Burl, his constant companion, was there, too.

"She's fine, aren't you, Jukie Juke." Liz rubbed her face against the purring cat. There truly was no place like home. And home was where the cat was. At least, that was what she'd always believed. But now, with Alex standing next to her, she longed for another home, a home that included him.

"Where do you want these?" he asked, nodding to the bags he was still holding. "Can I take them to your room?"

"No need. I can take them later."

"They're heavy. I can take them now."

"You are such a gentleman," she teased.

"Yes, I am."

She led the way down the hall to her bedroom. "Just set them anywhere." Her bedroom was not spacious. There weren't many places to set two bags, even bags as small as hers were. As she moved over to her bed, to be out of his way so he could maneuver her bags into the room, Julia leaped from her arms onto the bed, then onto the floor to greet Burl.

She half expected Alex to set her bags on her bed, but he set them down by her dresser. Then he turned to face her. Was it her imagination, or did he look a little flushed? She couldn't tell. But she felt herself grow warm, too. Their gazes met and held. And held. And held.

Liz could feel her blood coursing, could feel her heart pounding. She could feel her need grow and build and tower above any other thought, any other desire, any other mere want. A hunger that had nothing to do with food, but everything to do with being fed. She needed Alex. She needed to be part of him, and to have him be part of her. And feeding her need was the message she could read in his eyes, that his need for her was just as great.

They came together in a rush, in a jumble of arms and mouths. Straining to hold each other ever closer and closer. Liz lost her coat and Alex his parka. Alex ripped off his sweater and his shirt, leaving the warm smooth expanse of his chest for Liz to explore madly, wildly. To press her lips into, her cheek into, and feel the beating of his heart, listen to his soft groan. Liz pulled her sweater over her head and tossed it onto the pile of clothes at their feet. She shuddered as Alex trailed tiny kisses down her neck and between and around her breasts. He reached around her back and fumbled for a moment until he had unfastened her bra. Slowly he drew the straps down her shoulders, then off her arms.

"You are so beautiful," he whispered.

"You're beautiful, too," she whispered back before reaching up for his kiss.

He clasped her to him, and she shivered at the feeling of his chest pressed against hers, of the feeling of his hands against the skin of her back and of hers on him. What a wonderful first course this was, she thought absently. *Bon appétit.*

Finally he broke off the kiss and pulled back just far enough so she could read the question in his eyes. Yes! she answered, knowing he would understand her reply. *Yes!*

"I haven't done this is in a long time," he whispered.

"Neither have I," she whispered back.

"I don't have a condom."

The vulnerability in his eyes touched her in a place deep inside her heart where she'd never been before, a place she hadn't known existed. She reached up to touch his cheek tenderly. She closed her eyes and settled closer against him. She had a condom. A ribbed, pink fluorescent condom. But somehow that would seem cheap and tawdry. There was nothing cheap and tawdry about Alex. "It's okay," she said softly against the hollow of his neck. "We don't need one."

"Why not?" he asked against her hair as his hands continued their reverent exploration of her body.

"I can't get pregnant." She'd said it without thinking.

His hands stopped exploring. His heart stopped beating. He stood still. "Why not?"

Oh, no! She hadn't meant to say that! She hadn't meant to spring it on him like this. How dumb could she get! She closed her eyes again, this time in a silent prayer that everything would be all right, that he'd understand, that he'd forgive her, that he wouldn't put her aside. She didn't think she'd be able to bear it. Not again. What in the world could she say to him?

"Why can't you get pregnant?" he asked again, and though his hands were still on her, they were no longer there sensually.

"Because many years ago I had to have a hysterectomy." She almost choked on the hated word, and she squeezed her eyes more tightly shut. "It was a long time ago. I can't ever have children."

He felt like he'd been punched in the gut. "What do you mean, you can't have children?" he asked stupidly. It came out harsher than he expected it to. He tried again. "What do you—oh, hell!" he swore softly. He took a very deep breath and let it out. Suddenly, all the desire he'd felt was gone. He felt empty. He felt wooden. He felt . . . nothing.

But she was still in his arms. They were, both of them, half undressed. Mumbling some sort of an apology—he wasn't sure exactly what he said—he gathered up his clothes and shrugged them on while he was walking down the hall to her front door. At the door he stopped. He'd forgotten something. Burl. He whistled. The big dog ambled over to him congenially. "Let's go, boy," he said in a voice that felt as raw as it sounded.

Somehow he got outside and into his truck. Somehow he fumbled the key into the ignition and backed out of her driveway. Out of her life.

272

Chapter Fifteen

He pulled into his driveway, turned off the engine, and sat in his truck for a moment. He ignored Burl, who was pawing at the door to get out. Burl knew he was home.

Finally, Alex got out of the truck. Burl scrambled out after him. Alex raised the garage door and went into the darkness. He called Burl, then lifted an ax down from its hook on the wall, and together he and his dog headed into the backyard. Burl immediately found some interesting tracks to nose. Alex strode to the back of the backyard, where there was a woodpile. He needed to chop firewood. Lots of it. Even though he already had a cord stacked next to the house, he needed to chop more. It was the chopping he needed, not the wood.

Alex chopped and split wood until it was too dark to see. Until he'd pounded out all his anger. Until he felt empty and drained and his arms burned with a fiery ache.

Then he and Burl went inside. It was cold. He turned up the thermostat. It was dark. He turned on the lights. It was quiet. He turned on a CD. Then he turned it off again. From the kitchen, Burl barked. Alex went into the kitchen and poured fresh water in Burl's bowl. That made Burl happy. The big dog swished his tail as he stuck his nose down in the bowl to lap noisily. Burl always drank from the bottom of the bowl.

Alex wandered back into his living room and sank down onto the sofa. He stuck his feet straight out in front of him and stared out at nothing.

She can't have children! The thought went round and round in his mind like a whirligig in the wind. It wouldn't stop. It just went round and round and round. And every time it went round, he felt it cut more deeply into his heart, like his ax into the firewood.

The phone rang, breaking into Alex's silence. He didn't want to talk to anyone right now. Didn't want to have to form coherent words and sentences. And after all, that's what answering machines were for.

"Hi, big brother," came Sharon's cheerful voice on the phone. "Just called to let you know we—Shelby and I— think Liz is great, and you should most definitely bring her back again. And tell her that the cookies were simply superb. I use the past tense because they're all gone. Give me a call when you get home. Love you a lot. 'Bye."

Still Alex sat, unmoving, staring out into the glooming of the sky. Burl clambered up onto the couch beside him to offer comfort by putting his head in Alex's lap

274

and emitting a series of long and low grunting sounds. Alex reached out and scratched Burl's head.

"It's gonna be okay, big guy," he said. "It's gonna be okay." But he knew that was a lie. Nothing would ever be okay again.

The light came on. "Liz!" Kathryn cried. "What are you doing here sitting all alone in the dark?"

Liz squinted at the light. "Hello," she said in a dull voice.

Kathryn stooped down in front of her and peered into her face. "Are you all right?"

"Not really."

"Are you sick or something? You look awful."

"Thank you for those kind words. No, I'm not sick."

"Is Julia—"

"Julia's fine. She's eating. If you listen carefully, you can hear her crunch her cat food. She's fine. You took excellent care of her. I am forever in your debt."

"That's what friends are for." Kathryn dropped her coat and sank to the floor, settling herself cross-legged, as if she was planning on being there for a while. "So, uh, what's the scoop?"

"There is no scoop. No news. No nothing. Except that there is no more Alex and me."

Kathryn's eyes grew big and round, and her mouth made an *O* shape. "What happened?" she breathed.

"He knows. I told him. At the worst possible moment."

"You told him?" Kathryn's voice came out as a squeak.

Liz nodded, keeping her eyes focused on the bookshelves lining the walls behind Kathryn. Not out of any immediate and significant interest in books, but to keep the tears from rolling down her cheeks. "Yup. I told him I was barren. *Sans* uterus. That I had a hysterectomy."

"You used the big *H* word?" Kathryn sounded incredulous.

Liz nodded again. There was a silence between them. The silence of friends, between whom words are not necessary. In the distance, Liz could hear Julia continuing to crunch her cat food. She concentrated on the sound. It was a way of keeping herself from screaming.

"I gather he did not take this news well," Kathryn said at last.

"Nope. He put on his clothes and left." She could imagine the question forming in Kathryn's eyes. "No. We didn't. Almost, but not quite."

"And let me guess—the reason you didn't is because you told him."

"Give the little lady a cigar," Liz said with a sigh.

"Other than that, Mrs. Lincoln, how did you like the play?"

Liz struggled to twist her lips into something vaguely resembling a smile. Kathryn was trying to make a joke. Trying to cheer her up. That's what friends were for. Julia chose that moment to leap up on her lap and curl up for a loud purr fest. Liz rubbed the little bulging belly and thought of holding Alexis. "I had a great time. A wonderful time. Alex has an incredible family. His sisters and his mother and father are all as incredibly gorgeous as he is."

"Must be a dominant gene," Kathryn said, nodding her head wisely.

"And they're nice. They're the most nondysfunctional family I've ever met. I kept expecting June and Ward Cleaver to show up, carrying a casserole or something."

"Ozzie and Harriet to pop in for a neighborly chat."

"Robert Young and Jane Wyatt with Bud and Kitten and—oh, what was the oldest daughter's name?"

"Princess," Kathryn supplied.

"Anyway, you get the idea. Talk about Norman Rockwell. The Hogans must have been his prototype. When Alex says he wants a family, this is the kind of family he wants." She finally looked over at her friend. "I don't mean to sound so bitter."

"I know you don't. It's just that this is the kind of family you always wanted to have. It took me until I was an adult to understand why you used to watch all those reruns all the time. It was because you wanted to have that kind of a family."

Liz listened to Julia purr for a moment. Kathryn was right, as usual. She'd always wanted to be part of a family like that. But evidently it wasn't going to be that way. She sighed. "Well, you know that old Rolling Stones song. They're right. You can't always get what you want."

"Screw the Stones." Kathryn waved her hand dismissively. "What do they know about functional families anyway?"

"What do I know, for that matter?"

"You know a lot," Kathryn said softly. "You know not to take them for granted. You know how special they are. And how rare."

"And then when I go and find myself one, a realio, trulio functional family that I think I might just maybe be able to be a part of, even in an in-law sort of way—not that I'd turn down Alex, wherever he came from, but his family was the icing on the cake. The meringue on the lemon pie. Those little silver balls on the iced sugar cookies." She stopped for a moment. She'd lost her train of thought. "And then what happens? Whamo! My body screws me once more. You know what I hate most about this?"

Kathryn shook her head.

"It's never stopped." And then the tears spilled over, coursing down her cheeks. She sniffed loudly and indelicately. After all, Kathryn was the kind of friend one could sniff and snort in front of. "First I have to have the damned surgery. Then Richard leaves me because of it and finds himself a fertile Myrtle to have babies with. Now Alex has left me because of it. Because he, too, wants children more than he wants me." She smeared the tears from her cheeks. "When is it going to stop? When is it going to go away and leave me alone?"

Kathryn rummaged around in the pocket of her coat and came up with a crumpled tissue. She held it out. Liz took it and blew her nose. "But in a way, it doesn't even matter. Because I quit. I've lost two incredibly wonderful men because of it. Two is enough. I think I'll go and be a hermit somewhere."

"If they were so wonderful"—Kathryn's voice was low—"if they were so wonderful, they wouldn't have left."

Liz sniffed loudly.

"Don't try to make them out to be more than they are." Kathryn shook Liz's knee. "Look, don't get me wrong. They're both nice men. But they're not perfect."

"That's what Sharon said."

"Sharon?"

"Alex's sister. I told her I was afraid Alex was too perfect. She said he wasn't. She should know."

"Sisters don't tend to have the best perspective on their brothers. Either they're too partial, or they're too prejudiced. Hardly ever unbiased."

"No one seems unbiased when it comes to Alex Hogan."

"Well . . . " Kathryn stood up. "You need more tissues. Cheer up. The fat lady has yet to sing."

"I suppose you have a fat lady in mind?" Liz asked, snuffling. Her eyes burned. They did that when she cried.

"Connie Hewitt. She has the part of the Mother Superior. You know. 'Climb Every Mountain.' Huge woman." Kathryn spread her arms out and rolled her eyes. "But she has the most incredible voice. When I grow up, I want to be able to sing like Connie Hewitt."

Liz struggled out of her chair, trying to keep hold of Julia all the while. Kathryn pushed her back down. "I'll get you tissues. I know where you keep them."

Liz leaned her head back and closed her eyes. "What would I do without you, Kathryn?"

"You'd have a runny nose."

"Cookies!" Kendra crowed. "Look everyone, Liz baked us cookies."

It was Monday morning at the library. Liz deposited the foil-covered platter on the table in the staff room and shrugged out of her parka. "Just some sugar cookies. Nothing special."

"Listen to that," Kendra teased. "Nothing special. Who're you trying to kid?"

"I'm not trying to kid anyone," Liz protested with a grin. "Sugar cookies are nothing special. Now, if I'd decorated them with icing and sprinkles, that would be special." Liz hung up her coat and tried to make her escape before the questions started.

"So, how was your weekend?" another clerk asked.

No escape. Liz decided to brave it out. She'd tell the truth. About the weekend, that is. "I had a wonderful time," she said firmly. "Alex has a lovely family and everyone was very nice. And now," she said as she unwrapped the cookies, *"bon appétit!"* She said it in a determinedly cheerful, Julia Child sort of voice. It was time to change the subject. "Has anyone seen the desk schedule this morning?"

"It's over here," someone called.

Liz left the clerks with the cookies and made her way to her desk. She had a lot to do this morning. Too much to do to spend her time telling everyone about her weekend. Too much to do to let herself dwell on Alex Hogan and the look in his eyes when he left her house. Too much to do to think about all the babies she'd never have.

Alex suppressed a huge yawn as the kids trooped off the bus that morning. "Good-bye, Mr. Hogan," they called. Until Joshua Martini stopped the line.

"Hey, Mr. Hogan, what do you call a boomerang that doesn't come back?"

Alex tried, for the kid's sake. "I don't know. A boomerisn't?"

"No," the little child said with a chortle as he clomped down the bus steps. "A stick, Mr. Hogan! A stick!" He leaped off the bottom step with a war cry, brandishing an imaginary stick. Or maybe it was a sword.

A stick. Where did that kid come up with these things? Sticks. Wood. Rocking chairs. The image of the rocking chair he'd been making for Liz floated tantalizingly into his mind. He'd done some preliminary carving on the back of it. Carved into the headrest was a line of tumbling kittens and books. He'd planned on carving a baby on one side of the headrest and a big Burl-type dog on the other. Obviously custom-made. Obviously for Liz. Maybe he could turn the books into something else. Boxes, perhaps? Then it would be more generic and he could sell it. But no. He knew he'd never sell it. There was too much hope in that piece of wood. Too many dreams carved into each knife stroke. He'd have to put it away.

There was a brief honk behind him. He snapped his eyes open. The kids were all in the school and he was still sitting in his bus like a fool. No wonder the bus driver in back of him had honked. Alex waved to the other driver, checked the mirrors, then pulled out of the school driveway and headed back to the bus lot.

Her mood was as gray as the day. Liz had to force herself to smile at library patrons, force herself not to scream when the umpteenth person asked where the tax forms were, force herself to get up out of her chair and take a little girl over to the aisle where the books on pet rabbits were. On her way back to the desk, Liz looked out the window at the sky, a sky that was not anything like the skies she'd grown up under. This one was thick and gray. She did not want to be here.

But where did she want to be?

The phone rang. She forced herself to answer it.

"Can you tell me the price for a used car over the phone?"

"Certainly, sir. I can look that up for you in the current N.A.D.A. What year is the car, and what make is it?"

From their perches at the checkout desk, Liz could feel the clerks staring at her. They'd been staring at her all day. Evidently, they hadn't believed her when she'd said she'd had a wonderful time, but they weren't rude enough to ask her any more questions. Not even Kendra, and Kendra was usually not afraid to ask anyone anything. Except Attila.

A movement caught her eye. She watched as the library director as if on cue, emerged from the door to the staff room. In his usual measured strides, he made his way through the study area to the windows, where he turned and, hands clasped behind his back, he faced the library. He just stood there, gazing over what was his domain. Like a vulture. Liz thought. Or Edgar's nevermore raven. Attila always observed what went on, but never seemed interested in it. He never seemed interested in anything. Talking to Attila was like talking to someone behind a wall. He was totally unapproachable.

For the first time, Liz felt like that also. Maybe, she thought, she was turning into Attila. Well, good. She didn't want to be approached. In fact, she'd just as soon lynch the next kid who came up and asked for the bug books. And lynch the teacher who'd assigned the report in the first place.

Attila, having evidently seen what he wanted to see, moved towards the reference desk. Liz reached for

Chase's Annual Events, one of her favorite books, and tried to look busy. Attila didn't stop. He moved past her and Liz watched surreptitiously as he moved down to the other end of the library where once again, he took up his watch.

"What's he doing?" Carol, the other librarian, back from a reference question, whispered.

Liz shrugged. "Whatever it is, it looks sort of ominous."

"He looks like a vulture looking for roadkill." Carol echoed Liz's previous thoughts. Then she cheered up. "Speaking of roadkill, I think a potluck is in order, don't you? You have *Chase's* open. Let's find a day to celebrate and celebrate it. How about National Dump Your Significant Jerk Day. That's coming up, isn't it?"

Liz grimaced.

Carol gasped. "Oh Liz, I'm sorry," she apologized. "I've really put my foot in it."

"It's okay. Really. Don't worry about it."

Carol started to say something else, but just then an impatient-looking man wearing an important-looking suit came up to the desk. "Where's your *Value-Line*?" he asked her. Oh well, there went finding an appropriate holiday.

Still, Liz decided that she'd still bring in chocolate chip cookies later this week for the staff. Even without anything to celebrate. After all, it wasn't their fault she was miserable. But what *did* they expect? she asked herself. She'd told them there was nothing between her and Alex. They didn't believe her. Maybe now they would.

Alex hustled Burl into the house. At least, he tried to hustle Burl, but Burl moseyed on in his own way. After his walk, much longer than usual today, the big dog was in obvious need of a nap.

Alex headed into his workshop. The chair for Liz was in front of him. No escape from it. He picked up one of the spindles and rubbed it, the smooth wood sliding across his fingers like water. He set the spindle down again. He didn't want anything to do with the chair right now. He rummaged around in a storage cabinet until he found a cloth tarp. He draped it over the unfinished chair. He'd deal with it later.

Right now he had a puppet stage to finish. The show must go on, he told himself. Think of lonely goatherds yodeling high on a hilltop. He unrolled the plans Carl Petersen, the shop teacher, had provided and carried them over to the sawhorses where he'd set up the wood for the puppet stage. He studied the plans. Very simple structure, actually. All the decorative details would be painted on. He pulled out the tools he'd need and found himself humming the tunes from the show. It reminded him of the year the family had gotten a VCR for Christmas. That year Santa also gave Sharon and Shelby a copy of *The Sound of Music* on video, and they'd watched it every single day after school until he'd stolen it and hidden it from them. He, of course, had insisted he knew nothing about the missing movie. It stayed missing for a very long time, but the songs remained, etched in his brain, he was afraid, forever. He looked at the note stuck on the plans for the puppet stage. They needed it by the next weekend for rehearsals. No problem.

"Hello, sweet Julia," Liz called as she dropped her book bag on the kitchen chair. Julia came trotting into the kitchen to stand by her empty bowl and yell.

"More food for the babies," Liz said as she poured yet more cat food. Dr. March had said to free-feed Julia, adding a can of wet food in the morning and evening. "Which reminds me, little one, we have to take you in and have you weighed. Make sure you're healthy, all those little baby kitties swimming around inside."

Julia was more interested in her food.

Liz dialed the clinic number. "Hi, Suzette. Can I bring Julia in on Friday for a checkup? Sure, ten o'clock is great. See you then."

Liz sat down on the floor next to her cat. "They'll be pleased with how well you're doing," she said.

Julia, intent on her food, didn't answer.

"We need to get a box set up for you pretty soon. I brought home a box from a load of copier paper, and lots of newspapers. I'll put in some soft old sheets to make it comfy for the babies."

Julia looked up from her food. There was a questioning look on her face.

Liz chuckled. "Yes. Babies."

Julia left her bowl and climbed up in Liz's lap. She butted her face into Liz, promoting herself some heavy-duty petting. She rewarded Liz with her purr.

"You don't care if I have a uterus or not, do you?"

Julia most certainly didn't. As long as she got enough food and love, she was happy. Cats were such wonderful creatures. The best on the earth.

Liz held Julia up so she could see her nose to nose. "I used to say you were lucky the day I brought you home. But you know what? I'm the lucky one." She set the cat down and got to her feet. "Let's make supper and curl up with a good book and read."

Julia was willing. Especially the supper part.

Tuesday afternoon, Liz looked up from the reference desk to see Kathryn. "If it's any consolation," her friend told her, "Alex looks like hell. All the teachers have been talking about him. Since it's widely known that you and he have been . . . uh . . . spending time together, they wonder if something is rotten in Denmark. Just thought I'd let you know."

Liz sighed. "So I'm—once more—the topic of gossip?"

Kathryn nodded. "Much speculation."

"And what has been your role in this speculating?"

"*Moi?*"

"Yes, *toi*. And knock off that look of feigned innocence."

"I've been telling everyone that the two of you are friends. Nothing more. So there's no need for nasty rumors. Maybe Alex stayed up too late, you know, like maybe he couldn't sleep for some reason. I told everyone that you look fine. Yes, I lied. I said that certainly if something horrible had happened that you'd look like hell, too." She looked at Liz critically. "You need some more foundation to cover those purple bags under your eyes."

"You're such a comfort," Liz said sarcastically.

"I try. Say, can you go out to dinner on Thursday night? It's the only night this week that I don't have to be at rehearsals."

Liz thought for a moment. "Thursday. Sure." Then she truly looked at her friend. Kathryn looked different. "What's going on with you?" Liz asked.

Kathryn blushed.

"You and your shop teacher?" Liz guessed.

Kathryn nodded. "Things are going well."

"Well, why didn't you say so?"

"I didn't want to interrupt your wallowing."

Liz rolled her eyes. "Please. We've been friends for too long to let a little wallow in self-pity come between good news. Promise you'll spill it all on Thursday?"

"Promise."

Then Liz had to help a fourth-grader find a biography of a famous Ohioan.

Wednesday morning, Alex unsnapped a CD case to put it in the player while he got ready for work. It was from the library. He set the CD in the player and turned the volume up. Then he noticed the due date stamp on the slip. It was due today. Since he usually checked out several CDs at the same time, that meant that a bunch of them were due today. He sighed. Well, he'd have to gather them up while he ate.

Later, after his morning route, he nosed his truck into the library parking lot to return the CDs. On Wednesdays, Liz usually didn't come to work until noon. Her car wasn't parked in its usual spot. Nor in any other spot, he saw, as he glanced around the parking lot.

It wasn't that he was avoiding her, he told himself. He just didn't think he could see her right now without—without what? Getting angry? He didn't have anything to say to her. He felt betrayed.

He set his parking brake, gathered up the CDs from the front seat and counted them to make sure he had them all. Then he took a deep breath and went into the library.

Even though he knew she wasn't there, he walked quickly past the reference desk. Without a word he set the CDs on the return counter and hurried past the checkout desk. He could feel the young women watching him. He made his way to the end of the library where the CDs were shelved. Flipping through the racks of them, he quickly selected several. He wanted to be out of the library. Out of her world.

On the way up to the checkout desk, he tried to avoid looking at the clerks by gazing around the library. His gaze landed on a book display. On the table, a child-sized rocking chair was draped with a baby blanket. Sitting in the middle was a teddy bear with a book in its paws. It was surrounded by several books—each one, so the sign proclaimed, an excellent choice to read to your child at bedtime. But Alex didn't have any children to read to. At bedtime, or any other time. He wondered if he ever would.

"May I help you?" a clerk asked.

He handed her the CDs and his library card.

"These will be due in three weeks," the young woman told him with a beaming smile. An overly bright smile that bordered on awe.

He nodded. "Thanks," he muttered and made his escape into the cold air.

He'd have to find another way to borrow his CDs. He didn't want to do that again. Not ever.

Thursday evening when she got home from work, Liz stood staring at Julia's bowl. There was still food in it. Not only that, but Julia didn't seem the least bit concerned about it. Liz scooped up the kitty and held her out so she could look her in the eye.

"So, what's going on? Who are you and what have you done with my cat?"

Julia closed her eyes and purred.

"Is it getting too crowded in there for much food?"

Julia continued to purr.

"Well, you're going to see Dr. March tomorrow, so we'll see what she says. In the meantime, I'm going out to dinner with Kathryn. So there better not be anything wrong with you."

Julia wiggled. Liz put her down. Julia stalked regally down the hall, her tail held high. Then Kathryn arrived and Liz headed out the door.

"Let's do Chinese," Kathryn suggested.

Liz looked at her curiously. "Since when have you developed a taste for Chinese? You've always hated it."

Kathryn shrugged. "So? You think I can't change my mind?"

"But the question is, *why* are you changing your mind?"

"I had some good Chinese food."

"When?"

"Carl Petersen took me to this new place up by the movie theater. I liked it."

Liz leaned back in her seat and smiled. "Then let's have Chinese. But only if you tell all."

"There's not much to tell. Yet."

"Then we'll celebrate the possibilities."

"Are you sure you don't mind?"

"Are you nuts? You're my best friend. The closest thing to family I have."

"Families don't always get along."

"Well, we do."

The Chinese restaurant was dim and uncrowded. They were seated immediately and served a pot of tea.

"What do you like about Carl?"

"He's steady. He's calm. Nothing seems to fluster

him. At least, nothing I've seen so far. The man teaches high school, for pete's sake. He's got to be calm."

"Is he divorced, never married, what?"

"Divorced. No children. Says he's had hundreds of teenagers over the past fifteen years and that's enough for him."

"Sounds perfect."

Kathryn sighed. "I wish I could give you my uterus. I certainly don't want it."

Liz chuckled. "I don't think they do transplants. Besides, I've decided I'm working out some karma. Maybe I was W. C. Fields in a past life, and this is nature's way of getting back at me." She picked up the small, squat teapot and poured, offering a cup to Kathryn. "So, he's taken you out to dinner. What else?"

"Nothing else."

"Yet."

"Yet. But I'm keeping my fingers crossed. And I see him at play rehearsals." She took a sip of tea. "He's not gorgeous, like Alex," she said thoughtfully. "But then, no one is gorgeous like Alex. But you know"—she cocked her head—"he's a regular nice guy."

"The world needs more nice guys," Liz agreed.

All through dinner, Liz learned about the nice guy, Carl. They drank two more pots of tea, until finally she glanced at her watch. "Oh, my. It's almost time for 'Mystery.'"

"Then let's get you home. You don't miss 'Mystery' for nothin'."

As they paid their check and left the restaurant, Liz

looked up at the sky. "Actually, I've missed 'Mystery' several times these past few weeks."

Kathryn stopped and stared.

Liz kept walking. "I was spending most of my spare time with Alex. I wasn't reading much, either. Now that I'm not going to be seeing him anymore, I'll have time to read again."

Kathryn caught up with her. "Are you sure you're not using books as a way of escaping from life?"

Liz shook her head. "Nope. Books are a constant in my life. Always have been, you know that. Sure, they're an escape. But I don't use books as a people substitute."

"You've given up the idea of being a hermit?"

Liz nodded. "That was just a version of ranting and raving. I like being around people too much. Even when they're pains in the neck."

The next morning, Liz woke at her usual time. No sleeping in for the weary, she told herself. Even if she'd woken up half a dozen times each night ever since she'd told Alex. She couldn't sleep.

"Well, Julia," she told her kitty, "we get to go see Dr. March today."

Julia snuggled deeper into her covers, refusing to open her eyes. But she did start her motor, so Liz knew she was awake.

"Good morning, Suzette," she said as she let the clinic door close behind her.

"Good morning, Liz. How are you today, Julia?"

After a short wait, she and Julia were ushered into one of the exam rooms.

"Hiya, Liz." Jessie breezed into the room. "Melissa'll be here in a jiffy." She leaned down to rub noses with Julia. "You're sure getting big. We'll have to get a sign to hang around your neck that says 'Wide Load.' "

Julia sat her little wide self down and yelled.

"I think she likes that idea."

Then Melissa came in. "Let's see how you are today, little one," she said. "Hello, Liz." She listened to Julia's insides with the stethoscope. "Sounds good inside." She looked at her eyes, and inside her mouth. "Color's good." She finished her exam, then turned to Liz. "She seems to be in excellent health for a pregnant kitten. How's her appetite?"

"She's not eating as much."

"That's normal. Not enough room inside for much food." She thought for a moment. "Has she been overly restless lately?"

Liz shook her head. "Is there a problem?"

Melissa smiled. "Not as long as you have a box ready for her."

"Box, newspapers, old clean sheets, two-ml hypodermic syringe without a needle, cotton swabs, scissors that have been boiled, dental floss, small bottle of iodine. Oh, and scales. And a book from the library on playing midwife to a cat."

Jessie whistled. "You've been busy."

"Sounds like you're prepared," added Melissa.

Liz sighed. "As ready as I think I'll ever be." Then she grinned. "I also still have your phone numbers on my speed dial."

Melissa chuckled as she rubbed Julia's head. "Don't be afraid to holler if you have any questions, or if there's any problems. Anything at all."

"I won't," Liz promised. She knew Melissa meant it. "I think everything will be fine. Sally Foster and Kathryn Leslie have both offered to play midwife if I need the moral support. So has Jessie."

The vet smiled again. "Then it sounds like you'll be set. Now, you know that her temperature should drop two or three degrees shortly before labor starts. But she should be fine." She bent down to nose-to-nose the cat. "I expect to see you with little itty bitties soon."

But it was while she was leaving the clinic that Liz saw Jessie again, out in the parking lot, pooper scooper in her hand.

"Okay," she said. "Out with it."

"Out with what?" Jessie looked innocent.

"You keep staring at me."

Jessie shrugged. "I don't mean to stare at you."

"And this is the first time in several weeks that you've not asked, no, bullied me, about Alex Hogan."

Jessie stubbed her toe into a speed bump. "It's really none of my business."

Liz grinned. "I know it isn't. But don't you dare tell me you're not curious."

Jessie's head shot up. "Sally says that Alex looks like a zombie, and you have these purple bags under your eyes, as if you're not sleeping. Curious? Of course I'm curious." She planted her fist on her hip. "But I'm not going to bully you about it. I promised Sally I wouldn't."

Liz looked at her friend. When she'd first moved to Hartley, she'd lived in the apartment next to Jessie. Jessie had accosted Liz as she was carrying a big bag of kitty litter in from the moving truck. They'd been friends ever since. "I kept telling you all that nothing was going to happen between me and Alex," she said. "I guess you all thought I was being coy or something. But it's the truth. Because Alex wants to have lots of children. It's no secret."

Jessie nodded. "Everyone knows that," she said. "Well, everyone who matters."

"But I can't have kids."

Jessie frowned. "Why not?"

"I don't have a uterus. You ever hear of endometriosis?"

Jessie's eyes widened in surprise. "Sure. It's sort of like the human version of pyometra. More common in dogs than in cats, but the best solution is to—" She stopped and stared at Liz while her eyes grew big and round. Then she whistled low and long. "You were spayed!"

Liz leaned against her car, Julia and carrier in her arms. Trust Jessie to put things in their proper perspective. "Yes, I guess you could say I was spayed."

Jessie nodded. "It is all clear to me now. Why Alex and you are both looking horrible." She looked up at Liz, sincerity shining in her eyes. "I'm really sorry."

Liz shrugged. "Just one of those things. Kathryn said I could have her uterus but I don't think they do transplants."

Jessie shook her head. "And I don't think I've ever heard of a prosthetic uterus. Other than a petrie dish. Gee, Liz, this really stinks."

"Well, I wanted to let you know. So you'd understand that this isn't something that can be fixed."

The two of them stood in silence for a moment. Then Liz shifted the weight of the cat carrier. "Well, I've gotta go. I should get Julia home, and out of the cold. See you later, Jess."

Jessie nodded somberly. "See you later."

Chapter Sixteen

As soon as Alex pulled the package out of the mailbox and read the return address, he knew what it was. Pictures. Dave was consistently obsessive about recording, on film, all the events of their lives. And Sharon was just as obsessive about taking the film in to be developed immediately. He tossed the unopened package on the table, where it lay staring at him, taunting him.

He opened the back door and called Burl in for supper. He fed Burl. The package still stared at him. He made himself a sandwich and turned on the evening news. Still the package stared. Dared him to open it. Dared him to look at the photos inside.

Alex stared back.

Then, with a great sigh, he reached for the package. He was right. They were photos, along with a note from

Sharon, reminding him to bring Liz back for another visit. Especially Liz with cookies.

He flipped through the pictures. Liz holding a sleeping Alexis. Alex, his arm around Liz, holding her close, kissing her on her cheek. Liz reading to the terrible trio. Joshua James, the littlest of the trio, holding onto Burl's neck to pull himself up to stand. Liz and Shelby doing dishes at his mother's house. And Liz looking at one of Mom's innumerable photo albums. Sheesh! Liz had no problem with poring over those old albums. In fact, she'd seemed to enjoy it. He thought that was what finally won his mother over, the fact that Liz was actually interested in all the old photo albums. Alex found himself smiling slightly at the memory. He turned to the last picture. He and Liz, their faces filling the photo, smiling into each other's eyes. Dave had snapped it at the last instant before Alex had kissed Liz. It was a kiss that had gone on and on and on, causing woo-woos from the guys. A forever kiss. A kiss that had given him hope for a future.

"C'mon, Burl, let's go pound some wood."

Burl heaved himself up from a nap and lumbered after Alex into the workshop.

"Say, Kathryn, can I borrow your camera?" she said that night on the phone.

"Sure." Kathryn's voice was slightly bewildered. "Why do you want my camera?"

"Photo albums."

"What about them?"

"They're all over the place at Alex's mom's house."

"What's in them?"

"Pictures of Alex and his sisters when they were little. All of their lives, actually." Liz didn't have any baby pictures of herself. She didn't think her mother did, either. "I don't have any pictures of Skillet. I want some of Julia. And all the little Juliettes."

"Why this sudden interest in photography?"

"I guess photographs remind you of all the good times. So I want to take pictures of Julia, and then when we're eighty-seven we can sit in our porch swings and look at them and remember Julia and her kittens."

"Sounds good."

"So, are you and Carl doing anything special this weekend?"

"Dinner and a movie tomorrow night. Do you want to come?"

"Thanks, but no. You know what they say about three."

"Sure. Three is a prime number. Three sides of a triangle. Three coins in the fountain. Three little pigs. The three fates."

"You're being purposely obtuse. They say that three is a crowd." Liz yawned. "Tomorrow I'm going to come home from work and curl up with my cat and a good book."

"Sounds boring."

"Sounds perfect." Maybe if she said it firmly enough, she'd begin to believe it herself.

Saturday morning, Alex and Burl were just home from their walk when the phone rang. It was Carl Petersen. "Say, Alex," he said, "how's that puppet theater coming along?"

"Just fine. It's all put together. I just need to do the painting."

"Good, good. Say, I was wondering if you could bring it over to the school auditorium next Thursday night for rehearsal."

Alex thought. "Sure. What time does rehearsal start?"

"Have it there at seven. Oh, and Alex, I really appreciate this. Remember, we'll put your name in the program, and on opening night there'll be two tickets for you at the box office."

Two tickets, Alex thought glumly as he hung up the phone. What could he do with two tickets? "Say, Burl, do you think you could pass?"

Burl, hearing his name, came wagging his tail to investigate.

Alex grabbed the big dog and gave his back a knuckle scrubbing. "Nah, you'd look silly in a dress."

Burl grunted in pleasure. Burl loved having a back scratch.

"Can you help me?" the woman asked. She looked very long-suffering.

"Sure," Liz replied. "How can I help you?"

"My daughter needs an insect identification book for school. She has to identify some bugs."

Liz pursed her lips in thought. "Eighth grade?" she guessed. "We've had dozens of eighth-graders coming in for insect books, and all our circulating books are checked out. We do have some things over here in the reference section, but you'd have to use them here."

A bored-looking teenager sauntered up to stand next to the woman. This was obviously the daughter. She was chewing gum and looked like she had something on her mind, and identifying bugs was definitely not it. "See, Gail," the mother said. "All the books are checked out. I told you that you should've come in earlier."

Liz took pity on the girl. She remembered her own middle-school bug identification project. "Some kids have been bringing their bugs into the library and identifying them here using the reference books. You're welcome to do that, too."

The girl looked irritated and popped her gum. "I'll just make up some names."

"Gail!" her mother protested.

"Well," the girl said defensively, "she's only a biology teacher. I mean, how smart could she be?"

Liz left them with the reference books. At times like these, she was glad she didn't have children.

When she reached the reference desk, she purposely swiveled her chair so she wouldn't have to look at that blasted display Cecily had put up. Books to read to your child at bedtime. Maybe she should bring some books home to read to Julia. Julia'd been unusually affectionate and cuddly the last couple of days. She'd probably like a bedtime story. Liz set herself to looking up titles of picture books about cats. Ah, here was one. Liz read the synopsis. A stray kitten has a variety of adventures until she finds the perfect home. This looked like a book Julia could identify with.

Brush in hand, Alex stood back to eye his work critically. From a distance it could pass for an expensive puppet theater. The wonders of paint. All it needed was a coat of varnish.

He set the brush in a jar of solvent for cleaning.

Then, turning, his gaze snagged on the chair for Liz. It was still shrouded, as if apologizing for being. For a moment, Alex stared at the drop cloth covering the chair of his dreams. Should he try to rework it? Or should he use the parts to make other chairs? He had an order for a Boston rocker for a woman up in New England. He could use the spindles for her chair. But no. He didn't want to think about it right now. He had to finish this puppet theater and then work on a selection of cradles for a woodworking show coming up in the spring. He turned his back on Liz's chair.

Later, that afternoon, while he and Burl were circumnavigating the neighborhood, they saw little Joshua

Martini. The little boy had bright red cheeks and nose. Burl loved Joshua Martini, who often had interesting things to eat in his pockets.

"Where's your hat?" Alex asked.

Joshua shrugged. "I dunno. It's somewhere." He looked up from hugging Burl. "Say, Mr. Hogan, who was purple and conquered Asia?"

Alex pretended to think for a moment. "I don't know."

"Alexander the Grape!" the child chortled. "And guess who they found in his grave?"

Alex sighed. "Who?"

"Alexander the Raisin!"

Alex chuckled in spite of himself. Burl, getting into the spirit of things, added his deep, powerful bark.

"Hey, Mr. Hogan, the guy on the TV said it was gonna snow tomorrow. Can we make snowmen?"

"Sorry to disappoint you, Joshua, but I don't think there will be enough snow for snowmen."

"But if there is, can we?" He sounded so very excited at the prospect. But Alex, for probably the first time in his life, wasn't in the mood to make snowmen.

"We'll see" he hedged.

Joshua frowned. "When my new mom says that, she usually means no."

Alex looked up into the sky. Oh, he hated disappointing kids. They were so often disappointed by life itself, it seemed criminal to add to it. Alex figured he had an obligation. "Well, Joshua, I'll tell you what. If there's enough snow tomorrow, you come over and we'll make snowmen. Okay?"

"Goodie!" The child bounded up in the air. Where did he get his energy? "And can Ms. Hadley come make snowmen, too?"

Alex forced his face into a neutral expression. "I think Ms. Hadley probably has other plans tomorrow."

"Oh." Suddenly, Joshua Martini lost all his bounce. Alex knew just how he felt. "Well, we'll build some terrific ones, and then she can come over and see them later. I gotta go now, Mr. Hogan. See ya!" And he darted off down the tree-lined street, dodging imaginary enemies right and left, making machine-gun noises as he ran.

Alex was left, standing with Burl. He'd always imagined himself with a little boy like Joshua Martini someday. Enthusiastic, energetic, a great builder of snowmen. Well, not now. "C'mon, Burl. Time to head home." Suddenly home seemed like a very long way away.

Liz felt herself struggling to not snap at patrons. When a middle-school student came up and asked for bug books, she wanted to scream, *The assignment is due on Monday; what makes you think there are any bug books left?* But she mashed down her irritation and managed to calmly explain that all the circulating books were checked out, that there were some insect guides in the reference collection, but they had to be used at the library.

"Honestly," she muttered to Cecily, who was scheduled on the reference desk with her. "Why do all these kids wait till the last possible moment to do their reports and expect us to still have everything they need?"

Cecily stared at her. "Are you feeling all right?"

"Fine," Liz said shortly. "I'm absolutely fine."

Cecily snorted softly. "Like I believe that." She shoved her chair back. "Look, Liz, you're the one who never gets irritated with the patrons. Not even with kids when they're noisy, or when they're banging on the keyboards. And you've been short with staff, too. What's going on?"

Liz looked down at her hands. "I'm sorry," she said quietly. "I guess I have been grumpy this week."

Cecily brightened up. "But this week is almost over. In one hour and seven minutes we'll be closed and we can go home. Next week will be better."

"I'm sure it will." But she wasn't sure at all.

That evening, curled up in her comfy chair, with Julia purring on her lap and a book unopened on the table beside her, she was sure next week would not be better. For she now knew what she was missing. She was missing Alex.

She rubbed Julia's head, and under her chin. Julia did the closed-eye purr. She stroked Julia's belly, that bulging belly. Julia stretched languorously and yawned a wide-mouthed yawn. This cat was going through a total personality change. This cat was turning into a lap cat, a cuddle cat, an I'll-play-later cat. From within

Julia's belly, one of the kittens rolled over, the movement rippling down Julia's side. What an incredible thing, she thought, to have babies growing inside. "Oh, there goes another one. Are they playing tag in there? Does it tickle?" she asked Julia. Julia's only answer was an expression that was at once both smug and wise.

Liz sighed, and as she reached for her book, she happened to glance out the window. Snow was falling. Light snow. Dusting Hartley, Ohio, with powdered sugar. Not enough, though, the weather forecaster had predicted on the evening news, to make snowmen. Snowmen. She'd never again be able to hear the word *snowmen* without thinking of Alex. Thinking of Alex, and of what she had lost.

Sunday late morning there was a knock on his door. It was Joshua Martini. "Hey, Mr. Hogan, is there enough snow?"

Alex surveyed the three or four inches of white stuff in his front yard. "I don't know, Joshua," he said. "Let's go take a look." They wandered out onto the lawn. Alex scooped up a handful of snow and patted it to try to form a ball. "What do you think?" he asked Joshua.

Joshua peered at the crumpled snow in Alex's hand. "It doesn't pack," he said mournfully.

"I think you're right."

Joshua shrugged expressively. "Oh, well. Maybe next time."

"You have a deal."

"I guess it's just as well that Ms. Hadley has something else to do today."

"I guess so," Alex said lightly. He was going to have to get used to people saying her name. Have to get used to that empty spot in his gut. An emptiness that had nothing to do with food.

"Well, see you later, Mr. Hogan."

"See you later, Joshua."

He watched the little boy trudge, shoulder slumped, down his driveway. He looked so dejected. What could he do to cheer him up? "Hey, Joshua," he called. "I have a knock-knock joke for you."

At the end of the driveway, the child turned eagerly. "What is it?"

"Okay. You start."

"Knock-knock," Joshua called.

"Who's there?" Alex asked.

Silence. Then little Joshua Martini erupted into gales of hilarity. "Oh, I get it! That's a good one, Mr. Hogan." Alex could hear his laughter continue as he trotted down the street toward his home.

Children were so resilient, Alex thought. They bounced back so quickly from life's many disappointments. All it took was a corny knock-knock joke to help Joshua feel better. But it wasn't the joke itself, Alex realized, it was the understanding that no matter what happens, no matter how bad things get, there will always be a new joke. "I need a new joke," he said to the dry clumps of snow in his hand. "Maybe it's time to put that rocking chair away."

In his workshop he pulled the tarp off the chair parts. The pieces of wood looked vulnerable and raw. He picked up the headrest and ran his fingers over the carved kittens. He wondered how Julia was doing. Her kittens were due pretty soon. He set the piece of wood on a workbench and began sorting the spindles. Short ones for the arms, longer ones for the back, thicker spindles for the rungs. They went in his spindle rack. The seat he hung up on the wall with the other waiting chair seats. That left the rockers. He scraped at a tiny spot with a fingernail. This was an excellent set of rockers, he thought. They would make an excellent chair.

Putting the chair away made him feel good. And hungry. Hungrier than he'd been in days. He wandered into the kitchen and opened the cupboards. Nothing. "Burl," he called, "we have to go to the store."

She decided to make *pots de crème*. It was sufficiently decadent. She was ready for some decadence. She also wanted to buy some special cat food to try to tempt Julia's fading appetite. "Imagine that," she told the cat on her lap. "I'm trying to encourage you to eat."

Julia merely purred.

"Then cream, eggs, gourmet cat food." Liz pulled her purse across the kitchen table and brought out a pen and a piece of paper to begin a list. "What else? I should bake something to take into work on Monday. And something to take to the vet clinic to thank them for all the care they've given you."

Julia continued to purr.

Liz thought and wrote. At last she had a grocery list. Julia, though, did not want to move from her lap. "Here you go, sweetie," Liz crooned, settling the cat in the corner of the couch. "All comfy. You take a nap now. I'll be back in a bit."

The streets of Hartley were wet and sloppy. Liz's windshield wipers clunked grudgingly back and forth, smearing the yucky slush instead of wiping it. The joys of Ohio in the winter, she thought. She turned on the radio, singing along to the oldies station out of Columbus, songs of unrequited love and heartbreak. "That sounds about right," Liz muttered to herself. A passing car splattered muck on her windshield. The joys, the joys.

Then she pulled into the perpetually crowded parking lot at Abernathy's. The cars were parked haphazardly, the painted lines slightly obscured by packed-down snow and gray guck. Shoppers struggled to push loaded grocery carts to their cars, the little metal wheels almost useless. Liz drove slowly up and down the drunken rows, looking for a parking spot. She saw one, over in the next row next to that—next to Alex's truck.

Liz stopped. So Alex was here. She didn't want to go in. She didn't want to see him, didn't want to see that he looked, as Kathryn said, like hell. And if he didn't look like hell, she really didn't want to see him. She didn't want him to see her. She didn't want to see him see her and turn away.

She fumbled in her pocket for her grocery list. What should she do? She needed the cat food, but the other things weren't crucial. Maybe she wouldn't bake today. Maybe she should do other chores. But she'd done all her laundry last night, after she'd scrubbed her kitchen floor. No, she wanted to bake. She would drive across town to that new grocery store. She'd been wanting to see it, and this gave her the perfect reason.

Alex was settling down to a late supper of pasta with garlic sauce when the phone rang. He told Burl, who, with a look of pure innocence, was leaning toward the table, to stay away from his plate, and scooted his chair back. He picked up the receiver.

"Alex." It was Dave, sounding long-suffering. "Your sister is standing right beside me. She made me call. She's worried. And you know Sharon when she starts to worry."

"About what?"

"She doesn't know. That's the problem."

"What's going on?"

"Alex." His sister's voice came over the phone. "You haven't answered the phone when I've called, and you haven't called me back, even after you got the pictures. You did get the pictures didn't you? So I was worried. I mean, you might've gotten into a car wreck on the way

311

home last weekend or something, and how would we ever know?"

Alex grinned to himself. Sharon's worrying was legend. "If I'd been in a car accident, believe me, you'd've heard about it."

"So, anyway, why haven't you called me back? I kept leaving messages on your machine."

"I've been busy."

"Out with Liz, I'll bet?" It was asked innocently, Alex knew. "Oh, can you ask Liz for the recipe for those cookies?"

Alex didn't know what to say. Didn't know how to say it.

"Alex? Are you there? Is everything all right?"

"Yeah. Sure."

"You sound funny."

"You sound irritating."

"Now I know something's wrong. What is it?"

"Liz. We're not seeing each other anymore."

Sharon gasped. Then was silent.

"Alex." Dave's voice came over the line. "What's going on? Sharon just handed me the phone and told me to deal with this. Then she stomped upstairs."

Alex shook his head over his sister. "I told her Liz and I aren't seeing each other anymore." It was easier the second time he said it.

Dave whistled. "Sharon's spent the whole week waiting to talk to you so she could invite the two of you back."

Alex shrugged. "Liz can't have kids." It was better that his family know the truth; otherwise they'd spend years speculating and wondering. His mother would never come right out and ask, but Sharon would. So would Shelby. They had no shame when it came to his life. They'd hint and pester like they'd always done. "She had an operation a long time ago. I didn't know."

"Oh, no." Dave groaned. "That sucks."

Alex heard Dave speaking to Sharon.

"Alex?" It was Sharon again. "She can't have kids? Why not?"

"She had an operation a long time ago?"

"What kind of an operation?"

"A hysterectomy."

"Why?"

The question stunned him. He'd never thought to wonder.

"Alex, why?" his sister persisted.

"I don't know," he admitted.

"You don't know?" Sharon's voice sounded incredulous. "She tells you something like this and you don't ask her why? You dummy. You men are all alike. Someone should teach you about women."

"You sound mad."

"You're right I'm mad. You're so in love with Liz that you can't see straight. And she tells you this and you don't even ask her why? You're so stupid. You are such a man." She hurled the word at him as if it was an insult. "If you weren't in Ohio, I'd throw something at you. How could you do that? I suppose she told you and you just stomped off?" Sharon huffed. "Well, is that what you did? And don't lie to me. I know that's what you did."

"If you know that's what I did, then why bother asking me?"

"To hear you admit that you did something incredibly stupid."

"I didn't feel stupid at the time."

"Well, then, what *did* you feel at the time?" she asked sarcastically.

"I didn't feel anything," he admitted.

"You men," she fumed. "You're nothing but a bunch of single-cell organisms. I don't know why we women put up with you."

"Because you love us?" he suggested.

"It's obviously some flaw in our basic design." Her voice was back to normal. Evidently she was over her venting. "So what are you going to do about it?"

"Do? There's nothing that I can do."

"I'm not going to get upset at you again. I'm really not. But you are not being very smart here. You can't make a decision until you have all the facts."

"I have all the facts." His sister could be so obtuse at times. "Liz can't have children. I want children. End of story."

"Then change your story."

"I don't want to change the story. Look, Sharon, I love you, but you're being difficult."

"*I'm* being difficult? You're being a *man* about this, and you accuse *me* of being difficult?"

"Quit bashing men."

"Then start behaving. Go over to Liz's house and ask her about this operation of hers. You need to know why she had it, and how it made her feel, and—stop groaning. Women have feelings and need to express them, and if you men have a problem with that, then you can go—oh, Alex, I don't know what you can go do, but I know that it can't have been easy for Liz to tell you. She does this really hard thing and you walk out on her. I wouldn't blame her if she never speaks to you again."

"How do you know it was hard for her?"

"Because she knows you want kids. And because she is so in love with you that she can't see straight. Didn't you know that?"

He sighed in relief. "No, Sharon, you've got it all wrong. She agreed to pretend to be my girlfriend to get your friend Cindy off my back."

There was blessed silence for a few seconds. Then, "Sorry, brother mine, but you are very, very wrong. She was not pretending. Women know what it looks like when someone's pretending to be in love, and what it looks like when they really are. You know what they say—you can't fool all the people all the time because half of them are women. And buddy, that was the real thing."

Once again, Alex was stunned speechless. "Are you sure?" he finally asked.

He heard Sharon snort. "That question doesn't even deserve an answer. Look, you think about it. Then do the right thing. The right thing, Alex, not the wrong thing. I'll talk to you later. Remember, we all love you."

"I love you all, too," he mumbled.

Love. He used it as a swear word as he hung up the phone. The word was tossed around and around so much in today's world that it had almost no meaning anymore. We proclaim to love the right peanut butter, or a particular brand of laundry detergent. We love motor oil, or a new kind of tires. But what about people? How, he asked himself, can you use the same word to refer to peanut butter and to garbage can liners and your spouse? It was impossible. Love for a person was a total and undying commitment. He knew it was possible to have that. His parents had it. Sharon and Dave did. He would settle for nothing less than his own definition of love. It was also Sharon's definition. And yet she'd used that word to describe his feelings for Liz, and hers for him.

Did he love Liz? The question was not a simple one. If he did, he'd have to give up his dream of children. Everything he'd done in his adult life was done to prepare for the children he'd someday have. Rocking chairs and cradles. He could not imagine life without children around him, growing, becoming. That was the way the world was supposed to work. That was the way he wanted the world to work. His world, at least. How could he give it up? He couldn't.

316

How could he give Liz up? He had to. Didn't he?

Alex sank back down at the kitchen table. Alone at the kitchen table. He looked at the food on his plate. He could warm it up in the microwave. He didn't feel like eating. "Burl, would you like some pasta and sauce?"

Monday morning, Liz carried the foil-covered platter of cookies into the staff room and set it on the table.

"My, my, what have we here?" Cecily asked in delight. "Liz has been baking again," she called out into the workroom.

Liz hung up her coat and turned around to see the staff crowded around the table. "Can we look?" a newer clerk asked. It was an unwritten rule that only the person who brought the food was allowed to unveil it. Peeking, while officially unsanctioned, was a common and furtive occurrence. However, to sample a dish before it was officially unveiled was on an equal footing with spitting in church.

"Sure," Liz said, unwrapping the foil. "You can even taste. Yesterday I went to that new grocery store across town and was inspired by their baking section, which is very nice. So I made chocolate crinkle cookies. Nothing special. Why do you all always act as though anything I bring in is the crown jewels?"

"Because it usually is," answered Cecily. "And chocolate crinkle cookies are the very best. Liz, you can get inspired any time. Say, has anyone made coffee?"

Liz slipped out of the room. Away from their chatter. She had an errand to do. She dropped her book bag off at her desk and checked her mailbox for any new epistles from Attila. Then she strode purposefully out to the 636.8s, the number Dewey reserved for books about cats as pets. She scanned the shelves. Cat breeds, litter box training in a day, the history of cats, cats for kids, cat health for pet owners. Breeding your cat. That's what she wanted. She pulled the book out and flipped through it. Yes, there was a chapter on queening and taking care of newborn kittens. This was exactly what she needed.

Later that morning, during a lull at the reference desk, she opened the book to the chapter on pregnancy. Near the end she found the section on signs of impending labor. Queens often became more affectionate, she read, as they neared the end of their pregnancy, and they often lost interest in their food. Yes, she thought, Julia was certainly more affectionate, and as for loss of appetite—even the gourmet canned cat food wasn't doing the trick. Nesting box, yes; when Julia wasn't on Liz's lap, she was curled up and purring in her nesting box. It looked like Julia was going to have her kittens very soon. The only thing that was missing was a drop in her temperature.

"It's cold out there!" the young woman exclaimed as she breezed through the door and came to a stop in front of the reference desk. "I would like," she said, a twinkle in her eye, "books on quilting. It feels like we're in for another ice age."

Liz made an attempt to smile at the woman. "Do you want to know about the history of quilts, or do you want books of quilt patterns, or how to make them?"

The young woman's forehead creased in thought. Decisions, decisions. "How to make them, I guess."

"We have books on making quilts over here." She led the young woman to the 646s.

"Oh, this is marvelous," the woman exclaimed. "Just what I wanted."

Liz grinned at her obvious enthusiasm. "If you don't find exactly what you need, let me know," she said. But on the way back to the reference desk she averted her eyes from the section on human pregnancy and labor and delivery.

Then she stopped. She was being silly. Memories of second grade floated into her mind. She'd refused to touch a picture of a spider in her science book. Even on a double dare. But that was when she was a child. Now she was an adult. It was time to face the things that made her squirm. *Only when you stare them down,* she told herself, *will you see they have no power over you.* She was beginning to sound like one of Kathryn's self-help books. But still, she pulled out a book on newborn babies and stared at the photograph on the cover. Double daring it to bother her.

Later in the morning, the library started to fill up with preschoolers and their parents. Cecily had story time this morning. She had thumped her basket of books and things on the reference desk while she trotted over to

319

refill the display. Liz watched, fascinated, as a little girl came into the library dragging her coat by one sleeve. The little girl was dressed in a frilly pink tutu, pink tights, and cowboy boots. Followed by her tolerant-looking mother, she scuffed her cowboy boots all the way into the meeting room.

"Wonder what Cecily's reading to the little varmints today," Carol said dryly.

"I just heard you refer to my preschoolers as varmints," Cecily said cheerfully. "I keep telling you, they're rugrats."

"Rugrats, varmints, what's the difference? So, what are you reading to them today?"

"Stories about snowmen," Cecily said with a great big grin. "I'm doing some positive thinking. I want another big snow."

Another big snow, Liz thought. Snow meant snowmen. Snowmen meant Alex. Kathryn was right; all roads did lead to Alex. *We are not,* she told herself firmly, *going to go there.* "What great stories do you have about snowmen?" She forced herself to ask the question in a cheery voice, as if snowmen didn't bother her in the least. It was another double dare she was going to win. Make herself think of the good times, not of the ending.

That afternoon, Liz was in the stacks, going through the shelves, looking for books that needed to be replaced or mended. It was contemplative work. Peaceful work after the rush and bustle of working on the reference desk. Liz looked at the book she'd pulled off the shelf. As she turned to place it on her book truck, she came face-to-face with Sally Foster, the kindergarten teacher, a big brown paper grocery bag in her arms.

"I brought you a present," Sally said, setting the bag down on the book truck. "Lots of old cut-up blankies and towels and sheets for Julia's kittens. Birthing kittens is messy."

Liz peered into the bag. "This is wonderful. I was going to cut up some more sheets."

"No need," Sally said with a shrug. "These have had bunches and bunches of litters of kittens born on them. That's the only thing they're used for. I loan them out to special people."

Liz smiled at her friend. "Thank you. I truly appreciate it."

"Do you have a good scale?"

Liz frowned in thought. "I have a scale, but I'm not sure how accurate it is."

"I'll loan you mine. It's a retired postal scale and is accurate to the whavevernth of an ounce. Perfect for newborn kittens. Remember, you have to weigh them at the same time every day, and if they're not gaining weight, call Melissa immediately."

"You're mother henning," Liz said with a grin. "One of those kindergarten teacher traits."

Sally grinned back. "Exactly. Now remember, if you want me to come help midwife, just give a holler."

Chapter Seventeen

Tuesday morning at the school bus office, Alex found a note in his mailbox from Carl Petersen, reminding him to drop the puppet theater off at the high school on Thursday night at seven. Alex pocketed the note. The puppet theater was finished.

When the children trooped off the bus that morning, Kathryn Leslie stuck her head around the door. "Hi there, Alex."

"Kathryn." He liked the cheerful music teacher. "Your turn to herd them in this morning?"

She nodded. "Don't know if you'd heard, but I'm also the music director for the community theater show."

"The Sound of Music."

"That's right. Carl Petersen said you had volunteered to make the puppet theater."

Alex chuckled. "I was volunteered, yes."

"That's wonderful. We're going to be doing a music run-through Thursday night. He said you'd have it to us for rehearsal that night."

"It's finished now. I could drop it off tonight if you'd like."

"No!" she said hastily. "No. Thursday is when we'll need it. I just wanted to make sure you'd be able to deliver it."

"Seven o'clock."

"Great." It was spoken with lots of enthusiasm. "Well, I'll see you then." And she ducked out to shoo the children up the steps into the school.

What was all that about? Alex wondered. She was probably making idle conversation. Still, it was a bit odd. Shrugging, he pulled the bus out of the school's driveway and headed back to the bus lot.

Wednesday afternoon, Kathryn stopped by the library. "Hey, best friend," she said. "I need a favor."

"Sure."

"My car started making some strange noise this morning, so I called the shop. They said to bring it in tomorrow—but I might need to leave it overnight. Now, tomorrow night, *after* rehearsal I can get a ride home with Carl. But he can't pick me up. So, I was wondering if you could give me a ride."

"As long as Julia isn't in labor. And if she is, you can borrow my car."

Kathryn beamed. "Oh, wonderful. I need to be there

about a quarter to seven. And if you're not doing anything, I want you to stay and hear Connie Hewitt sing. She's going to be second on the list, so you won't be out late."

"This is that wonderful voice you were telling me about?"

"Yup. This incredible voice here in Hartley, Ohio." Her friend rolled her eyes. "What is the world coming to?"

Liz shook her head at her friend. "You're a snob," she said with great affection.

"Yeah, I know. So, you'll pick me up at about six-twenty? That'll give us plenty of time to get there. And then you can stay and hear Maria sing about the hills being alive and all that, and Connie Hewitt's incredible voice, and then you can go home and watch 'Mystery' while your pregnant cat gestates. I'm counting on you."

"Don't look so earnest. I'll pick you up tomorrow night at six-twenty."

"And you'll stay to hear Connie Hewitt sing. Promise me."

"I promise" she said lightly.

Kathryn's face lit up. "Great. It's gonna be great."

"Here we go." Kathryn, her arms full of music, ushered Liz into the building.

"We have the elementary-school teacher bit down pat, don't we?" Liz asked.

"Sure do. And I'm a professional. Do not try this at

home. Now, I have to be up on the stage with the piano, so I'm going to settle you down here in the seats—oh, look. There's Ray. Sylvie is the oldest Von Trapp, you know. Quite good, and she really looks the part, as long as she doesn't get too big before the performances."

"I heard."

"I thought you had. So, go sit next to Ray. Remember, you have to stay to hear Connie Hewitt sing." Kathryn breezed down the aisle.

Liz shrugged out of her winter coat and hung it over her arm as she scooched along the row of seats. High school auditoriums were not noted for the generosity of their leg room.

"Hello, Ray."

He turned, and his eyes lit up when he saw her. "Hello, Liz. What brings you out on a night like this?"

"I had to give Kathryn a ride, and I promised her I'd stay long enough to hear Connie Hewitt sing. Can I sit next to you?"

"Of course."

"I haven't seen you at the library recently. I wondered if you'd dropped off the planet."

"Just busy."

"I guess there's a lot to do to get ready for a new baby." Liz struggled to keep her voice even.

"More than I ever imagined," Ray agreed. "Sylvie is painting the walls of the baby's room."

"Dragons?" Liz guessed.

Ray chuckled. "She calls them draclings. Baby dragons for a baby person." He shook his head, an expression of wonderment on his face. "She amazes me."

Liz stared down at her hands. The expression on his face was almost too much for her to bear. "I'm sure it will be lovely. Her artwork is very beautiful. I've always thought so."

An attention-getting piano chord rang throughout the auditorium. Kathryn was ready to begin her music rehearsal. Liz glanced up on the stage. She could pick out the teacher who played Maria, and next to her was an immensely large woman. That must be Connie Hewitt of the incredible voice. The entire cast was on stage, watching Kathryn as she led them in vocal exercises.

Ray leaned toward her and pointed. "There's Sylvie." Sylvie was with the other Von Trapp children, all standing straight, lined up by size. All singing scales.

Suddenly, Liz had to know. She felt she'd known Ray long enough to ask such a question, though it was quite personal. "What was it about Sylvie that made you fall in love with her?"

If Ray was surprised by the question, he didn't show it. Instead, he took it for the serious question it was. As Liz knew he would. He was quiet for several moments. Then, at last, he said, "I'd never felt as comfortable with anyone as I did with Sylvie. The better I got to know her, the more I wanted to know her. She's not perfect, and I'm certainly not, but we're right for each other."

"What if," Liz said, her voice low, her eyes on the

actors gathering on the stage, "there was something that was in the way, something keeping you apart, something that couldn't be changed?"

He was silent. So silent that she risked a glance at him. The compassion she saw in his expression brought tears flooding her eyes. She blinked rapidly. He reached out and put his arm around her, comforting her, as a big brother. "It's going to be all right," he said softly. And she didn't have the heart to argue with him.

Alex pulled his truck up next to the sidewalk. He didn't want to carry this puppet theater any farther than he had to. It was one heavy puppy. Carl hadn't been specific about where to bring it, so he'd have to find him and ask. He climbed out of his truck and locked the door. The doors to the school were unlocked, and the doors to the auditorium were open. He could hear a group of people singing scales. He stepped inside the darkened auditorium and stood still at the back for a moment, allowing his eyes to adjust to the dim light. He saw Kathryn up on the stage, pounding out chords on a school-quality piano. But he didn't see Carl. He looked carefully at the few people scattered throughout the seats of the auditorium.

Then he saw her. Saw her sitting next to a man, a man who had his arm around her shoulders. And she was not protesting. In fact, she was leaning slightly into the man. Pain clenched his gut, clawed its way up through him. Liz was with another man. He could not bear to see. He could not bear to look away. As he watched, the man said something to Liz, she nodded, and he removed his arm, which was a good thing, because Alex was ready to rip it off him.

Alex sagged against the back wall, breathing hard. Never, in his whole life, had he wanted to do violence to another human being. What was worse, now that his vision had cleared the red from the edges, and the man was sitting up straight again, he could see who it was. It was Ray Novino.

As quickly as his rage had come, it was gone. It was replaced by a feeling of incredible loss. And it was then, standing in the back of the darkened auditorium, while Kathryn had the entire cast of community players sing "Edelweiss," that he realized he was, inextricably and unmistakably and forever, in love with Liz Hadley.

For a long moment he watched her watching the action on the stage. He could tell, by the way she was nodding slightly in time to the music, that she was humming along with it. He wanted, more than anything, to be next to her, listening to her hum, feeling her closeness, her warmth. Then, as if she could feel him watching her, she turned around in her seat. He knew the instant she saw him. Could see her sudden stillness. And for an instant her expression was unguarded, was real and open. And he knew that she loved him, too.

Liz whipped her head back around and fought the urge to run. He was standing by the door. If she ran now, she'd have to go past him. What was he doing here? she

328

asked herself wildly. He had every right to be here, she reminded herself. It was a public school. This was community theater, open to everyone.

"Are you all right?" Ray whispered. "You're shivering. Are you cold?"

Liz grit her teeth. "I'm fine. Someone just walked over my grave," she lied. Though, the way she felt, it was almost the truth. Then she noticed Carl Petersen, the shop teacher, hurry up the aisle to the back of the auditorium. Carl Petersen, Kathryn's new friend, who was in charge of the sets. Oh. She remembered now. Alex had told her he was making the puppet theater for the Von Trapp children. He was probably delivering it, and if he was delivering it, that meant that Carl knew he was delivering it, and that meant that Kathryn probably also knew. Which meant that Kathryn had lured her here under false pretenses. She had been set up.

"There's Connie."

"What?" She dragged her mind back to the present.

"You said you wanted to hear Connie sing," Ray explained patiently, ignoring the fact that she'd probably sounded startled. "They've finished with the chorus and now it's Connie's turn."

Sure enough, the pianist played the first chords of "Climb Every Mountain." Kathryn, schemer or not, had told the absolute truth. Connie Hewitt had a Voice with a capital *V*. For the first time in her life, Liz felt she understood the song. A song that was sung so often it was almost a cliché. Sung by Connie Hewitt, it was not a cliché. It was—"She's amazing," she breathed, not able to take her eyes off the woman on the stage.

"And to think," Ray said quietly, so as not to disturb the rehearsal, a teasing tone in his voice, "she's hidden away, here in Hartley, Ohio."

"Hartley, Ohio," Liz whispered back. "Where there are no mountains to climb."

"Only the mountains we make for ourselves."

"Out of molehills?"

"Or our fears. Those are the mountains that we probably need most to climb."

"That's right," Liz said, grinning at her friend. "You've been reading the history of psychology." But it was an astute comment, she thought. Was she making mountains of her fears? Was she using all of this—her relationship with Alex—as a reason to turn into an old maid? Was there a way she could find something positive in it all? Something she could grow from?

"I never answered your question." Ray interrupted her thoughts again.

"What question?" she asked.

"You asked what I'd do if there was an insurmountable problem between Sylvie and me. She and I would do whatever it took to find a solution. Because, as someone once told me, for every problem you should be able to find a hundred solutions. A hundred and ten, if you're bright."

Liz nodded slowly. "Thanks, Ray." He'd given her lots to think about. He and Kathryn were both right—it was a together kind of thing. He and Sylvie would work on a problem together. Kathryn said that if Alex had been perfect, he wouldn't have left. Therefore there was no use in moaning and groaning about it all. It was, in the long run, probably a good thing. With a deep sigh, Liz stood up and shrugged her arms into her coat.

"Leaving already?" Ray asked, reaching out to help her find her sleeve.

"I have a mountain to go climb," she said lightly.

A mountain to climb and something decadent to bake. She settled into her comfy chair with one of her well-thumbed and spattered Julia Child cookbooks. "Something without any nutritionally redeeming value whatsoever," she told Julia, who had appropriated her lap for some industrial-strength purring. "Preferably chocolate." Liz passed the pages of pies and biscuits and concentrated on cakes and cookies. She finally chose *le marquis au chocolat*. She had all the ingredients, and she could have the cake part in the oven by nine o'clock—when "Mystery" came on Public Television. Then she could assemble it. It would be a late night, but this was very worth it.

She had just slid the cake pan in the oven and was licking the beaters, an old habit, when the telephone rang.

Alex! she thought, her heart leaping. No, she told herself firmly. It wasn't Alex. It was probably Kathryn, apologizing for setting her up. It was neither.

"Hello, Elizabeth," came the familiar voice.

"Hello, Mother."

"Your father and I were having dinner and wondering how you are."

"I'm fine. I'm baking something to take in to work tomorrow."

But her mother didn't seem to be interested in what she was baking, or anything about work. "We saw Richard and his family at church last week. He has such lovely children."

"I'm sure he does," Liz said. She propped the phone between her ear and her shoulder and set the pan of *crème au beurre a l'anglaise* over moderately low heat. She stirred.

"Have you decided when you're coming home, dear?"

"I'm not. I'm staying here."

"Oh, come now. Aren't you getting tired of all that cold? There's another snowstorm coming your way. What will you do with all that snow?"

Liz held up the filling and dripped it from the spoon. Not quite thick enough. "Why, Mother, I'll build a snowman. In fact, if we have enough snow, I'll build an entire snow family."

"Elizabeth, this is not a joking matter. Your father and I both think living up there in all that winter weather isn't safe for you. After all, you were raised in Arizona."

"Which is why I appreciate the cold so much. Mother, I am forty years old. I can make my own decisions about where I live, and right now I live in Ohio, and I like living here." She heard her mother's outraged gasp, but she ignored it and went on. "I'll be happy to talk to you about what I'm doing, about my life here, my job and my friends. But I don't want to continually listen to your comments about Richard and his lovely family. I have to go back to my cooking now. I'll talk to you later. Give Daddy my love."

She hung up and stared at the telephone. She'd done it. She'd spoken her mind to her mother. She'd wanted to do that for twenty years. It felt good. It felt exhilarating. It felt like she was standing on top of a mountain.

Julia rubbed around her legs, purring mightily. Liz scooped up her cat and looked her in the face. "I am terrific," she announced.

Julia squeezed her eyes shut and purred.

"This is it," Liz warned the next morning as she unwrapped the cake. "So you'd better enjoy it."

"This is what?" Kendra asked. Any time there was the slightest hint of food, Kendra was always the first one in the staff room. "Ohmigod! It's gorgeous. What is it called?"

"*Le marquis au chocolat*. It's the last treat until all the kittens are in their new homes. Having kittens is a lot of work, you know. I can't see spending time baking when I have babies to take care of."

"This is, what? Couple of weeks?"

Liz rolled her eyes. "Kittens aren't ready to go to new homes until they're at least eight weeks old. Assuming they have homes to go to. Eight weeks from the day they're born, and they're not born yet."

But Kendra wasn't paying attention. She was staring at the cake on the plate on the table. "Get out the paper plates and the napkins and dig in," Liz invited with a grin. Kendra looked like she'd found manna.

"You know," Kendra said in a trance-like voice. "I've heard there are people who don't like chocolate."

Liz chuckled. "Remarkable," she teased.

"I don't think they're human. Everyone likes chocolate."

Everyone, Liz thought. Everyone on the staff, certainly. But—what about Attila? She wondered. She didn't know. Attila rarely took part in their food-fests. Which was just as well, because he would probably put a damper on the activities. Maybe, the thought insinuated itself in her mind, he knows that. Maybe he knows he's not liked. Maybe—maybe he's so distant because he knows the staff doesn't like him. Maybe he's really not unapproachable at all. Maybe he's just shy. Then again, maybe she was full of hogwash. But still—what if . . .

Guilt washed through Liz like a spring flood, rising higher and higher. She had to do something about it. Quickly.

She reached for the knife as Kendra put it down. Then she reached for a plate. Just because Attila wasn't friendly towards the staff didn't mean she shouldn't be friendly back. That would make her as low as he was. She cut a piece of the chocolate cake and set it carefully on the plate.

"Hey," Kendra exclaimed. "Where are you taking that?"

"If everyone likes chocolate, that means Attila does too."

"Attila? Talk about pearls before swine."

But Liz merely smiled as she grabbed a paper napkin and a plastic fork and whisked herself down the short hall to Attila's office. The door was closed. That was no surprise. She didn't think she'd ever seen it open. Liz knocked.

"Come in." His voice sounded surprisingly human, Liz thought as she balanced the plate on one hand and opened the door.

"I made some chocolate cake, Mr. Hunnicutt. I brought you a piece before it was all gone."

The surprise in Attila's eyes was a palpable thing. "Why, thank you, Miss Hadley."

Then she didn't know what to do. Evidently, Attila didn't know what to do either, because they both seemed to stare at each other.

"I'll put it here, on your desk."

"Yes. The desk."

The rich sensual chocolate looked completely out of

335

place on the expanse of naked desk. In fact, the whole office was much without soul. Most librarians' desks were decorated with little slips of paper that held book titles, or call numbers, or hastily scribbled notes. Most librarians' offices were piled high with books to be read, reference logs to be examined, and—in the case of Cecily the children's librarian—puppets used for story-times. But Attila's office was strictly utilitarian. There was, however one hint of human interest. The latest edition of that new travel guidebook series for Europe sat squarely on top of Attila's briefcase.

"Well," Liz muttered nervously. "I'll get back to work now." She turned to make her escape.

"Miss Hadley." His voice stopped her.

She glanced back at him. He was still staring at her. For the first time, he actually seemed to see her. She wasn't sure if this was a good thing or not. "Yes?"

"Thank you. I will most certainly enjoy your cake with my lunch." His features cracked and he smiled. It wasn't much of a smile, but then, he probably didn't have much practice smiling. Maybe he didn't have much to smile about. Now where, she wondered, did that thought come from?

"You're welcome." And she found it was true.

"All these people have to have their videos before the storm hits," Carol, the other librarian scheduled on the reference desk that afternoon, muttered sarcastically. "Just think, they might have to be locked up in their houses with their kids. Whatever will they do?" She shuddered dramatically.

What must it be like, Liz mused, to dread being shut up with one's children. "What do you do with your kids when it snows?"

"We all read. I make a big bowl of popcorn and we read in front of the fireplace."

"No videos?" Liz asked curiously.

Carol grinned. "Sure. After I've read *In the Rain with Baby Duck* fourteen times I'm ready to let them veg out. And I'm ready for some adult input. So what are your big plans for the weekend?"

Liz glanced out the window at the thick gray sky. "I am going to wait for kittens to be born. Say, Carol, are your kids old enough for a kitten?"

Carol looked thoughtful. "I've been thinking about it. Let me talk to my other half and I'll let you know." Then she looked smug. "I'm honored that you think I'm worthy of one of your kittens."

"Yes," Liz said absently, "I think you're worthy." But her mind was on the phrase Carol had used to refer to her husband. Her other half. Having another half was well and good, Liz thought, but she was whole. She was going to stay whole. She had a great job—except for Attila, she thought automatically. Then she stopped herself. If she kept telling herself that Attila was the bane of their life, then it was bound to be true. A self-fulfilling prophecy. So, she told herself. Let's begin again. She had a great job, a lovely little house and now a perfect cat. Yes, this was a much better way of thinking. She could make her own decisions, do whatever she wanted to. If she wanted to spend the whole day in front of the fireplace, reading a book in her pajamas, well, no one would bother her. Maybe that was what she'd do tomorrow while she was waiting for the kittens. Take home a good, thick book to read. She already had plenty of wood on her back porch, thanks to Alex.

Alex stacked the wood in the fireplace and struck a match. "Don't stick your nose in it," he told Burl. "It's a match. It'll burn."

Evidently, Burl was suitably impressed, for he lowered himself to the floor and plopped his great big head on his front paws.

When the fire was burning brightly, Alex settled back on the couch. But there was no Liz to help him enjoy the fire. He patted the seat next to him. Burl took the hint. "Well, bud, it looks like it's just you and me."

Burl's eyes turned mournful.

"Sorry, guy. There's nothing I can do. I love her, but that doesn't mean I have to act on it."

Burl closed his eyes and groaned.

"What would you do?"

But Burl didn't answer.

What to do? Alex thought. What to do. It was like a flaw in an otherwise perfect piece of wood. Sometimes he could cut or carve around it, sometimes he could make the flaw part of the design, but sometimes he had to find a different piece of wood. Speaking of wood, he should be working on that cradle he was making for Sylvie and Ray Novino. But this was Friday. He was tired after a long week. He didn't feel like working with wood. He wanted to stare into the fire.

The next morning, Alex and Burl went out into a white world. Not enough snow for snowmen, but enough for a few snowballs on their walk. This morning they walked farther than usual. They walked through the neighborhood until they came to the street where little Joshua Martini lived. And where Karen Matheson lived—the woman who'd rescued Burl.

Passing her mailbox, Burl stopped and looked up the long drive to the white house. He stared at the house and barked.

"You want to go visiting?"

Yes, Burl most certainly did. Karen was known to have lots of goodies for dogs to eat, and she was fully in favor of sharing them. And when Karen answered their knock, Burl wiggled all over in anticipation.

"Well, good morning!" she exclaimed. "How nice of you to come for a visit." Though her words were directed at Alex, she was busily rubbing Burl all over, including his itch spot. His hind leg started pumping in time to her scratching. "Come in," Karen invited.

For Burl, Karen's house was a second home. Karen's dogs were family to him. He trotted into the kitchen.

"He knows where the dog food bowls are," Karen commented wryly.

"He's not the least bit shy," Alex agreed.

"You've done well with him."

"He's a terrific dog."

"Well, come on in and see the rest of my terrific dogs," she said, beaming as she and Alex followed Burl into her kitchen. Karen was very proud of her dogs. "They're in the backyard right now, all but my newest child—Goldie."

"You named a Newfoundland Goldie?" Only Karen would do such a thing.

"Her name is Golden. I decided she needed a very good new beginning. She's not in very good shape."

In the kitchen, Burl had given up on the dog food bowls and was prancing around at the back door. He wanted to go see his buddies. Karen looked at Alex. "May he?"

"Of course." And Burl was allowed to race out the door and romp with his own kind.

"Goldie is in the crate room, napping right now. I've only had her for a week. She's much like Burl was when I got him. When she's feeling better, I'd like you to meet her."

The two of them wandered out into the backyard, where they were immediately surrounded by a surging mass of Newfoundlands. Nine of them. Alex petted and patted for a few minutes, until they dispersed. Burl discovered a three-foot piece of thick rope, knotted at each end, which set him to prancing proudly over to one of the other dogs. He dangled the rope in the other dog's face. The other dog took up the challenge. Tails wagging, the two dogs tugged at the rope.

Beside him, Karen smiled beatifically at the dogs. "Once more, Alex, I have to thank you for giving Burl an excellent home."

"He's a wonderful dog. Anyone would be lucky to have him."

"Not everyone," Karen said, her voice grown thoughtful, "is willing to take on a rescued dog. In fact, most people aren't. Jessie and I were talking about this very thing last night. Most people want a puppy, one of known parentage, known breeding. Known breed, for that matter." She shrugged. "It takes a special person to open his home and heart to a grown dog, one who probably comes with emotional baggage." She turned her smile on him. "Burl is very lucky that you were willing."

All the way home, as if they had a life of their own, Karen's words danced themselves around in his head. *Not everyone is willing to take on a rescued dog . . . one who probably comes with emotional baggage. Most people want a puppy. Most people want a puppy.* Suddenly, he realized the words had changed. *Most people want a baby. Not everyone is willing to take on an adopted child . . .* He stopped short. Burl sat down beside him and looked up at him, a question on his furry face. Could he? Could he adopt a child? Would he? Yes, without a doubt. But could he?

Liz. Her name shot into his mind and pranced and whirled, like Burl with that rope. Liz. Liz couldn't have her own children, couldn't have his children. But the two of them, together, could make a home for other children. Their children.

Suddenly filled with hope, he scooped up a handful of new snow and formed it into a snowball. "Yo, Burl, think fast!"

Chapter Eighteen

Saturday morning, Liz slept late, waking only when Julia decided to pat her on the cheek and yell.

Liz peered at her cat. "What's the matter, Jukes?"

Julia muttered to herself.

Liz threw the covers back. "What's wrong?"

But there seemed to be nothing wrong with Julia, except that she was hungry. Liz watched her eat. She didn't eat very much. Liz made herself a cup of tea and some toast, watching her cat closely. She pulled out the book on breeding cats and munched her toast while she reread the chapter on the early signs of labor. When she was finished eating, she set her cup in the sink. "Now for your favorite part of the day," she told her cat. "It's time to take your temperature." Julia was not impressed. But her temperature had dropped! It was 98.4 degrees. Almost two and a half degrees lower than it had been last night. Liz stared at the thermometer in wonder. "Look, Julia, according to the cat book, it means that sometime in the next twelve hours, you'll have kittens."

Julia sent her a withering glance. "Well, duh," she seemed to say.

Liz cleaned the thermometer and put it away with the kitty first-aid things. Time to get everything ready. She brought out Sally's postal scale and set it up on her dresser next to a pad of paper and a pencil. She had to weigh each kitten soon after its birth. She brought out the extra bedding for Julia's nesting box, and made sure she had everything she was going to need. Iodine, dental floss, and the blunt-nosed scissors and hemostat forceps she'd boiled for fifteen minutes yesterday. Just in case. Just in case. Julia, stretched out on Liz's bed, watched without much interest.

Finally, when her bedroom had been turned into a kitty nursery, when there was nothing else she could do to prepare, Liz sat down next to Julia. "If I sit here and watch you, I'll go crazy." She stroked the furry face, under the chin and gently down the bulging belly. "So you can stay here and rest. I'm going to go cook something."

Julia's answer was to shift her position on the bed, trying to get more comfortable.

In the kitchen, Liz called Kathryn. "Hi, Kath," she told the machine. "You're not home, but Julia's temp dropped, so it's going to be any time. Give me a call.

Oh, and thanks for trying on Thursday night. I'm not mad at you, but you should've known that it was no use."

Sally wasn't home either, so Liz left another message on a machine. Neither was Jessie. "Where is everyone?" Liz muttered to herself. "Is this a conspiracy?" She called Dr. March's answering service and left a message asking her to please call.

She got out potatoes and stuck them in the microwave to bake. Then she got out her soup pot. Baked potato soup. Comfort food. Right now, she needed all the comfort and calm she could get. Maybe she should also bake some bread pudding.

While she waited for the potatoes to bake, she trotted down the hall for a quick check on Julia. The cat wasn't on her bed. Liz quickly scanned the room— and found Julia in her nesting box. "Are you all right?" Liz asked, crouching down to pet her. Julia shifted her belly and stared up at Liz. She looked uncomfortable. She got to her feet and out of the box. Evidently it wasn't time yet. She followed Liz into the kitchen.

The phone rang. It was Dr. March. Liz told her that Julia's temperature had dropped. "I just wanted you to know, in case something goes wrong. She still looks awfully small, you know."

"You've taken excellent care of her," the vet said reassuringly. "In all probability she'll be absolutely fine. But I'm glad to know that she'll be in labor soon. Be sure you call me at home if you need help. Don't bother with the answering service; call me anyway. I'll stop by tomorrow to check them all out. It's better for the kittens if they're not exposed to the world just yet. Congratulations, Liz. You're going to be a grandmother."

Liz hung up the phone feeling a little less alone than she had before.

Liz made soup. Liz made bread pudding. Liz made a fire in the fireplace. But still no kittens. Liz curled up on her couch, in front of the fireplace, with a book in her lap and her cat beside her.

That afternoon, Alex stopped his truck in the street in front of Liz's house. Smoke drifted casually up from her chimney. Lights were on in her living room. She was home. He pulled in front of her house and turned off the engine. "You better wait here, guy," he told Burl. "She might not want to see us. Especially me."

Burl thumped his tail on the seat.

Alex took a deep breath and let it out. Slowly, he told himself as he walked toward her house. Slowly. She hadn't shoveled her driveway again, Alex noted. Or even the walk leading up to her porch. There weren't even any footprints. Maybe she was sick.

He knocked.

The door opened. He watched her face immediately shift from greeting to wariness as she stood there, in her hallway, looking at him through the glass of her storm door. She was wearing what she called her comfort clothes, ratty gray sweatpants and a very red, very oversized sweatshirt. Though he couldn't see her feet, he knew that she was wearing pink fuzzy slippers. But he could see her eyes, and in them he saw something he'd never seen before. Something deep. Suddenly, the realization of what he'd done, how he'd hurt her, shot through him. He hadn't known, hadn't let himself know. He'd only thought of how he'd felt betrayed. Now he could see hurt in her eyes. It was disguised, but he could see it. He was responsible for it. He felt deflated. He'd been all ready to tell her he would marry her anyway, and they could adopt children. He'd expected her to jump up and down, clap her hands for joy, and all would be well. He silently swore at himself for his stupidity.

Still, she stood in the door, neither welcoming nor turning away. Waiting. It was up to him.

"Can we talk?" he asked. His voice was clogged, so he cleared his throat and tried again, a little louder this time. "Can we talk?"

"This isn't the best time." Her voice was neutral. Even through the glass of the storm door.

He shoved his hands in his pockets and shuffled his feet. Then, behind her, he caught sight of Julia, coming toward the door. "Look at her!" he breathed.

Liz whipped her head around. Then she turned back to him. "She's all right. Her temperature dropped."

He frowned. "Temperature? Has she been sick?"

"No. It means that her kittens are due any time now. It's a matter of hours, rather than days."

So this was why, he hoped, it was not a good time for her to talk. Julia raised up, her front feet on the door, to look at him. She opened her little mouth and yelled.

"Hello, kitty," he said, stooping down to see her.

The cat rubbed her face against the glass of the window.

He looked up at Liz. She looked down at her cat, resignation on her face.

"You might as well come on in. For a few minutes."

It wasn't what he'd expected—in his stupidity, he pointed out to himself. Still, it was a beginning. Liz bent down and held on to Julia with one hand while she held the door open with the other. She shivered as she stood up, wrapping her arms about her. She looked past him, out to the street.

"Is that Burl in your truck?"

"Yes. I told him he needed to wait."

She considered this for a moment. "It's pretty cold outside." Her voice was, still, resigned. "Why don't you bring him in? As long as he doesn't bother Julia."

"He'd like that."

She nodded. "So would Julia."

Indeed, when he opened her front door for Burl, a minute later, Julia trotted over to the big dog and rubbed herself against his front legs. Burl leaned down and gave her a great gusty sniff. She batted at his face.

He wagged his tail. At least the critters were happy to see each other, Alex thought forlornly. He again had the feeling that this was not going to be as easy as he'd thought it would be.

Liz led the way to her living room. She sat in a chair, not the couch, where, from the look of the blanket and book on it, she had been sitting. It was a subtle hint. He, also hinting, sat on the couch and leaned over to see the title of the blue bound volume with a bookmark stuck in the middle. *"In This House of Brede.* Good book?"

She nodded. "Very good," she said briefly. "It's about a woman who leaves everything behind to be a cloistered nun."

He felt put in his place. He tried again. "Nice fire. It feels good after being outside in the cold." But he felt cold without the warmth of her friendship. And, he realized now, her love.

Still she was silent. Tolerating his presence. Here he was, sitting in front of a fire, with Liz this time, yet more without her than he'd ever been. If there was going to be a change, he thought, he'd have to be the one to bring it about. He took a good look at her, and his insides lurched. She looked weary through and through. As if she hadn't had sleep in a long time. Her sparkle was gone. She looked older than she had. She also looked thinner, as if she hadn't been eating. He hadn't been, either. He cleared his throat.

"Maybe," he said hesitantly, "maybe I shouldn't

have come. But I didn't want to leave things the way they were."

"How were they?" she surprised him by asking. Her voice was serious. She certainly was not making this any easier for him, he thought. But then, why should she?

He shrugged. "You know. Abrupt. Sudden." He stared into the flames, not seeing them. "I guess that was my fault."

"You were the one to leave," she agreed.

Burl chose that moment to plod over to the fireplace and lower himself to stretch out in front of the warmth. Julia followed him across the room. She curled up under his chin and set about giving herself a bath.

It gave Alex something to look at, other than the fire. Looking at Julia and Burl was safe. Looking at Liz was not. Yet there was nowhere he wanted to look more. He was so hungry for Liz. "I'm sorry."

There was silence. Then, "For what?" she asked.

"For the way I behaved."

"How was that?"

He quickly looked at her, but she seemed to be serious. "I didn't behave well."

"No," she said evenly. "You didn't."

"I'm sorry for that."

"I am, too."

Frustration bubbled up inside him. He stood up and began to pace her living room. He was aware that Burl and Julia were watching him. But Liz wasn't. He turned around and stopped right in front of her. Still she did not look at him. "Do you want me to grovel here? I'm trying to make an apology."

"You don't have to grovel," she said carefully. "I just want to be very sure what you're apologizing for."

He knelt down on his knees in front of her. He took her hands in his and looked up into her face. "I shouldn't have acted like that. Shouldn't have left like that."

"How should you have left?" She slipped her hands from his.

He reclaimed her hands, more firmly this time. "I shouldn't have left at all." He thought he saw a flicker in her eyes, a lowering of the wall between them. Please, he begged her silently. Please. But the flicker was gone again, the wall back up. And he still held her hands. He rubbed the back of them slowly with his thumbs.

"No," she said gravely. "You shouldn't have."

"I did. But I came back."

"Why?"

He did not know if she meant why he had left, or why he had returned. He answered both. "I left because I didn't know what I know now. I came back because I love you. I need you. Forever." Saying it was a liberation.

He watched her eyes fill with tears. He watched her struggle valiantly to keep that wall in place. She shook her head. "It could never work between us."

"Yes, it could. It can. And it will. If you let it." Of this he was sure.

"I can't ever give you children. Not because I don't

351

want to, but because I am not able to. I should have told you that a long time ago."

"But we could adopt children. As many children as you want."

A lone tear slid slowly down her cheek. She gently shook her head. "No."

"Why not?" The words burst from him. He dropped her hands and reached for her, pulling her to him. He pressed his lips on hers, wildly, madly, trying to make her understand. She didn't respond. He released her. "Yes," he told her fiercely. "It would work. I would make it work, and so would you. You know that, Liz. You know that."

She nodded, her eyes lowered. "I know you would try," she whispered.

"I would not merely try. I would do it." Then a thought suddenly struck him like a hammer. What if he was wrong? "Is it . . . you . . . don't you love me?"

She jerked her head up, her gaze finding his. "It's not that," she admitted. He could breathe again.

"Then what is it? I need to know!"

She sighed, a long, slow sigh. She glanced away from him, over to her cat. His gaze followed hers. Julia was still curled up with Burl. Julia now purring, Burl now snoring. "They're noisy, aren't they?" she said with affection. He glanced back at Liz. She had that Madonna expression on her face again as she watched over her cat.

Alex got up from his knees and started for the front door.

"Where are you going?" she asked.

"The fire needs more wood." And he needed a chance to think. A brisk wind had picked up and the biting air cleared his head. He hefted an armful of logs. This would keep them for a while longer. Long enough for her to tell him what was going on, at least. She hadn't said she didn't love him; but then, she hadn't said she did, either. It was like carving wood. The pattern was in the wood already, and the carver had to carve away everything that was extraneous until the pattern was revealed. Liz had the answer, and he had to clear away all the junk until he found the truth. He could do that. While he wasn't an expert carver, he had a fair hand.

But when he got back inside with the wood, she wasn't in the living room. "Liz?" he called, depositing the wood on the hearth. Burl startled at the crash. "Just me, old guy," he told his dog as he stacked the wood neatly. Burl put his head back down. "Liz?"

"I'm in the kitchen," she called back.

Alex opened the fire screen and set another log carefully on the pile. He considered it, reached for the poker and rearranged the burning wood, then added one more log. There, he thought with satisfaction as he closed the firescreen. That would burn nicely.

"Soup," Liz announced. He turned to see Liz set a

tray on the coffee table and smile slightly at him. "I thought," she said, "you might be hungry for some baked potato soup." She held a bowl out to him. It was a peace offering. The proverbial olive branch.

He accepted it. "Thank you." He also understood that while they ate, there would be a ban on all talk about their relationship. "How soon should her kittens be born?" he asked, to make conversation.

Liz glanced at her watch. "Any time," she said doubtfully. "But you'd never know it, would you? She's acting like nothing out of the ordinary is happening."

"This soup is the best."

"I was so nervous earlier today that I had to cook," she said. For a moment, the old Liz was back. Then she bit her lip.

He grinned at her. "I'm glad." Glad she'd cooked. But more glad that she'd been able to let down her guard, if only for a moment.

She blushed. Burl snored, Julia purred, Liz ate her soup. Alex leaned back, full of soup and a feeling of peace and comfort. Everything was going to be all right. He realized he was smiling. He rose, picked up his bowl and set it on the tray. "I'll take these into the kitchen. Otherwise Burl might be tempted."

"Thank you." But her smile, genuine this time, was his thanks.

She was going to have to tell him. He deserved to know. She clenched her hands together in her lap. It was difficult enough to talk to Kathryn about it, and Kathryn had been there. But Alex was here. He didn't know. So when he came back into the living room, she said, "I want to tell you." He looked suddenly unsure and very young. Her heart went out to him. He was such a good man. He deserved the very best.

He stood in front of her and held out his hand. "Come sit next to me."

She shook her head. "I'd rather not." She didn't want to be comforted while she told him.

"Please." And she realized that maybe he was the one who needed the comfort. So she took his hand. They sat together on her couch. Close, but not quite touching, their shoulders and knees automatically slanted toward each other. She stared down at her hands, but she knew he was watching her closely.

"After I graduated from college, a long time ago," she began, "I married a guy I'd dated all through high school. His name is Richard. He was a wonderful man. A lot like you, actually. He wanted the family and the car and the house with the picket fence. The whole bit. We were going to have that." She stopped for a moment, gathering her thoughts into a coherent form. She didn't want to start blathering. She wanted to— needed to—make him understand. "But then I came down with something called endometriosis. It's a uterine disease. It was pretty awful. The doctors tried lots of things, but finally, they recommended that I have a hysterectomy. So I did.

355

"At first, Richard was very supportive. We decided we would adopt children. We went through all the screening processes, filled out a million forms, took personality tests, that kind of thing. We were put on a waiting list. But the closer we got to the top, the more nervous Richard became. The more unsure. I thought it was just normal new father nervousness, so I turned our spare bedroom into a nursery, put up a crib, bought teddy bears." She tried to keep all emotion out of her voice. It was as if it had all happened to someone else—not her.

"One day, the social worker called us and told us about a baby. A baby girl. She was three days old. The birth mother was a high-school student who'd gotten into trouble. She wanted to go to college and didn't want the baby. I was ecstatic. But Richard wasn't. Finally, he admitted he didn't want someone else's child. Someone else's mistake, he called it. He wanted his own child. He wanted his own. It ate away at him, and our marriage, until there was really nothing left. When we finally divorced, I think it was almost a relief. I went to library school, worked in Arizona for a few years; then Kathryn talked me into moving to Hartley. Richard married a very nice woman and they now have three children and another on the way. From what I hear, he is an excellent father. End of story."

Alex had been very silent through all this. She glanced at him again. He was staring into the fire, evidently very deep in thought. She relaxed back into the couch and let him think. After a minute, he scowled at her. "I don't understand. You married some jerk who didn't want to adopt children, so you got smart and got divorced. What does all this have to do with you and me?"

She blinked at him. "What do you mean, what does it have to do with you and me? It has everything to do with you and me."

"What?"

"You want children. I can't have children."

"I know that. I still want you. We can adopt children."

"Richard said that, too. In the beginning. And then he changed his mind."

"I'm not Richard. He was a jerk."

"No, he wasn't a jerk. He just didn't want to raise someone else's child."

"He was a jerk."

A chuckle bubbled up and escaped. "Kathryn says the same thing."

"Very astute woman, your friend Kathryn." He paused for a moment. "What does she say about me?"

She decided to tell him the truth. "That if you were so wonderful, you wouldn't have left."

A tinge of red washed over Alex's cheeks. He looked down at his hands. Then up at her, his face open and honest. "She's right. I shouldn't have left."

Was it possible? Liz wondered. Could Alex really be willing to accept her as she was? The only way she'd ever find out for sure was if she trusted that it was so. Yes, it involved risk, but that was what life was all about—taking risks. She reached out to touch his cheek gently, softly. "You shouldn't have left," she whispered. "But you came back."

"I came to stay." He spoke the words with quiet determination, without hesitation. "If you'll let me."

If she let him? Liz gazed wonderingly into his eyes and felt herself begin to melt like chocolate in the sun, becoming all soft and gooey. Her eyes drifted closed as he drifted nearer and nearer until their lips met and melted together.

"Did you know," she whispered at last against his mouth, "that a passionate two-minute kiss burns fifty calories?"

"Where did you hear that?" he asked, his tongue doing delicious things along the curve of her cheek all the way to the shell of her ear.

"It was a reference question yesterday."

"How many calories," he said between tiny kisses across the bridge of her nose, "can you burn up in a lifetime of passionate two-minute kisses?"

"I suppose it depends on the length of the lifetime," she said, struggling to keep her mind from turning into mush.

"My lifetime. Your lifetime. Forever." He captured her lips again with his as they burned fifty more calories. Then fifty more.

Her drowsy reverie was interrupted by a snort. Burl, she thought muzzily from within Alex's arms; Burl was snoring. She opened one eye to check up on him. The big dog was sill stretched out in front of the fire, but he was not relaxed. His head was up, his eyes alert, his ears cocked forward, listening, waiting. Then she realized what was missing. "Julia!" she gasped. "Where's Julia?"

Alex opened his eyes. "Julia's gone?"

Liz didn't answer. She struggled to her feet. "Julia," she called. "Jukie Jukes. Where are you?" There was no answering *mrrow*. She looked in the kitchen. No Julia. She caught sight of Burl disappearing down the hall into her bedroom. She hurried after him, almost colliding with Alex, who was also after Burl.

Alex reached her room first and stopped abruptly in the doorway, so that she almost crashed into him again. He reached behind, to pull her in front of him. "Look," he whispered.

She looked.

Burl was sitting still in front of Julia's nesting box staring into it, a look of intense curiosity on his face.

Then Liz was next to the box, looking in, too. And Alex. "Oh, look," Liz whispered in awe, tears springing into her eyes. "Look."

"Four," Alex said.

"And she did it all by herself." Liz reached into the box to scratch Julia under her chin. Julia, curled around four itty-bitty kittens, gazed back at her with a decidedly smug expression, and purred. "Can I pet your babies?" Liz asked. The kittens were so tiny, so new, so

359

scrawny. Their eyes and ears were closed. One of them was barely dry. But they had each found a nipple and were nursing aggressively. Liz reached out one finger to stroke a minuscule body.

"Don't drool on them," Alex cautioned Burl. "They're babies. You can play with them when they're older."

Julia stood up and stretched, shedding the kittens, who tumbled into a squalling heap. Ignoring them, Julia hopped out of the box, trotted past Liz and Alex and headed for the door.

"Where are you going?" Liz asked her.

Julia didn't answer.

"Stay here with the kittens," Liz told Alex before she followed her cat to the kitchen. Julia sat down in front of her empty bowl, glared up at Liz indignantly and yelled.

An hour later, Julia was fed, the nesting box refilled with clean towels. The kittens had all been checked over and weighed, their weights, marking and other information noted on a kitten chart. There were three girls and a boy. They each had the appropriate number of fingers and toes and each one had a tail. "They're perfect," Liz said with great satisfaction as she set the last one back into the box. Julia checked her baby over thoroughly before allowing it to nurse.

"She's going to be a good mother," Alex commented, wrapping his arm around Liz's shoulders and drawing her close. "So will you."

They stood together, their arms around each other, watching the kittens breathe. Until the phone rang.

"I just got home and got your message," Kathryn said breathlessly. "Is everything all right? How's Julia? Do you need me to come over?"

"Everything's as perfect as perfect could be," Liz told her. "Julia has four kittens and Alex and I are going to adopt."

There was silence on the other end. Then Kathryn gave a whoop and a holler so loud and long that Liz had to hold the phone a foot away from her ear.

An hour later, Sally called. Then Jessie. Then Liz called Dr. March, who promised to come over the next afternoon.

"Is there anyone else in town who you have to talk to before I can have you all to myself?" Alex asked with a teasing grin.

Liz felt her insides go all melty again. She shivered in anticipation. "No."

"Good."

They left Julia curled up with her kittens, and Burl, who had appointed himself official nanny, stretched out next to the box.

Alex rearranged the logs in the fireplace so they'd give off the most heat. It was cold outside. But inside, they were warm. His family. His Liz. He'd marry her tomorrow if she'd let him. Or the next day. Or the next. He rose from the fireplace and wrapped his arms around her, holding her tight. He loved the feel of Liz in his arms. He would never let her go. When two trees were planted close together, they grew into each other, becoming part of each other. That's how his life with Liz would be. They would be part of each other. They were part of each other. Their children would grow to be part of them, too. It didn't get much better than this. "All we need is our two-point-five children."

"If you don't mind," she answered, "I'd rather have three."

He closed his eyes and sent thankful thoughts to the formerly stray kitten who had brought them together.

"I'm older than you are," she told him late that night, in her bed, their bed, her head nestled against his shoulder.

"I am aware of that." He settled his arm about her. He had never in his life felt as satisfied as he did right now.

"Does it bother you?"

"No." He cuddled her into him more closely. "Does it bother you?"

"No." She was silent for a few moments, her fingers trailing up and down his arm. Then she spoke again. "You're really willing to adopt children?"

Without opening his eyes, he smiled into the darkness. "Yes. Are you?"

"Yes."

"Good." Oh, yes, he felt good. He felt very good. In fact, he felt so good that he had to share the good feeling with her. "Liz, my love," he said, reaching for her, "there's just one more thing."

"What's that?"

"Are you willing to spend the rest of your life burning calories with me?"

"You bet." And she proved it to him.

Christmas means more than just puppy love.

"SHAKESPEARE AND THE THREE KINGS"
Victoria Alexander
Requiring a trainer for his three inherited dogs, Oliver Stanhope meets D. K. Lawrence, and is in for the Christmas surprise—and love—of his life.

"ATHENA'S CHRISTMAS TAIL" Nina Coombs
Mercy wants her marriage to be a match of the heart—and with the help of her very determined dog, Athena, she finds just the right magic of the holiday season.

"AWAY IN A SHELTER" Annie Kimberlin
A dedicated volunteer, Camille Campbell still doesn't want to be stuck in an animal shelter on Christmas Eve—especially with a handsome helper whose touch leaves her starry-eyed.

"MR. WRIGHT'S CHRISTMAS ANGEL"
Miriam Raftery
When Joy's daughter asks Santa for a father, she knows she's in trouble—until a trip to Alaska takes them on a journey into the arms of Nicholas Wright and his amazing dog.

___52235-7 $5.99 US/$6.99 CAN

THE MAGIC OF
Christmas

Emma Craig,
Annie Kimberlin,
Kathleen Nance,
Stobie Piel

"Jack of Hearts" by Emma Craig. With the help of saintly Gentleman Jack Oakes, love warms the hearts of a miner and a laundress.

"The Shepherds and Mr. Weisman" by Annie Kimberlin. A two-thousand-year-old angel must bring together two modern-day soulmates before she can unlock the pearly gates.

"The Yuletide Spirit" by Kathleen Nance. A tall, blonde man fulfills the wish of a beautiful and lonely woman and learns that the spirit of the season is as alive as ever.

"Twelfth Knight" by Stobie Piel. In medieval England, a beautiful thief and a dashing knight have only the twelve days of Christmas to find a secret treasure . . . which just might be buried in each other's arms.

___52283-7 $5.99 US/$6.99 CAN

CONNIE MASON

Tempt the DEVIL

"Her historical romances are the stuff that fantasies are made of!"
                                                    —*Romantic Times*

"Ye cannot kill the devil," whispers the awestruck throng at the hanging of the notorious Diablo. And indeed, moments later, the pirate not only escapes the noose, but abducts beautiful Lady Devon, whisking her aboard his ship, the *Devil Dancer*. Infuriated, Devon swears she will have nothing to do with her rakishly handsome captor. But long days at sea, and even longer nights beneath the tropical stars, bring Devon ever closer to surrender. Diablo is a master of seduction, an experienced lover who knows every imaginable way to please Devon—and some that she has never imagined. Devon knows she will find ecstasy in his arms, but does she dare tempt the devil?

___4366-1 $5.99 US/$6.99 CAN

Dorchester Publishing Co., Inc.
P.O. Box 6640
Wayne, PA 19087-8640

Please add $1.75 for shipping and handling for the first book and $.50 for each book thereafter. NY, NYC, and PA residents, please add appropriate sales tax. No cash, stamps, or C.O.D.s. All orders shipped within 6 weeks via postal service book rate. Canadian orders require $2.00 extra postage and must be paid in U.S. dollars through a U.S. banking facility.

Name_____
Address_____
City_____State_____Zip_____
I have enclosed $_____ in payment for the checked book(s).
Payment <u>must</u> accompany all orders. ❑ Please send a free catalog.

ANNIE KIMBERLIN

I came of age in Boulder, Colorado, during the Great Hippie Era. A circuitous path led me to the University of Illinois, where I earned my MLS. Today I'm a librarian in a large metropolitan library system. Though my early life was filled with cats, as an adult I became converted to dogs. My dogs and I have competed in breed and obedience, earning titles in both. One of my former foster dogs is the star of my 1997 Christmas novella *Away in a Shelter.* Currently I live with four dogs, a former stray cat, two teenagers and 1,800 rubber stamps. Part of my royalties from all of my books go to support The Company of Animals, a nonprofit agency that distributes grants to animal welfare agencies providing emergency and ongoing care to companion animals throughout the United States. Write to me at P.O. Box 30401, Gahanna, OH 43230, or abouricius@aol.com.

Hartley, Ohio, is a town where everybody knows each other's business. For its residents, there are few things that happen slower than falling in love . . . but when it happens, it's forever.

JULIA

Liz Hadley was a cat person, and since she didn't currently own a kitten, there was nothing that she wanted more. The stray that had been found in the snowy library parking lot was perfect; she couldn't wait to go home and cuddle.

AND ROMEO

Still, the arms that held the cat weren't so bad, either. The man her coworkers called Romeo apparently also had a soft spot for all things furry, though it appeared to be the only soft spot on his entire body. The man had the build of a Greek god and his eyes were something altogether more heavenly. And in the poetry of his kisses, the lovely librarian found something more profound than she'd ever read and something sweeter than she'd ever known.

52341

ISBN 0-505-52341-8

0 71145 00550 2

$5.50 US
$6.50 CAN
$12.95 AUS